HYDE

The
Angel of Meridian

Justin Hyde

Acknowledgements

Writing a book is such an incredible undertaking. It involves both excitement and frustration; and requires both passion and dedication. A few months ago, I was thrilled to begin the adventure again, and I could not have done it without the support of my beautiful wife and the inspiration of my 3 amazing kids. Tristan, Kailyn, Adaline and Emma, I love you all. This is for you.

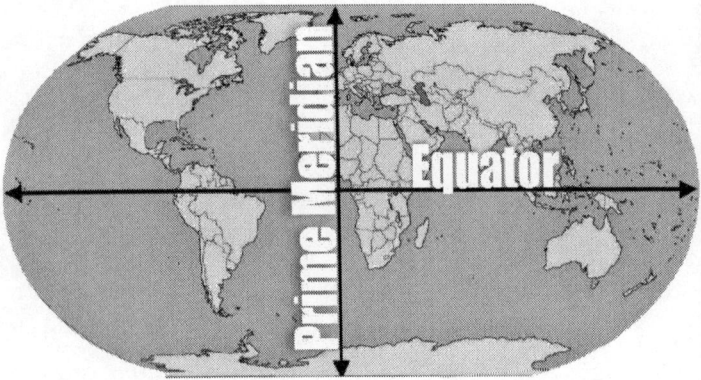

"With genetic engineering, we will be able to increase the complexity of our DNA and improve the human race."

— Stephen Hawking

"Science is dangerous. There is no question, but that poison gas, genetic engineering, and nuclear weapons are terrifying. It may be that civilization is falling apart and the world we know is coming to an end. In that case, why not turn to religion and look forward to the day of judgement, being lifted into eternal bliss, and watching the scoffers and disbelievers writhe forever in torment."

— Isaac Asimov

"In the beginning, after this earth was prepared for man, the Lord commenced his work upon what is now called the American continent, where the Garden of Eden was made. In the days of Noah, in the days of the floating ark, he took the people to another part of the earth."

— Brigham Young

Prologue

June 15, 2018
Latitude 22° N, Longitude 159° W

"Then the Lord God said, 'Behold, the man has become like one of us.'"

The man looked up from the book and gazed out from under the brim of his tan hat at the men standing around him. There were six of them. Several of them did not speak English, but they did not question him or interrupt. A bead of sweat dripped down the side of his face, but he hardly noticed.

Above them all, the sudden cry of an 'elepaio shook the canopy awake, and dozens of different species took off in a loud, startled flight. The men flinched and began whispering to each other. The 'elepaio was a sign. They considered it an 'aumakua—a spirit animal—born of a deceased ancestor whose soul had leaped from Pö to the land of the living. 'Aumakua's came to protect and warn.

The man in the tan hat did not take his eyes off the group when he began reading again. "He drove out the man, and at the east end of the Garden of Eden He placed the cherubim, and a flaming sword that turned every way to guard the way to the tree of life." He had spoken the verse from Genesis with passion and fire in his voice, and now the sweat ran down his face twice as hard. He pulled a handkerchief from his hip pocket and

Justin Hyde

dabbed his forehead.

The men around him were dark skinned, some thick bodied, others lean and muscular, but they all wore the bark-cloth tribal malos of their people. The humidity in the air did not phase them, and their bodies remained dry. Yet they trembled.

"Kekoa, let's keep moving," the man in the tan brimmed hat said.

Kekoa stepped forward and gave instructions to the rest of his men. He had the body of a warrior, and as the meaning of his named suggested, he was brave. But that was not true of all of them. He turned back to the man in the hat. "They are afraid," he said.

"Afraid of what?" the man in the hat asked with annoyance. "The bird?"

"No," Kekoa said. His English was good, but the words did not always come together right. "They are afraid of your God. My people do not worship Him, but they still fear. If what your God say true, there is an angel guarding here."

"I thought you said that your people knew the entire island?" the man in the hat said.

"We know from stories. The jungle is too thick here. 'Aumakua here. No one come here."

"Today we do," the man said back sternly.

What Kekoa had just said was not wrong though. If they were indeed in the right place, then one of Gods own warriors, an archangel, was said to be here protecting it. But it was not the Tree of Life that the man in the hat was after. Even if the Tree of

Life was here, what good would it be to him? The tree held no guarantee of wealth or personal glory, no actual potion for immortality, despite its name. Adam and Eve had already eaten the fruit and given man the knowledge of right and wrong that the tree possessed.

Slowly the group started making their way deeper into the jungle. Rare bursts of sunlight penetrated through the thick canopy overhead and cast thin lines of light onto the wet floor like laser beams. It wasn't surprising that the name of this place meant "overflowing water," and each man in the hunting party stepped cautiously.

"There should be a hill up ahead," the man in the hat said. He pointed in front of them. But the jungle was thick, and it was impossible to see more than 10 or 20 feet in any direction.

Using sticks and machetes, they weaved their way deeper and deeper into the rainforest and up the rise of the mountain. The air began to grow heavier around them with dew and the musky scent of wet vegetation. One of the men slipped on the mud and went down. His hands reached out desperately to find a saving grasp, but he landed hard on his backside and began sliding.

One of the other men reached out quickly to grab him but failed, and almost slipped as well. Finally, the man caught the root of a banyan tree and clenched his fist around it tightly. The sudden tug on the plant stopped him, but it shook the leaves above and a giant centipede dropped from the branches and landed on his arm. He yelled out in fright, and the nightmarish creature bit down, sinking its large venomous fangs into the soft flesh of his forearm. The man let out a terrifying scream. Extreme pain instantly engulfed his arm like a flame, and he flung the giant centipede into the surrounding rainforest, then writhed on the ground, grasping his wounded arm tightly with the other.

"The bite can cause dead skin," Kekoa said, not knowing the right word for necrosis. "If he has an allergic reaction, he will go into shock."

"Help him up," the man in the hat said, annoyed.

They continued up the hill, hoping that eventually the sky would break through the tops of the trees and free them from the green cocoon of the jungle. But it did not. This part of the island was dense. No one ventured here. Small streams and brooks winded and tunneled through the underbrush, making every step a treacherous one.

We must be getting close, the man in the hat thought.

A few more feet ahead they came to an abrupt stop. An unpassable tangle of jungle rose in their path. Somewhere beyond it was the sound of running water. The men stopped, clearly content with turning back.

"We cannot pass," Kekoa said. "What do you want to do, Makehewa?"

Makehewa took the tan brimmed hat off his head. He didn't particularly care for the name that

Kekoa had given him, but he had let it slide enough times that all the men were now familiar with it. If he resisted the name now, they would use it anyways, in secret, when speaking of him behind his back, so instead he embraced it. "Let me through," he said.

He pushed his way to the front of the group and studied the green wall. Something about it was different than the rest of the forest. The color seemed to be an odd shade different, and the vines and branches did not hang the same way that they did everywhere else in the jungle. Here, they looked as though they were purposely woven into this obstacle. They crossed each other and lay only at angles across a single plane—sometimes going up, sometimes going sideways, but never going out. It was both natural and unnatural at the same time.

As he leaned in closer to the foliage, he thought he could feel an energy coming from it, although he couldn't explain it. "Let me see that," he said to one of the men standing behind him.

The man handed Makehewa his long blade, then backed a step away.

Makehewa had thought briefly about using his own sword, the one hanging from his belt, but now was not the time. The men would question it. First, he had to be sure of this place. He tossed his hat to the man, then turned and raised the machete at the rainforest wall. With a strong swing he slashed at the vines and branches, but the blade slid over the tops of them like a skate on ice. He tried two more times to no effect, then lowered the machete to his side and stared at the tangle of green in front of him. The living wall seemed to be responding to the attack. Not with blood, or by falling to the ground in severed pieces as should have been, but almost as if it were tightening up on itself.

It's defending itself.

Slowly he reached out a gentle hand—moving closer to the wall with tenderness instead of aggression. As his fingertips reached the vines, the tightening stopped, and they began to loosen and slowly part until he was able to slip his entire hand into the wall without so much as touching a leaf. He turned to Kekoa and the men. "Follow me," he said.

But the men did not move. Even Kekoa remained where he was.

"Then stay," he said. He knew this was it. He could feel it. The rest of the men could turn back now for all he cared. They had gotten him here, and that was all that he really needed. Cowards should not share in his glory anyways, and he would end them all if need be. *Better for them to stay here and hide, then get in my way,* he thought.

He knew, or at least had reason to believe, that he was safe—that the angels of God had long ago left this world. Yet Makehewa still had a flashing moment of trepidation and doubt as he disappeared alone into the wall. Angels, he knew, were not the obedient, ever-loving divine beings that history often portrayed them as. Many of them were feisty and even scary at times. Satan himself was once Lucifer the archangel, before he rebelled against God and lost the great battle against Michael in heaven.

In the Book of Enoch, there were tales of angels coming to earth and having sex with humans, taking human wives, and even having children with them—the Nephilim. Sometimes the angels would lash out at humans when angered. Even the archangel Gabriel, when Zechariah did not believe him about the birth of John the Baptist, punished Zechariah by taking away his ability to speak.

Makehewa knew that all angels though, including the archangels, were restless beings, and would not sit still forever—even on God's command. Only Samael, the angel of death, was unwaveringly obedient to God—forever fulfilling His order to kill, without question. Still, all of the archangels were soldiers of a great army, with powerful weapons crafted in heaven. Most of them however, no longer needed their weapons in heaven, since the casting out of the fallen, and so they were often left behind. Stored where they *would* be needed. A tradition still upheld today by the many world armies who store nuclear weapons in underground storage vaults—strategically placed bunkers scattered all across the globe.

He reached down with his gloved hand and felt the heel of the short-sword on his belt. It had once belonged to the angel Phanuel.

But not anymore, Makehewa thought.

He had found Phanuel's short-sword in the ancient city of Capernaum, near the Sea of Galilee, where Jesus had performed his first miracle. Phanuel was considered the angel of exorcism and must have been there when Jesus performed the exorcism in the synagogue, casting out a demon from a possessed man in the crowd.

Stepping further through the wall of green, Makehewa suddenly felt a warm touch on his hand. He parted the vines in front of him, and a glow, like a cool reflection of the sun, swept over the horizon. It lifted, and Makehewa saw that he was no longer standing in a rainforest on the side of a mountain, but was now on a flat, sprawling field with an endless sky and sparkling sunlight shinning down upon him.

He took in a long breath of fresh air and found it tasteful and calming. Without control, his eyes closed, and he smiled. A beautiful feeling of love and acceptance passed through him.

Suddenly aware of all things, he recognized the weightlessness of his own eyelids and opened them into a dazzling brilliance of shapes and colors. Birds and mammals of all kinds sung and played through the lush green fields of the garden.

Then, without warning, it was all ripped away. A thunderous noise filled the sky and dark clouds converged above him. A voice he did not recognize as his own, spoke inside of him. The language was one he did not recognize. But its message was clear.

Do not proceed.

Makehewa looked around in fear. He was ready to run back through the wall. But in front of him, in the dark, there was a tiny cave. There it was. It was here. He ran towards it and ducked inside.

Across from him, at the back of the cave, was a pool of still water. At its center, a pointed rock stood tall, reaching three feet above the level of the water. Suspended above the rock, floating above it by no earthly means, was a sword—Uriel's sword. Long and heavy was the blade—burning with a yellow-orange flame that seemed to be alive. The fire danced and moved over the angelic steel.

Makehewa reached out for it, and the flames flared up and roared.

17 months later

CHAPTER 1

November 18, 2019
45° N, 7° E.
Elevation – 11,300 feet above sea level.

Crack!
The sound of the ice breaking was terrifying. It was the only sound for miles. A few small, frozen chips broke free from the wall overhead—passing through the fog of his breath in front of him as they fell. It would be almost a minute before they hit the ground below. He remained perfectly still. Too afraid to move. Then a louder *CRACK* and a huge two-foot sheet of ice above him broke off. The point of his ice axe had severed a vein in the frozen wall. It—the axe—would have fallen, along with the ice, had the strap around his wrist not caught it.

Cameron gripped tighter with his left hand on the other axe still dug into the wall as he dangled from the side of the precipice. Luckily, the crampons on his boots also bit securely into the cliff beneath his toes, and he paused for a minute while the sudden panic inside him calmed.

He listened for a moment, waiting for the sound of the heavy ice shattering at the bottom, but it never came. Not at this elevation. Slowly, he took in a long breath and flipped the ice axe back up into his right hand. The snowy peak seemed to extend equally as far above him as it did below. It stretched

Justin Hyde

up into the clouds like a massive stone wave reaching for the heavens. But with the sun beginning to creep down on the jagged western horizon, he needed to clear his head of those thoughts and keep moving.

The ascent was not an easy one, even for experienced climbers. Off in the distance to his right, Cameron could see the eastern face of the white pyramid—each of its four sides facing one of the cardinal directions, like a giant metamorphic compass. At its apex, he knew, was the iron cross. He had seen it firsthand, on another assignment 8 years ago. But on this climb, the famous summit of the Matterhorn was not his destination.

Three weeks earlier, the Swiss government had commissioned aid to find a hoard of Nazi gold rumored to have been lost somewhere in these mountains; shortly after the fall of Hitler's regime. After their defeat in World War II, the Germans had sent their remaining gold on a train bound for Austria. A stockpile and safeguard for the eventual Fourth Reich. But ongoing attacks from Russia had forced the train to reroute and hide. It was never seen again.

While most treasure hunters nowadays searched for the gold along the German-Austrian border, one group of fortune-seekers had recently been running illegal mountaineering and excavating operations in the Swiss Alps. Additionally, the group often became hostile when confronted, and even after several arrests, the group seemed to be growing in strength and number, rather than dwindling.

Swiss Parliament and the Federal Council were taking lead in controlling the group, but as a precaution against copycat organizations later invading the region, they had also requested a nonpartisan third-party exploration effort to simultaneously attempt to locate any signs that the gold may actually still be hidden there somewhere. Putting to rest the rumors—or perhaps proving them true.

Cameron Skull was that exploration effort. Two nights ago he had stayed at Iglu-Dorf in the town of Zermatt near the base of the Matterhorn. The hotel consisted of literal igloos, interconnected by a series of snow tunnels. He found little interest however in following the ascent up the Matterhorn with the other mountaineers the next morning. It was true enough, the Matterhorn did indeed contain treasure. But it was not the shiny kind of treasure that you could spend. It was the breathtaking, once-in-a-lifetime kind of treasure that you could only see and feel.

Instead, the next morning Cameron had ventured east, in the direction of Mount Monte Rosa.

Now, perched on the side of a near vertical cliff somewhere in the middle of the Swiss Alps, he swallowed and risked a look down. He couldn't see them from so high up, but railroads had traveled these passes below him for decades, and there was one route in particular that used to exist in this region that was said to have had a long tunnel going through the mountains. Supposedly the tunnel had collapsed shortly after the war. And it is whispered by some that the train carrying the Nazi gold out of Germany may have in fact been hiding in that tunnel at the time of its collapse. And that the collapse itself was likely the result of Russian bombs landing on the area.

Damn that's a long way down...

He needed to get to the other side of this peak though. Several modern rail lines still ran this part of the Alps, like the Gornergrat Train that he had taken to Zermatt a few days ago. Most of them however traced the outskirts of the mountains now, rather than going through them. But if the rumor of the collapsed tunnel was true, then it could be possible that it was buried somewhere in this very mountain beneath him—entombing the Nazi train within. But the northern face of this peak had been thoroughly searched many times over in past years, so any access that still existed to the tunnel—if an access did still exist—had to be on the southern side. And the only way to get to the virtually inaccessible southern side, was to climb over.

He looked up again. The mountain was formidable, and his muscles were weakening. He wanted a drink of water; and if it wasn't for the mask he had pulled back over his mouth, he would have licked his chapped lips, despite the risks of doing so. Pretty soon he was going to have to make camp for the night. But where?

All he really needed was a small, semi-level ledge, just big enough to hold his ultralight one-man arctic tent, but so far there wasn't one anywhere in sight.

Then, abruptly, a cold wind whipped past him and he shivered through his parka. The steam from his breath escaped, even through the wool of his face mask, and fogged the outer layer of his tinted goggles. It wasn't until the goggles cleared again that he saw that the wind had also blown some of the cloud cover above him. He gazed up, hopeful that his eyes weren't deceiving him. It looked as though there might be a small overhang some distance above. If he could reach it, and more importantly, get over it, he might be able to make camp on the ledge above.

The bottom of the overhang was not snow covered like the rest of the mountain. Once reaching it, Cameron hung the two ice axes from a carabiner on his belt and tucked them behind a leather bag full of powdered chalk. He carefully pulled off his gloves, exposing his bare skin to the frigid temperatures, and reached into the bag, coating each hand and sifting the white powder through his fingers.

With some effort, he reached above him and let the tips of his fingers find purchase on a narrow fissure on the bottom of the ledge. In order to make this maneuver he was going to have to let his feet leave the security of the wall and pull himself around with only the strength in his upper body.

He coughed once, a nervous tick, and tried to control his breathing to keep his heart rate down. Then, with a final deep breath, he swung his legs out from the wall, leaving his body dangling below him.

The underside of the ledge only protruded a few feet. With one or two swings and regrips and he should be close enough to reach around and start pulling himself around to the top of it. But just as he was about to make for his second hold, a sound resonated down through the rock. It was a shuffling sound, and Cameron almost thought he could feel its vibrations slightly through his fingers.

Then it got louder. And closer.

A small handful of loose snow fell from the edge above him. Then another, and another. Then a whole pile of snow came tumbling past him and his heart sank, and his feet scrambled to try and gain footing somewhere, but the cliff wall was now out of reach.

Avalanche!

Suddenly a very large dark shape appeared in the falling snow. It made a sound as it fell but was just an obscured black image in the midst of a plummeting white snowfall. Cameron was terrified and confused at the same time.

He watched it fall. No more snow followed behind it, and the snow that had fallen with it began separating and spreading out on the way down, leaving the dark object more defined.

Cameron's terror grew. The thing that had just fallen from the cliff above him—was a man.

—

Two thousand feet below Cameron Skull, Matteo sat comfortably in the seat of the heated train car, staring out at the beautiful landscape around him. His wife and two sons were also with him, occupying themselves with music and food. His oldest son, Ben, had just recently turned 16, and was sipping on a cold Quöllfrisch lager.

"It's so beautiful," his wife Emily said.

Matteo smiled at her, then lightly slapped his younger boy Adrian on the knee. "You're missing it," he said to him.

10-year-old Adrian pulled the headphones out of his ears and the music blared out into the train car loud enough to turn the heads of the people in the row over. "What?" he asked.

"Look," Matteo said, pointing a finger out the window.

Alongside the train, snowdrifts banked the edge of a narrow, unfrozen stream. The train followed the gentle curve of the river around a bend, while the setting sun cast reflections of the mountain peaks off of the slow-moving water. A small, nearly invisible in the snow, white Mountain Hare jumped from a rock and disappeared into the brush beyond. The scene was magnificent.

Even Adrian paused in appreciation. "Wow. It's—"

SMASH!

The roof of the train car buckled in, and every passenger on board ducked and covered. Screams, and cries of "Oh God!" and "What's happening!" came from everywhere.

"Dad!" Adrian called.

His mother, Emily, grabbed him and pulled him close. "What was that?" she cried.

Matteo didn't answer her. He remained still; his head cocked slightly to one side. His eyes were unblinking—staring out the window in front of him.

The train came to a fast stop. Brakes squealed and the large steel wheels screeched as they tried to keep traction on the frozen track.

Emily followed her husband's stare and gasped when she looked out the window. One arm hugged Adrian tighter and the other came up quick as she put a hand over her mouth.

"Dad," Adrian said again, this time with fear in his voice.

Matteo inched a step closer to the window. Red streaks were flowing down it, some of them following the fractures in the glass, like a growing red river delta of crimson blood. A bare foot, dark-purple and rotten from frostbite, dangled over the edge of the roof—filling the center of the window with a horrid, deathly sight.

CHAPTER 2

60° N, 0° Longitude

Francesco Ferrari hung up the phone and sat back in his chair, staring absently at the unfamiliar clutter of paper on the desk. He was not the type of man who could operate efficiently among such a mess. But James Kestner, the Director of Alpha-Meridian, had called and asked him to look for an admissions form that he had left there.

Miraculously, Francesco had been able to find it.

As he stood and walked out of the office, he turned to lock the door and saw the name placard hung on the outside of it. JAMES KESTNER was engraved above his title, DIRECTOR, and it left Francesco with an awkward, almost uncomfortable feeling. He wasn't sure if he could ever get used to the new structure.

A year and a half ago, James Kestner had been General James Kestner—not Director. He had been the chief officer of a covert private military group known as Nightcorp International, based out of the United States. But due to the nature of Nightcorp's global involvement and influences, political agendas, and of course some large financial exchanges from several allied countries, pressured the United States into "sharing" one of their A-teams. But rather than just convert to a UN organization, which everyone despised the idea of, Nightcorp retained its affiliation and primary allegiance with the United States—although they had relocated to a newly commissioned U.S. owned territory in the North Shetland Islands in the Nordic Sea.

Also, along with the move, they had reinvented themselves and reemerged and were now one of the most unique and sought-after schools in the world.

ALPHA-MERIDIAN

A-M, or simply Meridian as it's casually known sometimes, is a college, of sorts. It promotes itself and focuses on "Hazardous Relic Recovery." And even though the first graduating class wasn't scheduled till next winter, there was already a waiting list to hire A-M alumni. Everyone from museums and private collectors, to corporate tycoons and even world governments had direct-hire requests on file. But acquiring students was a complex process. Admission to Alpha-Meridian is extremely selective, and students are considered by referral only. As well, even after a student has gotten a referral, they are still screened through multiple intense and strenuous aptitude and physical tests before given their admission papers. One surprise to most people though is that Alpha-Meridian does not background check its applicants. Instead, relies solely on the word of the referrer. Besides—many of the students probably wouldn't have passed a background check anyways.

Another irregularity of Meridian is that the curriculum is not optional or credit based, nor is it graded on a scale. You either pass, or you don't. It is a two-year study in which students are required to take, and pass, every class:

Relic Recovery and handling: Including two semesters of religious artifact identification, one semester of mythology and one semester of delicate handling techniques.

Operative training – Beginner and advanced: Including light weapons training for beginner level, and long-distance weapons and equipment for advanced. One semester of self-defense and close quarters combat and one semester of silent maneuvers.

Deciphering: Including one semester of code breaking, one semester of text identification, one semester of trig based mathematics and one semester of language basics and sign language—ASL.

Conservation and preservation - CP: Including one semester of geography and exploration, one semester of meteorology, one semester of zoology and one semester of biology. All classes focusing on the human impact on each subject.

And finally—field training. This is where each student is put through extreme scenarios to test and strengthen their skills. Field training pushes students to new heights—literally. As situations for graduates will often require them to face extreme environments, they are placed in precarious situations in Meridians 100-acre backlot, along with an instructor, and taught to mentally and physically handle things like heights, water submersion and isolation. Basically—Survival 101.

Each class is designed to be a deep-impact crash-course. Graduates will then complete a two-recovery internship. Any student who fails or drops out of the program is held by very strict NDA agreements regarding the campus and curriculum, signed on day one.

Francesco, or Frank as he is sometimes called, stopped outside a closed door and peeked through the small rectangular window at the top of it. Inside the room, Iris Wilhelmsson was teaching the small class of only 7 students. From the muffled voices Frank could hear coming from inside the room, he knew right away that Iris must be diving into the basics of Italian.

Iris may have been the campus language specialist, but Frank desperately wanted to open the door and flaunt his flawless dialect. Being born and raised in San Casciano in Val di Pesait, just outside of Florence Italy, it was Franks English, if anything, that could use a little work. But it was Iris' class and he would not undermine the teacher. Besides, Iris WAS extremely gifted when it came to languages and speech. In fact, ever since she had helped Cameron Skull decode the ancient languages on the lost pages of the Devil's Bible a few years ago, she was publicly recognized as one the top translators in the world. Her first language was her native Swedish, with English and Italian being just two more of her eleven total fluencies.

She caught Frank looking at her through the window and he lifted his wrist and pointed at a make-believe watch. She held up her index finger as a traditional "one minute" answer, and Frank was appeased enough to walk away. Generally, when men stared at her like that, it was with perverted eyes. But Frank never made even one inappropriate gesture at her. Even though, with her long athletic legs and blonde hair, she could have been the cover of any men's magazine. She looked at Frank like a brother, but her eyes were for another man.

"Alright," she said to the class. "Tomorrow we're going to talk about how to cross-communicate French and Italian by using related articles of speech." She held up her right hand and ran through the beginning letters of the American Sign Language alphabet. "And don't forget to practice your ABC's."

She walked back to her desk and took her phone from the top drawer before leaving the room. Down the hall she found Frank in his office. "Hey, Francesco," she said, being one of the few people who preferred calling him by his full name.

"Hi, Iris," he said back. "I wasn't sure if you remembered our call with Director Kestner in a few minutes."

She sat down at the desk opposite him. "I

remember. I hope he has some good news."

"I think he also wants to talk about…" The phone rang, interrupting him, and he leaned over and hit the speaker phone button to answer. "Director," Frank said. "I've got Iris here with me. How's everything going? Are they still running tests on you?"

"If I have to sit through one more x-ray, I'm going to lose my shit. But other than that, I'm fine," he answered. He sounded a little out of breath and Frank and Iris looked at each other, wondering if it was from the deterioration in his lungs or if the docs had just run him though another cardiac stress test. He'd had two already this week, but he still wasn't ready to give up his Cuaba cigars. "I can't wait till we get the hospital wing finished over there," he added. "Oslo is a nice city and all, but I've had enough of this lab rat treatment. Anyways, Frank, were you able to find that paper I asked about?"

"Yes," Frank answered. "I've got to tell you though, James. This guy seems like a bit of a hothead if you ask me."

"He is," Kestner admitted. "But he's nothing Ethan can't handle. Can you scan his application and email it to me?"

"Sure," Frank said hesitantly. Although he knew that Kestner was right about Ethan. James Kestner was an intimidating man himself in person. He was big and black and muscular. His collared shirts always fit tight around his biceps and chest, hiding the tattoos on his arms. He had a shaved head, and his dark scalp gleamed in the light like he was polished. On his rare days off he was a beer drinking, barbequing, cigar smoking American. But even he wouldn't want to tangle with Ethan Price.

"How's the rest of the construction going?" he asked.

Iris interrupted, wanting to get to the point. "Director. Have you heard from Cameron yet?

"Not yet," Kestner said without expression. "Professor Skull has a bad habit of going MIA on occasion though. Have either of you two heard anything from the DHA?"

"I got an email this morning from someone at the Federal Archives," Iris said. "They're pushing for answers, but they are well familiar with the Professor's reputation, so they aren't pushing too hard. From what I can tell, we have a little time still anyways. It seems like the Department of Home Affairs, who controls the Federal Archives, is having some internal issues with this as well. The FOEN, the Federal Office of the Environment, feels like their toes are being stepped on apparently, and issued a temporary suspension to FA's request for non-citizen dig permits. If we can get some kind of an update from Professor Skull that he has reached the mountain, we can use the suspension to our advantage and turn the tables a bit to buy him a little more time."

"Sounds good," Kestner said. "Hopefully a *little* more time is all he needs."

CHAPTER 3

Aboard the *Glacier Express*

Matteo continued to stare through the icy, blood-streaked window at the gruesome leg dangling from over the crushed edge of the roof. The rest of the train was in a state of panic, and a crazed woman bumped him hard as she ran for the forward exit of the car. He spun around, looking immediately for his family. They were all there, and he could see Emily trying to hold back her frightened tears.

Matteo lifted his hands, palms up in an open gesture for embrace. "Come here," he said. "It's alright." But the assurance in his voice was unconvincing. A man had just fallen from the cliffs above and landed right on top of them. Only God knew how far the fall had been.

Adrian and Emily buried themselves into his chest, but Ben, a curious adolescent with years of gore-stricken video games and bloodthirsty movies embedded in him, couldn't take his eyes off the window. He took the final swig from his beer and tossed the empty glass onto the floor as casually as throwing a feather into the wind. "Whoa." He began to take a step forward when the blood-streaked purple and black foot outside jerked and twitched in a single kick, then went still again. Ben let out a scream and jumped back, colliding with several other passengers and taking them all to the ground with him.

"Ahh! It moved!" he yelled.

A man beneath him pushed and twisted trying to free himself from the pile of people. "What?" he shouted blindly.

"What moved, Ben?" his father asked. "What are you talking about?"

"The leg!" He pointed his finger. "The leg moved! I saw it!"

Matteo glanced momentarily over his shoulder. All was still except for the red trails of blood slowly slithering further and further down the cracked glass. "That happens sometimes. It's not anything to be afraid of." Although inside he was curious. *What if he's still alive?* Suddenly the panic started all over again. *We need to help him! We need a doctor! His back is surely broken. I'll make a stretcher. How can we stop the bleeding?* Thought after thought after thought in rapid succession.

The front door of the train car slid open and a man came in. He was wearing the uniform of the railroad and everyone turned to him for answers. "Is anyone hurt?" he asked loudly.

Dozens of voices erupted from the car, each new voice just encouraging the next voice to be louder, in a never-ending battle to be heard, until finally the commotion was nearly worse than the panic. Matteo had to do something. He moved a man aside and stepped up to the conductor. "I don't think so," he told him. "What about the man who fell? What if he's...?" The somber look in the conductor's eyes was enough to let Matteo know that what he was about to ask was impossible. His head drooped a little and his voice got quieter. "How about in the other cars?" he asked, redirecting his question. "Is anyone hurt there?"

"No. the other cars are fine, just confused," the conductor said. "Can you help me? We need to get the body off the roof—right now, before this gets worse." He gestured to the crowd of people looking at them.

"Of course," Matteo said.

The conductor nodded at him. "Thank you. There are two other men outside who can also help. I'll stay in here for a minute and try to calm everybody down and keep them distracted while you three remove the body. Take it to the rear of the train and I'll meet you there. We can put together a makeshift box for him…" He paused. "For, the body. That should work till we get to St. Moritz."

Matteo zipped up the front of his coat and turned to Emily. He could see her between the heads of a few other people. "I'll be right back," he called. "Going to go help with something real quick. I'll be right back."

A worried look flashed over her face, but she knew that her husband would never refuse a chance to help people. He had grown up a devout Evangelical Christian, and all his life he considered the chance to help other people more of a blessing for himself than for them.

Even the first day that the two of them met—

Emily's sister had introduced them after service one Sunday morning at the Reformierte Kirche church in Grindelwald, the town where they had both grown up, and Matteo had walked away from her right in the middle of a sentence to go help an elderly woman when he saw that she was struggling trying to scrape off a layer of ice that had formed on the windshield of her car. Since then they had married, had children, and moved to Italy, just coming back to Switzerland a year ago when Matteo lost his job. His endless desire to help people was one of his best qualities, but right now, at this moment, Emily secretly wished for once he could ignore it—but he couldn't, so she feigned a smile.

Outside the train, darkness was quickly creeping in. Only a sliver of sunlight still remained—squeezing through the peaks to the west and casting a narrow beam of light across the train car in front of them. Matteo was thankful that the remaining light was not laid across the body. He preferred the darkness now rather than having the evening sky highlighting their grizzly task. Although, the sun took the temperature with it as it dropped out of sight, and Matteo blew a warm breath into his cupped hands as he jumped off the steps and into the snow outside.

"Hello," a voice said. The man speaking shown a flashlight onto Matteo's face. "Are you coming out to help us?"

"Yes," he answered, squinting against the light.

The other man outside spoke up. "One of us should climb up onto the roof and try to slide the body down to the other two."

"Do we have anything that we could put in front of the window first?" Matteo asked. "I think we should try and hide this from the passengers if we can." He looked around him trying to get a feel for his surroundings. "Also, do you think we need a fourth person? It might not be so easy for one person to get the body over the edge by himself. The impact may have..." His sentence trailed off.

"Let's see what we can do with just the three of us for now," the man with the flashlight said. "Who wants to climb up?"

"I'll do it," Matteo answered. He was not a huge man, but Matteo was in decent shape and fairly strong for his age and size. He felt like he had as good a chance as any of them at being able to move the man.

"Okay then." The man tossed Matteo another flashlight and said, "Me and Thomas will stay down here and catch the body as you lower him down. We'll also try and cover that window with something while you're climbing up to the top. But we shouldn't spend all night on that, so if we can't find something in the next couple minutes, I say we proceed anyways just to get this train moving again."

Matteo didn't disagree, so he turned and walked away, scanning the train for an access ladder to the roof. He shone his flashlight over the back of the train car—nothing. So, he turned and made for the forward end, struggling a bit to pick his feet up out of the snow with each step.

At the front of the car he found the ladder. The flashlight was too big for him to hold in his teeth, so he stuffed it awkwardly into his front pocket, leaving the beam shining straight up against his side, and began the climb up.

Once reaching the top rung, he pulled the flashlight out and set in on the roof before hauling himself over the edge. He stood and brushed the loose flakes of snow off his pants and picked the flashlight back up. Ahead of him, the light illuminated the darkness, but revealed nothing. All he could see from the end of the car was the roof of the train and a light dusting of snow that was starting to fall from above. The body should be just a little more than halfway down the length of the car, he knew. So, he cautiously started walking, keeping the beam of his light focused a few feet in front of him. An acrid stench began filling his nostrils and he held back a sudden urge to gag.

After a few more steps, he began to see the wrinkles of the roof where the metal had started to collapse. Then abruptly the wrinkles dipped into a crushed depression that sunk down nearly two feet. The cave-in was exactly the size of a body. But— there was no body.

"What the..." Matteo quickly raised the beam of light and swung it first in front of him then to each side and over the edge of the train. Then he pointed it back into the hole. Blood covered the stretched and bent metal but there was nothing else there. His heartrate spiked. "Hey! Did you guys pull him down already?" he called to the two men below.

The man below retuned a flashlight beam to Matteo. "What?" he called.

"Did you guys pull the body down already?"

"Pull the body down," one of them said confused. "No. We're ready when you are."

"Thomas," the other man said. "Look." He changed the direction of his light from Matteo to the empty V-shape now in the roof where the body had been.

Matteo was filled with fear and confusion. Maybe the man had been alive after all and had somehow managed to move. If so, he had to still be up here on the roof somewhere—or possibly on the ground just below. He must be badly injured though and certainly couldn't have gone far.

"Check all around the train," Matteo said. He raised his beam of light and slowly started scanning the roof in front of him. Nothing. Changing directions, he let the light sweep over the snow-covered field on the left side of the train, beyond the two men down there. The river was about 30 yards out, and past that, the base of a mountain peak. Matteo could see nothing.

Then he turned. On the right side of the train was another snowy field, although shallower. It only went out about 20 feet, then got consumed by brush and cottonwood trees.

His heart pumped, and a drop of sweat

appeared on his forehead, even in the cold, and ran down the side of his face. The last tiny sliver of the setting sun cast a thin line over the area, and in the white of the snow, he saw—not a pattern of footsteps like he had been leaving—but a jagged, uneven path of powder with a raised bank on each side and streaks of red, as if something had been injured and drug, leading away from the side of the train and disappearing into the forest beyond.

The sunlight faded out.

Justin Hyde

CHAPTER 4

60° N, 0° Longitude—The Prime Meridian

A few minutes before the sunset, the small outline of a distant cargo ship traveling the Northern Sea Route was barely visible from the coastline just outside of Meridian. It was probably too early in the season for the route to be iced over, but the big unstoppable ships were capable of smashing through layers upon layers of ice in order to reach their destination.

Frank admired the determination of the crew and the strength of the vessel, and wished he could hear the sound of the mighty ships horn bellowing as it came into port in a few weeks. It was still an awesome sight to see though, even from so far away. Although the chill carried by the evening breeze was sharp in his throat, and he suddenly yearned for a hot cup of coffee.

It was from this very sea that Alpha-Meridian arose. Even the symbol of Alpha-Meridian was a dedication to the Viking past of these waters. A time when open sea wooden longboats and dragon-carved double-keeled warships powered by strong, hard men ruled the seas. Today, the legacy of the Vikings lives on in Meridian—in dedication, if nothing else. The ancient Norse Runic alphabet left behind by these people is where the symbol for A-M spawned. The rune for A, and the rune M

Joined together to form—*Alpha-Meridian*

Alpha: representing the beginning. The schools beginning, the first of its kind, and the beginning of each student's journey. Alpha, for the power and assertiveness for which all who passed through Alpha-Meridian would excel. In numerals, Alpha is number 1.

Meridian: for the Prime Meridian on which the school resides. The center of two halves. The connecting line between sides. In Chinese culture, meridians are known as Jing-luo—pathways for invisible energy. They are fundamentally crucial to one's wellbeing. In fact, they are of such importance that all acupuncture points lie on a body's meridian.

Frank watched the top crest of the sun as it faded out of sight, then turned to walk back to his cottage. Several of the full-time staff members at A-M were given their own private cottages just outside campus. Mainly built from repurposed local materials until new, more permanent cottages could be made. Actually, the main school building itself was currently the only fully completed structure of Meridian. Construction efforts continued almost nonstop, but resources and manpower were hard to come by in such an isolated and remote part of the world.

The students at Meridian, and some of the other staff, stayed in dorms. Students sharing rooms in pairs in the student dorms, and single staff resident rooms in the staff dorms.

Once at home, Frank entered into his living room and dropped onto the couch. He probably should have gone back to his office for another hour or so this afternoon, as sunset on Shetland Island this time of year only meant that it was around 3:30, but he decided he could finish things up remotely today.

He glanced out the window to his left. A hundred feet away or so he could see Professor Skull's cottage. He could see the outside porchlight that was set to automatically turn on after dusk, anyhow. He thought again about how different things were a little over a year ago. *It hasn't even been that long,* he thought. *I guess Professor doesn't sound too bad though.*

Before the rise of Meridian, back when they still operated on their own as Nightcorp International, Cameron Skull was a colonel. Colonel Skull was the second highest ranked, and probably the most respected member of the team. *He's still the most respected,* Frank thought.

Now, *Professor* Skull was mostly a meaningless title. Cameron didn't teach anything. Well, not in a classroom anyways. He was the school's field operative. And until students graduated and could start filling positions, Cameron was basically contracted out through A-M, right now filling a request from the Swiss government. Eventually he would be in charge of the student's internships, but the school was still too much in its infancy for Cameron to assume his role. So instead, he worked mostly alone.

Frank knew that Cameron wasn't home tonight though. Even if the Professor hadn't been lost somewhere in the Alps at the moment, Frank knew that sitting on his butt in his cottage isn't where he'd be either.

Cameron spent most of his time back home in Benton County, Oregon. He had a 14-year-old daughter, Kendall, who he would never dream of leaving. Nor would he consider shipping her out to the middle of nowhere with him either. Sadly, Cameron's wife had been killed in a drunk driving accident on Christmas morning, almost ten years ago, when Kendall was four. The accident wasn't her fault, but it haunted Cameron deeply.

So, he had kept his home in Oregon, and got someone to stay with Kendall for a few days at a time whenever he had to leave. She was responsible, for a teenager, but he still didn't trust her home alone for undetermined periods of time. And unfortunately, this trip was gearing up to be his longest absence yet. But Jake Evans was staying at Cameron's house with Kendall till he got back.

Jake was Iris's ex-brother-in-law. And while a bit clumsy and awkward most of the time, he was trustworthy. Cameron had worked with him before, and Kendall liked him. She preferred Francesco staying with her, when he could—Frank was practically her uncle—but she liked Jake too. The only problem really was that Jake could be like a kid himself sometimes, so they got along well, but also bickered on occasion.

Frank turned his attention to the television, although didn't turn it on. Instead all he saw was himself—the image of himself staring back at him from the shiny black screen. Reflecting brightly on his chest was his pin. Made of a unique alloy of titanium and Inconel, it was the rune A merged into the M—a symbol that was worn by both students and personnel at A-M, showing their mergence with the school.

But Frank's pin was slightly different. His was one of the pins worn only by the elite founding members of Alpha-Meridian. The ones who had crossed over from Nightcorp. It was the rune A merged with the rune M. But not merged into one. On the pin of the originals—the Alpha stood above.

CHAPTER 5

45° N, 7° E.
Elevation – 11,300 ft.

5:45 p.m.—Cameron swung his leg over the top of the overhang. His pack was considered ultralight, by most mountaineering standards, but right now it felt like it weighed 100 pounds. All the muscles from his shoulders, through his arms and into his fingertips strained to pull him onto the ledge.

He undid the clips and pulled an arm through one of the straps of his pack, then immediately rolled over onto his back in the snow, grateful to be lying down. He pulled off his goggles, then the face mask, to let the cool air replenish his lungs without hindrance.

After a few moments he relaxed enough to notice the magnificence of the night sky. The stars and constellations filled the darkness of the universe with a blanket of twinkling lights. A shooting star whizzed by and Cameron made a quick, silent wish. Thinking about all the times he used to tell Kendall to make a wish upon a star, and wondering what she was doing right now?

Cameron knew how rare of a sight this was—to actually see the night sky, totally undiluted by any artificial light pollution. Even crossing the Grand Canyon, down into its lowest points, an almost constant stream of headlamps from thru-hikers brought distraction to the raw beauty of the Canyon after dark.

Something was wrong here too though, he suddenly realized. There was a faint yellowish glow coming from his right. He remained still, only shifting his eyes to the side. The glow was indeed there. For a moment he had thought, or hoped, that it could just be some kind of reflection, or maybe the effect of a natural phenomenon, like a prism. Starlight and ice, smooth and with the right angles could have caused it. But no. It was an electric bulb.

What the hell?

Very slowly he rolled to his side. The yellow light was dim—and distant. From below it had been impossible to tell, but the ledge he had just gotten onto was more than just a few feet deep on the topside like it was underneath. It was a plateau at the top of the mountain. There must have been close to 30 feet of relatively flat ground before the mountain shot up again.

With the moisture in the air from the falling snow, a blurry halo surrounded the glow, but from the looks of it, the light was hung directly from the rock, next to a man-sized rectangular grey metal door leading into the side of the mountain. Like a sealed off cave. There was a sign above the door, but it was too far off to read.

Instincts immediately went into high alert and Cameron's posture went from relaxed to on-guard. He kept himself low to the ground and shifted his body and his gear sideways till he was behind the cover of a small rock formation a few feet away. From his new vantage he could see how the mountain curved just past the steel door. Parked around the curve was a large snow vehicle. Cameron recognized it. It was a Ripsaw EV3 super tank. A light-weight dual track vehicle designed specifically for the harshest conditions—snow, above all. It could carry four passengers over or through nearly any terrain at almost 80 miles per hour. Equipped with over 1000 horsepower and ground penetrating radar to detect crevices and weak spots.

This extreme snow tank also appeared to have a trailer attached to the rear of it. The trailer was not treaded like the Ripsaw was though. Instead it appeared to be just a large sled. The bottom section being a smooth flat-bottom boat-shaped design, but the top was enclosed with a large steel cage. Several of the bars were bent slightly out, like some powerful animal had been captive in it—angry and desperate to escape.

This was very wrong. None of this should be here. There were no records of anyone being on this particular mountain in well over two decades. The last team of adventurers who attempted the ascent was back in the early 90's. But they did not acclimate properly and found themselves suffering from advanced altitude sickness early on, and were forced to turn back before ever reaching the summit. And there certainly were no records of any structures built here.

Cameron debated whether to try and radio

Meridian and let them know what he had come across. He always carried a compact Iridium satellite phone. But he didn't have enough information yet. Francesco had already done his research prior to Cameron's assignment. There were a number of man-made structures this high up in the Alps, mostly mountain huts and cable-car stations, but none of them were in this area. The only other thing this high up was the Sphinx Observatory, at almost 12,000 feet above sea level. But that was nearly 50 miles away.

And another question: How did that Ripsaw get up here? The super tank was built for the toughest terrains and environments, but there was a limit to even its capabilities. This peak was classified as a 5.13d on the American Yosemite Decimal System of difficulty. Which, even to expert climbers, basically meant—good luck.

Suddenly a loud—*tang*—came from the metal door. It opened inward and a small-framed man dressed in heavy white layers stepped out. He shouted something into the cave before closing the door and walking over to the Ripsaw.

It's a woman, Cameron realized. The voice was hard, but feminine. *Wish Iris was here*, he thought. She would have recognized the language the woman had spoken and known right away what she had said. But without being able to get his small digital translator out in time, Professor Skull had no idea.

The headlights on the Ripsaw burst on, but

the vehicle made no sound. It must have been the latest generation of the snow tank, which used a 3-phase induction motor. The same technology invented by Nicola Tesla, and used today in Tesla Motors high-end all electric vehicles.

Silently the treads began spinning in opposite directions and the Ripsaw spun around, swinging the caged sled dangerously close to the edge of the cliff as it did, then headed off around the curve of the mountain till it was out of sight.

Cameron picked himself up into a crouched position and watched for a minute, but nothing else moved. Leaving his pack stashed behind the small rock formation, he moved quickly and quietly towards the metal door and the yellow light hanging beside it. As he neared, the sign above the door started becoming more and more legible, but what he was reading so far made no sense to him.

Finally he was beneath it, standing at the front of the door. He leaned in and tried to listen for any sounds coming from within, but the soft whistle of the breeze outside was enough to blow away anything that he might have heard.

As he always did, Cameron decided to go for it. He reached a hand out and grabbed the cold cylindrical handle of the door, then gave it a small turn and a tug. It didn't budge.

Maybe I should call Frank?

But before he was able to reach for the satellite phone, the now familiar—*tang*— of metal on metal came from the door again and made

Cameron stumble back quickly. Had he been near the edge of the cliff, he would have fallen.

He scrambled back for the cover of a closer pile of small snow-covered rocks. Again, the door opened. This time, Cameron was closer to it, and he could hear a low awful noise coming from within the cave. It sounded like scratching and gurgling and moaning all in one. Then an angry, guttural roar.

What the hell was that?

The man who had come out, walked to where the Ripsaw had been parked. He glanced around the bend, then turned back to the cave entrance. But before entering, he stopped at the door and looked around.

There were obvious tracks in the snow from his retreat, and Cameron's hand went for his pistol in anticipation of a fight. It was very unusual for him to be unarmed. He rarely traveled anywhere without at least his Heckler & Koch VP9 on him. But even as a compact 9mm, the guns size and weight was an unnecessary burden in the Alps. Even a threat from wildlife was nearly nonexistent at over 2 miles up, so on this trip he had left it behind. *Damn*, he thought. He reached for one of the ice axes still hung from his belt instead, but luckily the man went inside and closed the door behind him before Cameron got it unclipped.

Not sure of what his next move should be, Cameron looked up again at the sign over the door. He still had an obligation to the Swiss government, but he was also unable to ignore this new discovery.

Inside, he knew, that whatever was going on here was not anything good.

On the small rusted sign riveted above the metal door, it read:

<u>**Cas9**</u>
CONTAINMENT FACILITY

CHAPTER 6

With the man back inside, Professor Skull decided to once again press his luck and try the door. He crept back through his tracks in the snow to the metal entrance. Again, reaching out for it, he grabbed hold of the cylindrical handle and turned, but just like the last time, it didn't move.

Why lock the door? Cameron thought. *Who are they afraid is going to come in, way up here at the top of the mountain?*

Then he remembered the sounds he had heard coming from within, and he realized something. Perhaps the door wasn't locked to keep people out. Perhaps the door was locked to keep something in. He realized something else as well. He had seen the door open twice now, so he was sure—the door swung in.

In nearly all non-residential construction, both ancient and modern, doors swung out. The direction of motion was intentional. That way, in the event of a fire or other emergency, someone running for the exit could charge the door and it would open, rather than having to pull the door towards themselves and retreat a step or two back into a possibly unsafe space.

It was now undoubtedly clear—this was a prison.

Containment facility.

But this realization did nothing to change his

situation. The door was still locked, and he still didn't know what was behind it. But he did intend to find out.

Another growling sound came from within, followed by a muffled voice and a loud bang.

There has to be a way in, he thought. If this place was meant just to keep something from getting out, then why risk an external lock? Why even make it possible to lock yourself out in the life-threatening cold of the mountaintop outside? He began to search around. He looked with his eyes and felt with his fingers, but nothing caught his attention.

Out of frustration he reached again for the handle. Nothing happened; however, this time his fingers felt something along the back of it.

A trigger.

Of course! His initial thoughts were right. The door could not be locked from the outside—BUT, it was designed to never open accidentally. It required two intentional actions to unlock. A double safety, similar to the way most machinery operated. The first action in this case was to squeeze the trigger on the rear of the handle. The second action, Cameron already guessed, was to pull the handle out. An outward pull was something that could not easily occur naturally. A falling rock would push the handle down. Likewise, an animal could push in or push down with a paw, or could even push up with their head. But pulling was only done with human intent.

His finger squeezed the trigger and he could feel it click in place. Then slowly he began pulling the handle towards himself. It resisted and he pulled a little harder till it hinged out and the clasp inside the door released—*tang!* Cameron kept pulling but the door itself didn't move. He had to keep one hand pulling out on the handle, and use his other hand to push the door in. It was an awkward combination of opposing forces, but another very efficient way of preventing accidental or unwanted openings.

One disadvantage of an inward swinging door though, at least it was a disadvantage for him at the moment, was that he could not peek in. Opening the door only a few inches did not give him enough clearance to see anything inside, whereas if the door swung out he would have been able to look through the cracked opening much easier.

He was going to have to just go for it. But he wasn't completely reckless. He stood motionless by the partially opened door and listened. Inside he could hear the low moans and shuffling sounds that he had heard earlier, along with some wet, slurping kind of sound. But more overpowering than the noise was the smell. It was like a bog, or a backed-up sewer, and he instantly wanted to gag, but forced himself to control it.

There were no signs of any people though. From the best he could tell, the only thing on the other side of this door, whatever it was, was not a person.

He stood up straight and swung open the door.

—

Immediately inside the metal door Cameron saw a terrible sight. A long corridor, straight and poorly lit—lined on both sides with bar covered cells. The back wall of each one was nothing more than a natural rock tunnel in the mountain. No concrete, brick or steel walls, just rock and dirt with a metal bar front.

What is this?

Immediately the noises inside grew louder. Not just from the door opening, but as a personal response to his intrusion.

Cameron looked into the first cell to his right. Inside there was a man, curled up on the floor in the fetal position near the back corner of the small space. The man's head was tucked into his knees and he did not look up at Cameron at all. He could have been sad, or asleep, or scared, or dead. Skull couldn't tell.

Similarly, in the cell opposite, the one to Cameron's left, was another man. This man however was clearly frightened. He also was curled up near the back wall of his dungeon, but he shivered at the sight of Cameron, and flinched every time Cameron moved. The man's clothes were tattered, and Cameron could see the white cotton of bandages underneath parts of his ripped shirt.

After a few moments though, the prisoner must have suspected that Cameron was not associated with the group who held him. "Help me," he said quietly. "Please... help me."

Skull walked a few steps further into the cave. There was nothing he could do for the man right now. Shifting his eyes he could see a light coming from somewhere up ahead, but without even moonlight coming in from the door behind him anymore, it was dark at this end of the prison, and Cameron wished he had unpacked his headlamp from his bag outside before entering.

Inside the next cell beyond the frightened man was another man, although in far worse shape. This prisoner in the next cell had been badly injured. Blood stained bandages wrapped most of the man's torso—but they were in desperate need of changing. Each of the bandages was crusted with dried blood and yellowish-green stained patches of festering puss. Surely the man had severe infections throughout his entire body now.

Opposite him was again another man, not quite as badly injured but much more malnourished. His dry skin clung to his bones and his lips were painfully cracked.

The whole place was a scene straight out of a horror film.

Suddenly, soft voices started echoing from deeper in the cave. This time Cameron had time, and he pulled a tiny, in-ear live translator from the breast pocket of his coat and pressed the device into his ear. After a few seconds the small unit detected the language and converted it to English in real time. Cameron clicked the volume up button, but half of the sound that was intensified was the moaning and scratching of the captives, and Cameron had to concentrate hard to hear the men speaking.

"It doesn't matter anymore how it escaped," the first voice said. "He fell off the damn edge!"

"Relax," said another voice. "I've already told you that there is nothing around for miles. He probably exploded into a puddle of guts as soon as he hit the bottom."

The first man responded back quickly, "You don't know that. These things aren't like us. If you're wrong, then this mountain is going to be flooded with..."

The tiny receiver in Cameron's ear cut out and filled with static. He scowled and returned it to his coat pocket.

After a moment's hesitation, he slowly crept to the next set of cells in the tunnel, in the direction of the voices—already afraid of what he would find there. And again, unfortunately, his instincts were right. A woman stood in the center of the next cell with her back towards him and her head hung to the ground. She was naked from the waist up and wounded, but no attempt had been made to treat her. An open gash ran up the length of her spine. The blood had tried clotting at some point, but looked more as though it had dried purely from prolonged air exposure rather than from the platelets in her body. The rest of her body as well was a purplish-green color.

Cameron took a step towards the bars on her

cell when again he heard the voices coming from the doorway down the corridor—from the same room where the light was coming from. He looked over his shoulder, then back at the woman. She was now facing him.

He jumped back in alarm. The abrupt move caused the two ice axes on his belt to cling off each other and the noise triggered whatever was in the cell behind him to react, and a hand reached through the bars and grabbed him. Cameron spun and grabbed the arm that was grabbing him—his fingers pushing easily into the decayed flesh until they actually punctured the man's skin, and dark, almost black, blood began oozing out.

Dear God.

Cameron shook himself loose of the man—if it was a man—and backed away, horrified. The creature looking at him was only the remnants of a human being. It was rotten and decomposing like a blackened month-old tomato, and smelled even worse. It growled and hissed and snapped it's jaws open and shut as it tried to get at him through the bars. It's wounds, and even the newly broken skin of its arm, seemed to be completely unnoticed by it.

It's a fucking zombie.

CHAPTER 7

41° N, 15° E.

**Basilica Santuario di San Michele Arcangelo
Mount Gargano, Italy**

The young boy looked up at the emblem on the priest's robe. It was a red and yellow circle with a wavy-bladed sword stitched onto the left-hand side. The boy, who was maybe 8 years old, had seen his mother wear something similar before, except her patch was blue and yellow, not red and yellow. All he knew was that it had something to do with the church.

The priest looked down at the boy and smiled. "Do you know what that is?" he asked him.

The boy shook his head.

"It is the emblem of the Micheliti Fathers. The guardians." There was pride in the priest's voice, and a matching spark of pride lit up in the boy's eyes at the word *guardian*. "Do you want to be one of us when you grow up?"

The boy nodded and the priest smiled.

"Where are your parents, son?"

Justin Hyde

The boy turned his head and pointed to his mother a few steps away. She was looking through some papers near the doors leading out of the grotto. The priest recognized her.

"Oh, is that your mother?" he asked. But before the boy could answer, the priest knelt down and spoke softer to him—but inside the cave cathedral, even whispers echoed. "Has she ever told you the story of this place?" he asked.

Once again, the boy responded without words. He shook his head from side to side and the priest wondered if perhaps the boy was mute. "Well," he began. "A long, long time ago, a very rich nobleman had a herd of bulls. One day, one of his bulls got out and ran away. When the man went to look for it, he found it standing at the mouth of this cave."

The priest gave the child a moment to look around at the giant space surrounding them. The church had been built right inside the rock. The altar itself, and all the adornments, were shaped to fit the natural curves and beauty of the stone without altering it.

"The man was angry at his bull for running away," the priest continued. "So, he took out his bow and arrow and was going to shoot the animal. But when he let loose the arrow, it did not pierce the bull. Instead, the arrow turned in the air and hit him!"

The boys mouth fell open.

"Well, the man was hurt, but he did not die.

He was very scared by what had happened. So, he went to see the Bishop, to tell him what had happened too. The Bishop listened to the man, and then after, he ordered three days of prayers to be said here. But the Bishop and his men were scared to come inside, so they all said their prayers right outside." He pointed over the boy's shoulder towards the entrance to the cave.

"Then what happened?" the boy asked. He was able to speak after all, and was intrigued and impatient to hear the rest of the story now.

The priest continued. "On the third day, Saint Michael came down from heaven and appeared to them. He told them that it was okay to go into the cave. He said to them, 'I am the Archangel Michael. And I am always in the presence of God. This cavern is sacred to me, and I have chosen it. There will be no shedding of blood here. Where the rocks open wide, men's sins will be forgiven, and what is asked here in prayer will be granted. So, go into the cave in the mountain, and dedicate this place to Christ.'"

The boy's mother walked over to them. "Padre Santé" she said in greeting. "How are you?"

Father Santé stood. "Isabella, good to see you. I didn't know you had a son. I was just telling him the story of the noble and the bull."

"I never get tired of that story," Isabella said. She ruffled the hair on her boy's head. "This is my son, Alberto."

"It's not just a story, though" Santé said. "It is the truth."

"And that is why I wear the crest of the Soure Michelite. To guard this place, same as you."

Father Santé brought his hands up to his chest, grinned and tipped his head to her.

Isabella reached for her son's hand. "Come now, Alberto. We should be going." She began walking towards the exit. "See you on Sunday, Father," she said over her shoulder.

—

Bastian Santé left the church an hour after Isabella and Alberto. But first, he had gone deeper into the cave—into the crypts—to the place that he guarded above all others. A place that only he and one other knew about.

The crypts of Santuario di San Michele Arcangelo dated back to the byzantine era and were abandoned sometime in the 13th century. They weren't rediscovered until the 1900's, but the excavations into the earth below the cave-church were not thorough. Much was missed. In fact, the crypts were made up of only two main rooms. In the larger of the two rooms were twin sarcophaguses, one of which has still never been opened to this very day. When excavating the crypts, most of the archeological focus had gone into deciphering the ancient runic texts that were inscribed on the walls, rather than into furthering the dig.

And while the presence of runes was indeed interesting, they were a distraction from the real treasure here. And so, Bastian Santé was able to uncover the small, secret chamber on his own—one year ago. At first, the opening to the hidden alcove was very small; less than six inches round, and easily missed. But with the help of one of his followers they made short work of enlarging the hole to a size just big enough to allow the width of his shoulders to squeeze tightly through.

Tonight though, he had not entered the antechamber. He had just stood at its opening and praised the miracle within.

He took in a final excited breath before leaving the crypt and heading up and out of the church. He was expected to be somewhere soon and was already going to be a bit late.

Outside, there was no actual parking lot for the church, but his car was parked along the street. He clicked the button on his keyring and the familiar two-beep tone of his Chrysler's doors unlocking sounded off, and the headlights came on automatically when he put the car into gear and drove away. Although, he really wasn't going anywhere. It was more just re-parking than anything. A hundred yards from the church was Castello di Monte Sant'Angelo.

The castle of Sant'Angelo was a dilapidated fortress that served no real purpose anymore. Its origins were largely unknown, and over the centuries it had been repurposed into everything from a prison, to storage facility, and eventually to nothing more than a backdrop for photographs. It was now owned by the municipality of Monte Sant'Angelo, and basically abandoned.

Father Santé had negotiated a lease of the property for church use, 10 months ago. He had spent the first 3 months making portions of the interior livable for the small staff that he intended to house there. The next 3 months following that was the construction of the research and anechoic testing labs. Finally, 6 months ago, he was able to start putting some of the repurposed castle to use— quickly finding out however that he was also going to need some isolation rooms. So, it was just in the last 2 months that things finally got under way. As expected though, there was going to be a lot of trial and error throughout the process.

He re-parked his car near the short front-entrance bridge leading into the main floor of the castle. The outer doors had been replaced many years ago with modern steel doors to keep out vandals and looters, and Bastian had a key.

Once inside, he made his way through the front room, down a hall and around the few turns that led to the testing rooms. Entering them required passing through a buffer room. Bastian opened the first door, entered the room and then pulled the door closed behind him—ensuring that it was fully sealed before reaching for the second door. It was designed so that both doors could never be open at the same time. Ever. One door needed to be fully shut before the other could open, ensuring the soundproofing of the interior room was never violated.

CHAPTER 8

44° N, 7°E
Luserna San Giovanni, Italy
11:13 p.m.

The moon was not full, nor was it completely gone. Two unsavory men used what little light it provided to sneak onto the homestead, unnoticed. The small farm was home to a restaurant owner and his family—wife, son, and daughter. The children were close in age, 10 and 12, and homeschooled by their mother.

Over the years, the 150-year-old farmhouse had fallen into a mild state of disrepair. The family grew olives but could not compete with the large organic olive oil groves of Tuscany, to which visitors and tourists flocked by the boatloads, so the man of the house supplemented the family income as best he could with his restaurant in town. But with him gone most days, and the mother busy schooling the children, the family often had to bring in help, in the form of foreign laborers, to help around the property. The temporary workers would tend the groves as well as aiding in upkeep and repair of the house, in exchange for room and board, meals, Italian lessons, and the experience of living a few months abroad.

The last of the workers had extended his summer stay though, and had only just left two days ago. Which is why the two men hadn't come for the girl last week. Tony, and his brother Sergio, were not homeless, technically, but were at the very bottom of the social classes and were always willing to do just about anything for some quick cash. Tony was wearing an Italian style wool flat-cap and a grey wool coat that night. He had a dark face, from both dirt and a weeks' worth of unshaven growth.

"Va Bene, lascia andare," he said to his brother.

Sergio nodded.

Slowly, they worked their way through the trees and up towards the house, keeping in the shadows and out of the moonlight as much as possible. The young girl, they had found out, had her own room on the second floor of the old home. Surely she would be fast asleep by now, as would the whole family.

"Maybe we should take the boy instead," Sergio said quietly. He was beginning to have some feelings of nervousness and doubt as the homestead came within sight.

Tony turned to him with an angry look that penetrated even the darkness, and Sergio knew better than to suggest it again. "We were told to get a girl, so we are getting a girl," he said.

"Yeah, but…" The last of Sergio's sentence never got further than his mind. *It doesn't have to be this girl.*

Their instructions had been very simple. Basically, just take a girl, any girl, under 13 years old— "Teenagers have lost their innocence," was the reasoning—and make sure that they did it far away. 600 miles seemed plenty far away, but now Sergio wished that he was a million miles away. *I shouldn't have agreed to this*, he thought. But the promise of a big payday later had made the idea sound good back in Monte Sant'Angelo two weeks ago, when they were first approached with the proposition. But now it was real, and he couldn't shake the already festering feeling of regret building up inside him.

Despite his feelings now though, he followed his brother through the trees, just like he followed him everywhere. Soon, the old two-story wood and stone house came within reach.

Tony paused under the last of the cover of the trees and looked with delight at the side of the building. Two of the outer walls were lattice and vine covered—ideal for climbing. And at the second floor above was a narrow balcony that stretched the entire length of the home. *This is going to be too easy*, he thought.

He signaled for Sergio to wait before following, then snuck over to the wall and grabbed a handful of the vine branches. They ruffled under his grip, but not loud enough to disturb anyone upstairs, so he slowly began pulling himself up. Once reaching the top, he struggled but managed to get a leg swung over the railing and hauled himself over. Then he waved a hand to his brother down below to follow.

Sergio hesitated. If he had a way out of this, he would take it. But without seeing one, he climbed the wall and joined Tony at the top.

The first window they came to on the upper floor was cracked open to let the fresh night air flow into the stuffy room. Both men peered inside. There was a queen size bed with two bodies asleep on it. *Mommy and daddy.* Tony took a small pointed dagger from the inside of his coat and spun the blade around loosely in this hand.

Sergio's heart raced. He was now scared, not just nervous. This was wrong, and he tried to hide the shakiness in his hands and knees as he watched his brother—not wanting to know what terrible thoughts were going through his mind, and hoping that he would not act on them.

Finally, Tony motioned with his head for them to keep moving. The floorboards of the old home squeaked under foot and he turned around and gave his brother another mean look. "Step to the edge," he said. He pointed to the corner where the floor and the wall met, then waited a moment for any signs that they had woken someone.

All remained silent, and a sense of confidence began building up inside Tony. He felt sure of himself now that this plan would go smooth, and that in a couple days he and Sergio would be heavy in the pocket and binging themselves on liquor and women. As much as his brother was a nuisance, he was still family. And in Italy, family was everything.

As the feeling of optimism continued to grow, so did his cockiness and his excitement, and he let the sharp blade in his hand drag and scratch along the top of the balcony handrail as he slowly walked to the next window.

—

Inside the room, little 10-year-old Becca slept peacefully—lost in a playful dream about the puppy her father had promised to get her for her birthday next week—and so she did not see the man appear outside her window. His round, dark figure, silhouetted by the moonlight, shown through the translucent curtains of her room, but did not enter. Her window was not left open at night like her parents.

Tony pulled lightly on the window frame, testing it. When it did not open, he placed the point of his blade between the window and the wall and was about to pry it when a hand with large fingers grabbed him by the wrist. He pulled away quickly and turned the knife to his brother's chest, burning with anger.

Inside the room, little Becca squeaked and rolled over onto her side. A smile traced the bottom of her face like she had just been licked by a waggy-tailed puppy. Maybe she had.

Sergio whispered to his brother, but Tony was disgusted by the pathetic pleading of his voice. "Tony, let's not do this. She's gonna wake up. It's not worth it. The whole damn house is going to wake up."

"Fogett'about'it," Tony said in his thick Italian

accent. "That's what you're here for." Then his voice got a little louder and he spoke with a casual tone. "I'll handle the girl." He looked back to the closed window. "And you handle the rest."

Sergio almost threw up. He was bigger and stronger than his little brother, but he didn't have the courage to challenge him, mentally or physically, and so he stood by silently as his brother popped open the window.

The room immediately sucked in the cool air and the curtains fluttered. Tony lifted his leg and stepped over the window ledge as easily as if he were using the front door. With the knife still in his hand, he paused at the edge of the bed. What did Bastian Santé want with a little girl anyhow?

He watched her—happy in her dream. Her curly brown hair was draped over her cheek, and the covers of her bed were pulled up just high enough to leave the bare skin of her shoulder exposed. Tony watched her some more. She wiggled. He thought about her. Bad things. Things that even he knew were bad. But then he thought—*Maybe Father Santé is even sicker than I am.*

Justin Hyde

CHAPTER 9

60° N, 0° Longitude

Iris continued banging on the front door of Francesco's cottage. "Frank!" she yelled. "Frank are you in there? Wake up. I need to talk to you. It's urgent."

Francesco rolled over and checked the time on the clock on the nightstand. Since cell reception was terrible in this isolated part of the world, he had gotten in the habit of just leaving his phone charging on the kitchen counter at night. The campus of Alpha-Meridian had its own amplifiers and booster tower, so as long as you kept your phone in field-test-mode, you could usually get at least -60dBm of signal, which on Frank's phone was a solid 4 bars. But just off campus it dropped to dirt and if he could get 1 bar by standing near his front door, he was lucky.

Why didn't she call the land line? he wondered.

The time displayed on the two-arm analog clock said midnight. Or close to it. He still had sleep in his eyes, and the exact minute wasn't important enough for him to spend time adjusting focus on.

"Hang on, Iris. I'm coming," he said, as he put one leg through his pants.

"Frank!" she yelled again.

She never, or very rarely, called him Frank, and he could tell now that something was more than

72

a little wrong. He quickly got his pants pulled up and buttoned, then went straight for the door, barefoot and wrestling a tank top over his head on the way. He pulled it open and saw Iris standing there. She was a mess. She had recently cut her blonde hair into a short, but long for the style, pixie cut, but now it looked more like a lawnmower cut. She had deep red around her eyes and on her nose, and Frank new that she had been crying.

He pulled her in and gave her a tight hug. "My God, what's wrong? What happened?" he asked.

Her sobbing got worse in his embrace. She cried for a second and then lifted her head from his shoulder. "Cameron is dead," she said.

Frank almost fainted. "Wh… what?

She pulled herself together a little bit. "A call just came in from the Cantonal police commander of Valais, in Switzerland. He said that a man fell from the mountain tonight." She paused. "Cameron was the only man on that mountain."

Oh no, Frank thought. That was true. He had done his research as well, and Professor Skull *was* the only man who should have been anywhere on that mountain right now. He swallowed hard. "What else did they say?"

Before Iris could answer him, Francesco's mind went to Kendall. *Oh God, why?* Kendall was now an orphan. How could she handle losing her father too, after only just losing her mother a couple years ago? Who would she turn to? Who would comfort her? No one could take the place of her parents. *I will do my best,* Frank thought. A tear escaped his eye.

This was going to be very hard on Iris too though. Over the last year, her and Cameron had grown very close. Their relationship started off rocky when Iris' ex-brother-in-law Jake was captured by Russian STB while working with Colonel Skull in the Czech Republic. Cameron could be rough around the edges at first and Iris had thought of him as a bit of a jerk when they first met. Then things got even worse and she was captured as well for her involvement and association with him. But Cameron had proved to be a very unique breed of man. He was rough and tough, but also, deeper down, kind and caring. But most of all, when he set his mind to something, especially if that something involved the safety of those he cared about, Cameron was determined and unstoppable.

Iris was already speaking when Frank started listening again. "...body landed on top of a train," she said. "They haven't found him yet though, but..."

"Wait," Frank interrupted. "What do you mean they haven't found him yet?"

She looked at him confused. Not because he didn't understand, but because she didn't. Why hadn't she thought that was strange earlier? "I don't really know," she admitted. But she cringed a little at her own next words. "They said that it looked like an animal or something may have pulled his body off the train car and drug him into the forest."

Francesco rubbed his chin, taking a moment

to digest the information. "No one saw that?" he asked. "What kind of animal?" Did they follow the tracks?"

"I don't know any of this," Iris said. "That's pretty much all they told me. I was too upset over the thought of him falling that I couldn't bring myself to think about the details."

Suddenly Frank felt a little guilty for pushing her. "I'm sorry," he said, and gave her another hug. Then he let go, unable to let the details die right now though. Something about this didn't make sense to him, and he couldn't just accept the fact that Cameron might be dead, without an explanation or understanding. "Did the police leave a callback number by any chance," he asked.

Iris nodded and wiped her nose on her sleeve. "I'll send it to you." She reached into her pocket and took out her phone, then hit a few buttons on the display and sent the Cantonal commander's number to Frank through a text message. But then she saw a little red circle with the number 1 on it, over the app logo of her email. She clicked the button and began reading.

"Thanks," Frank said. "Why don't you come in and sit down for a while?"

Iris started walking towards the couch in Franks living room, still reading through the email on her phone. "Frank," she said, as she sat down.

He turned and looked at her.

"Listen to this," she continued. She read the email out loud:

To: JKestner@alphameridian.com
CC: IWhilhelmsson@alphameridian.com
From: LAwapuhi@kpd.gov
November 19, 2019.
11:29 p.m.

Director Kestner,

My name is Lea Awapuhi. I am with the county of Kauai police department and Investigative Services Bureau. I have been tasked by my department, and the Hawaiian Department of Public Safety, to reach out for assistance in an outstanding case from June of last year. In short, a small hunting party went missing in the rainforest last summer. Two days ago, however, one of the men suddenly turned up. From the looks of him, he had been pretty badly hurt at some point. We don't think any of the other men that were with him survived, unfortunately. I will save you those details though. That's not the reason for my email. I am contacting you because the government of Hawaii is hoping to get some assistance in researching a lead that we got from the man's testimony, and possibly authorizing an excursion into the rainforest to investigate whether or not his statement actually holds any truth.

I cannot release any other details at this time, without acknowledgment from you and your staff confirming your willingness and ability to assist. We will of course have to hold you to a non-disclosure agreement, as this is a very sensitive matter.

Awaiting your response,

CSS, Lea Awapuhi

"I wonder what that's about," Iris said.

Francesco could see that she was doing everything in her power to keep it together. But the distraction of the email helped to free her mind of the painful image of Cameron. He sat down on the sofa beside her. "Cameron isn't dead," he said softly.

She turned to him with hate. How dare he even say something so hurtful. Was he trying to give her false hopes and prolong her suffering?

"I know you love him," Frank said. "You never say it, but everyone can see it. But he is my best friend. I am hurting too." He looked deep into her watery eyes. "I know Cameron. And I can feel it. Somehow, I just know he is okay." He didn't add the words, "They haven't found his body" but both of them were thinking that in the back of their minds.

"Let me take over with the Swiss," he continued. "You need to focus yourself on something else." He looked at the phone in her hands. "Get ahold of Director Kestner and see how he wants to handle this new situation. Without Cameron..." He paused. "With Cameron in the field already, we aren't prepared to send anyone else out. The students still have a long way to go."

She could tell that Francesco wasn't going to take no for an answer, so she nodded her head in agreement, and prayed that he was right.

CHAPTER 10

41° N, 15° E.

Bastian Santé opened the door to the Cas9 In Vivo testing room. Over the past two months he had played with dozens and dozens of people, all of them being disappointments in the end.

He walked past the naked form of his last experiment, still lying on the table. It was a woman in her 20's who he had had brought here from the back-alley streets of Rome. She wasn't the first to have died—but at the same time, she was. Most had simply—changed.

Not even glancing at her though, he went and picked up the test results from the stainless-steel table next to her and walked back out of the room. At this hour, all was quiet in the castle, and his footsteps echoed as he walked through the Great Hall towards the Castle Keep and the stairway that led up to his private rooms.

Bastian's rooms were a mix of office, laboratory and bedroom. He closed the door behind him as he entered, and immediately scowled at how cold it was in the room. The testing rooms downstairs were lined with acoustic studio wedge-foam to keep them soundproof—as people had a tendency to scream—which by chance also added a layer of insulation to them, typically keeping them at a semi-agreeable temperature. But the bare stone walls of the upstairs floor of the castle did little to insulate against the November chill.

He sat down at his desk and thumbed through the papers he had collected from the room with the dead girl—thinking back through all the different testing that had been done over the last few months, and wondering why none of it had worked the way he wanted it to yet.

What do I need to do? What am I missing?

CRISPR-Cas9 Genome Editing. Bastian had stolen the new technology from world leading scientists who were too concerned with abiding by conventional laws and regulations. The DNA restructuring premise of the Cas9 protein was so simple however, that Bastian was easily able to replicate it on his own. And to his own levels, and for his own purposes.

The acronym stood for Clustered Regularly-Interspaced Short Palindromic Repeats—CRISPR. In the outside world, it was facing heavy resistance from activist groups, media, and even some scientists from notable schools like Stanford. Even the Chinese government had recently launched a small war against it, despite some of their own trials with it.

Supporters of it however, argued that the benefits of being able to genetically alter living DNA was a major game changer in everything from agriculture to health and safety. Already, specific genome sequencing of crops like wheat and tomatoes were showing far superior nutritional values over any other produce in their class.

On the global health level, molecular biologists at Imperial College in London had shown successful results of treating malaria by using CRISPR technology to genetically modify the DNA of infected mosquitos. The results of the test also showed that female mosquitos became infertile, while the male mosquitos continued to pass on the mutated gene.

But it was the simplicity of CRISPR that really made it unique. Other similar technologies were out there, such as ZFN and TALENs, but they required complex protein engineering and were very costly and time-consuming to perform, and often inefficient. Whereas Gen2 CRISPR Cas9 used bacteria to transport RNA and simply redesign or clone already existing protein compounds. Basically, it made it possible to alter, add or remove genetic material in the genome of a living organism.

It worked by attacking a virus with bacteria carrying the Cas9 enzyme. The RNA segments held by the CRISPR arrays target specific areas of DNA. They then cut into the DNA strand and replace that section of DNA with the modified code.

But while the puppet scientists and biologists of the mainstream world were busy playing around with vegetables and bugs, Bastian Santé had bigger plans. To achieve what he wanted, things needed to go much further than that.

Human trials.

And even though there were a few subtle experiments going on with humans outside of Bastian's castle, most of them were much too passive to take the big leaps that were necessary for true greatness. Even in large respected places like the U.S. and Canada, some patents were starting to be awarded for treatments of human diseases like multiple myeloma, using CRISPR technology. Childs play in Bastian's mind. The only tests he thought that were being done that had any true value for the world were from a Chinese neuroscientist, who announced at last year's International Summit on Human Genome Editing in Hong Kong that he had successfully born twin girls from embryos that he himself had created. Genetically modified human babies with superior characteristics and immunities than anyone before them.

Bastian had thought about kidnapping the man and bringing him here to Monte Sant'Angelo. But eventually decided that the neuroscientist/anti-bioethicist was the only one of any real value to the rest of the world, and that maybe by simply following the progress he made on his own, Bastian could still benefit.

Still, even with all the resources and knowledge readily available, and the obvious exponential advancements it offered, no one dared to take delivery applications in humans any further than topical creams and edible capsules. One or two bold scientists out there somewhere may have toyed with injecting CRISPR through the ear canal, or even through skin grafts, but even the slightest mention of delivering the protein through any surgical method, even outside the body, was an abominable thing to say. Just the thought could strip someone of their degree and all credibility in the science world.

Father Bastian Santé however, didn't even see the reason to perform the process Ex Vivo, or even In Vitro. He did everything direct to the body— In Vivo. Cutting straight into a person and surgically delivering the enzyme exactly where and how he intended.

He stood from the chair at his desk and paced around the room. Maybe a drink would help relax him, along with some sleep. He checked the time on his wristwatch and saw that it was almost 2 in the morning. *A drink first.*

There was a small bar under one of the narrow windows in his bedroom. He unscrewed the top to a bottle of Fernet Branca and poured a small amount into a glass. The dark brown amaro was one of his favorites, and he sipped it slowly to savor its bitter sweetness.

Tomorrow we will try the boy, he thought. *I need a clean spirit. The souls of all the others are too poisoned with sin.*

That had to be the problem. He was sure of it now. And if the boy didn't work, maybe a girl would. He considered girls to be purer anyways. Those two idiots he had recruited a couple weeks ago should be back with one any day now. Little did they know however, that even though the two of them were filthy creatures, he would still use them in the end. *Might as well*, he thought. Then he laughed.

After finishing his drink, he set the glass down

and got into bed.

—

On the bottom floor of Monte Sant'Angelo Castle, a small violin spider watched through three pairs of glassy eyes at the sporadic flight of a fly as it buzzed in the quiet space of the chamber. The fly would land, then take to the air, then land again, far above the little spider.

The shy recluse twitched its legs a few times, plucking at a line of its unorganized web like it was the string of a banjo. It knew the web was useless though. The fly would not come to it. Nor did the brown recluse want it to. She was a hunter. She would go after the fly herself, when the time was right.

But this hunt would be her most challenging ever. She was not used to attacking insects with wings. She preferred the taste of cockroaches and crickets. Those that stayed to the ground and could be easily brought down by the speed of her attack. But tonight, she was starving. The cold, colorless room in which she had made her home did not provide for her well. Soon she would have to leave. But right now, the hope of a meal first set her body into motion. Her predatory instincts, and the raw need to hunt, and eat, pulled at her.

The fly landed again, out of sight, and the buzzing stopped. The recluse scurried away from her corner home and towards the giant reflective thing she had scouted that could take her up to where the fly was concentrating. It would be a long climb up, but she could do it quickly, as long as she was not seen while crossing the tile floor to get there.

She weaved left, avoiding a wet obstacle in her path that she had not seen before. The ground was slick enough as it was, but crossing through a puddle was not her style. She was agile and redirected her course easily to avoid it.

Up ahead, the shiny metal of the tower she would climb to reach the fly was getting near. The buzzing above her started again, and she picked up her pace and ran fast for the pillar.

Suddenly another drop of dark liquid exploded in front of her and she reared up on her back legs and bared her venomous fangs—ready to attack and defend herself. But the start wore off quickly and she dropped back into position and took another fast step forward.

Then she was dead.

The heavy purple and bare foot above her had crushed her body into the floor like she wasn't even there. Then another leg slowly swung off the table above, blood oozing down the long slender muscle of its calf. The leg was stiff from rigor mortis and did not bend well at the knee.

The naked girl on the table slowly started to sit up and rise. Neither of her legs worked in the way that was natural or convenient, but she had no memory of what they used to be like anymore, so it was learning to walk all over again. Simple actions

Justin Hyde

though seemed to just occur now on their own. Her body acted without her, and went through the motions that it felt it needed to do in order to fulfill its new desire.

To calm the rage.

CHAPTER 11

45° N, 7° E.
Elevation – 11,300 ft.

"Shhh. What was that sound?"

"One of them is just worked up about something," the other man said in French.

The first guard answered back, "They are like horses. They don't get spooked for no reason."

"Then go look," he said, dismissively.

The guard grunted. The notion of getting up from his chair was not appealing, but he stood anyways and pulled up on the waist of his pants.

Outside the room, Cameron had taken the translator out of his ear already and didn't know what the two men inside were discussing. But he had a suspicion.

Quickly he began looking for somewhere to hide, but there was nothing. The injured woman in the cell across from him was still facing him. She was calm and hardly moving, except for a slight sway in her posture—almost the complete opposite of the violent creature in the cell behind him, who was still reaching an arm through the bars to try and get at him. Further down the corridor, between him and the lighted room were several more rows of cells, with no telling what inside them.

Cameron ran back towards the exit. If he could get outside before the man emerged, he could hide out in the snow again.

"Stop!" a voice shouted.

Cameron froze. *Damn.* So much for that. He put his hands up to the level of his shoulders. To his right, the captive man who had pleaded with him for help a few minutes ago, looked at him through sad eyes. Cameron stared back at him, curiously. The sadness in the man's eyes was not for himself. It was for Professor Skull.

The guard approached him cautiously from the rear. He carried a Sturmgewehr 90 assault rifle. Standard issue for Switzerland armed forces. Although the man was probably either discharged, or the weapon was stolen. No way was this an honest government operation. If such a thing existed.

"Turn around, slowly," he said in English, somehow already suspecting that Cameron was an American.

Suddenly the professor in him was gone, and Cameron relapsed into his old familiar role of Colonel Skull. He did as the man asked, and slowly turned around. "My name is Cameron Skull. I am under the jurisdiction of the Federal Council Defense Minister. This mountain is currently prohibited to traffic of any kind by order of the Land Administration."

The guard hesitated only a moment, then raised the rifle to his shoulder. "How did you get up here?" he asked.

Cameron kept his arms raised but tipped his head in a downward motion to the pair of ice axes on his belt. "It wasn't easy."

Faking indifference, the guard motioned for him to move. "Let's go," he said.

The prisoner beside Cameron sucked in a breath. "You must get away," he whispered. Still on his knees in the cell, he reached out and wrapped his fingers around the bars. "Find a way."

"NOW!" the guard yelled.

Cameron slowly walked up to the guard and stepped around him in the confined hall of the prison tunnel. He was a good 4 inches taller than the man and suspected that the size difference was making the guard extra aggressive. A struggle to prove that his small stature did not make him weak. He shoved the barrel of the rifle hard into Cameron's back as he passed.

With his arms still raised, Skull walked slowly past the next series of cells. "If you're..."

The guard shoved the barrel into his back again, even harder this time, and Cameron was pushed forward. "Shut up."

Then the guard did something very stupid. He opened his mouth and tried shouting for his comrade. "Vale..."

Cameron could not allow him to signal his friend. He needed to keep them separated in order to deal with them safely. Before the guard could finish shouting the name, Colonel Skull spun and grabbed him by the shirt and swung him into the cage of the creature. Immediately the bloody dead hands of the man inside wrapped around him and tore at him like a school of piranhas, and the guard, frantic and terrified pulled with all his might to free himself.

Long sharp nails scratched at him through his clothes. One pierced the side of his face, tearing a line down his cheek. The guard tried to scream but the cut had gone all the way through the side of his face, and blood filled his mouth. Desperate for life, he pushed away once more, this time freeing himself from the deadly grasp. A dry, green fingernail caught in his shirt and ripped off the hand, keeping itself attached to the guard as he jerked himself away.

Cameron dodged out of the guard's way as the man scrambled on all fours and pressed himself as far away as he could manage from the creature. Against the bars across the corridor.

Slowly a figure moved up behind him, and Skull watched as the woman with the long open gash on her back bent over and quietly reached out of her cell. She grabbed the guard by the throat and squeezed hard, pulling and pinning him back against the bars. Her fingers pressed into the soft area around his neck until his throat was completely in her hands. She pulled, and the guard's larynx ripped out from his neck. Blood poured out like a river. The life in his eyes went empty and he stopped resisting, both arms falling limp to his sides. An awful sight.

Cameron looked up. Above and behind the man's body was the woman, still holding the organ in her hand.

She was staring at him.

—

Cameron stared back into the hollow soul of the woman. She made no expression.

But on the floor next to the body of the guard, was the rifle. Cameron kicked it away from the bars with his foot, then bent down and picked it up, checking the chamber and the safety before taking his eyes off the girl and pointing them down the hall.

As suspected, the other guard had heard the commotion and came bursting out of the room. He carried another of the military assault rifles, but Cameron fired first. Three rounds blasted from the gun. Two of them whizzed by the guard's shoulder and ricocheted off a wall somewhere down the cave. But the third round struck him. It splintered the bones near the man's collar, and he dropped his weapon and pressed a hand from his good arm over the wound.

It was a deadly strike. Blood ran like a fountain down the man's side. The bullet, or a bone fragment, must have struck his upper aorta, and they both knew right away that he was only minutes from death.

The man had not yet dropped though. He was still standing, but the threat was gone, and Cameron lowered his rifle. A bubble of blood came out of the guard's mouth like he was trying to speak. He could not. But then, he smiled.

Cameron's eyes opened wide. *What the hell*

is he... Then unexpectedly the guard used the final bit of his strength, before falling to the ground, to reach a hand inside the door of the lighted room where he had just come from. He grabbed hold of a lever on the wall just inside the room, and as his legs gave out and his body fell, he pulled the lever down with him.

A—*click*—followed by several more—*click click click click's*—echoed in both directions, up and down the prison tunnel. The moans and growling sounds of the prisoners increased, and then the squeaking of rusted hinges slowly swinging open filled the dark cavern. The cells were opening.

Oh fuck!

Immediately Colonel Skull turned and ran for the front exit. A set of bars in front of him opened and he shouldered it closed again as he sprinted past. Behind him, he could hear the sounds of pursuit, and ahead of him, more and more feral bodies came into his path. He raised the Sturmgewehr back to his shoulder but hesitated. These men were badly injured prisoners, and he did not want to shoot them. But it became quickly obvious that they were not on his side and had no intentions of letting him leave. He winced, but put two rounds into the heads of two of the men, then jumped over their bodies as he neared the door.

Remembering that the door swung in, Colonel Skull grabbed the handle and pulled it towards him. The door opened and he was about to take a step out into the escape of the frozen wilderness outside, when a familiar plea stopped him.

The man who had been begging for help, and then tried to warn him of the danger, was still sitting at the front of his cell. He looked up at Cameron with despair.

There was no question in his mind though about what he needed to do. Cameron would never leave a man like that behind. He let go of the exit door and grabbed the cell door to his right instead. It opened and he reached down, putting and arm under the man's shoulder and lifting him to his feet. He cringed in pain but did not resist the colonel's help.

"Come on," Cameron said. "I'm getting you out of here." He helped guide the man's arm around his neck. "Hold onto me."

Together they hobbled out of the cage and out the front door. The wind had picked up outside, and an icy chill hit them like an uppercut.

"We have to hurry," Cameron warned. Carrying the rifle still, and the wounded man, he could not reach back into the cave and pull the door closed behind them. And the sounds inside were getting louder. "Those things are right behind us."

Not only had the night grown colder and darker since he had entered the prison, but the snow had also begun falling harder as well, and each footstep was painfully difficult for both of them. Cameron needed his gear though. It was 30 feet out, still hidden behind the rocks. He pulled himself and the man clinging to him in the direction of his bag.

Halfway there, he stopped. The angry sounds behind them had changed. No longer were they echoing the way that they had been. They were now clear direct noises, and Cameron knew that the things had emerged from the tunnel and were now out in the open of the snowy mountain with them.

If he continued for his bag, they would be trapped. The rock formation and his gear were on the edge of the plateau, where he had climbed up from over the cliff below.

It was a hard choice to make, but Colonel Skull turned, abandoning his pack, and started making for the curve of the mountain where the Ripsaw had been earlier. If the snow tank could make it that way, so could he.

Some of the escaped creatures were now in their path though. Able to spread out, they made almost a wall in Cameron's way—many of them unfortunately blocking the chosen route.

"Leave me," the man said. He hardly had even the strength to get out the words.

"I'm going to pretend you didn't just say that," Cameron said back. "There *is* a change of plans though."

He pulled the man through the deepening snow to a different part of the mountain. There were no trees this high up, but this new area was rough terrain. There were jagged rock spikes shooting up from the ground, like a black and white stone forest, with narrow crevices in between them. Hundreds of options and routes to take. Cameron and the man could easily get lost in there.

They weaved through 10 or 20 feet of the stone woods before Cameron stopped them. He set the man down and leaned him against a rock wall. The sounds of moaning and growling were still out there, but further away now. The danger had subsided. The detour into the mountain maze had worked, and Cameron breathed a sigh of relief.

He turned to the man on the ground. "What's your name?"

The man looked up at him, bewildered. Why did it matter what his name was right now? But the gesture was one of friendship, and it was soothing in the midst of the chaos. "My name is Christian," he said.

Cameron extended his hand in proper introduction when a closer noise made him pause and look up again. The creatures were relentless. Instead of shaking Christian's hand, Cameron grabbed it and hauled him to his feet again. "We have to keep moving."

Christian nodded and tried to help move himself. They took the first few steps away from their hiding place, when the unthinkable happened.

Cameron stepped down and the snow beneath his foot fell away, exposing a hole. The two men dropped through the mountaintop, plummeting deep into the darkness within.

CHAPTER 12

45° N, 7° E.
Elevation – 11,100 ft. and dropping.

The mountain swallowed them whole.

Christian felt a panic like he'd never known. Even being locked in a prison with the other experiments, who were far worse than he was and would rip him apart if given the chance, didn't compare to the feeling of the ground being ripped from underneath him. One second, solid footing— and the next, a freefall into utter darkness. His body emptied itself from fear and the sudden sickness of his guts being forced up by his body being pulled down, and he vomited and urinated on himself in midair.

To his side, sharing the space of his fall, Cameron Skull flailed his arms in a desperate attempt to lock onto something stable. His body spun, and then bounced off a side wall of the subterranean tunnel. He grunted loud in agony as his shoulder struck rock—the sound filling the void with a rumble, like it was the voice of God.

The space was not unlike the tunnel that made up the prison above, except this tunnel was smaller in diameter and angled down. It had also been sealed off with snowpack rather than a metal door. The entire mountain must have been riddled with these tunnels. Finally, it leveled out a little and both men hit the snow- and ice-covered edge and continued their decent at a slide instead of a drop.

"Turn around!" Cameron shouted. "Get your feet in front of you!"

Christian had landed on his back with his feet pointing uphill and was now barreling deeper into the mountain—headfirst.

"Turn around!" Skull yelled again. There was just enough moonlight following them down the tunnel to make out Christian, but not enough to see what was up ahead. But Cameron knew that at some point they would reach an end. Whether that end was a wall, a turn or another drop, didn't really matter. It wasn't something you wanted to hit with your face.

Christian tried, but failed. He was too weak from the experiments, and then from his imprisonment, to even move on solid ground, so there was little chance of him controlling himself in this situation now. He moaned as he wrestled with himself and the surroundings—fingers scrapping across the ice trying to find a hold. Nothing was working. Then the angle of the tunnel steepened, and all hope was lost. He began to cry.

Cameron heard him but wouldn't give up hope. "Christian, you have to..." But then he felt the angle change as well, and his speed picked up rapidly.

After ten more feet, Christian hit the wall of a sharp, almost 90-degree turn in the tunnel. The impact crushed his weak body and he could feel bones breaking beneath his skin. He stopped fighting, closed his eyes and began to pray.

Next Cameron hit, feet first. His knees took the brunt of the impact and sent him spinning around the turn. It was only a second later when again the ground was lost beneath him and he went soaring over another edge.

This time the drop was less extreme than the first one—although terrifying nonetheless. Skull hit solid ground below and finally came to a painful stop. His equilibrium was so off balance that it took close to a minute for his head to stop spinning and acknowledge that he wasn't actually moving anymore.

He tried to lift an arm to rub the side of his head, but his shoulder erupted in pain. His eyes closed tight, and his head flung back.

After a few deep breaths he opened his eyes again. The center of the mountain could have been the center of a black hole with as little light as there was at its core, and he doubted if his vision would ever adjust enough to see anything. Blindness was something he had never trained for, and he made a mental note to add it to the student's curriculum at A-M.

He swallowed hard, then managed a whisper. "Christian."

He listened. There was no reply and no other sounds. His only senses that seemed to be working were his sense of touch—it was damn cold!—and his nose—it smelled minerally. The crystalline basement rock of the mountain had an unusual scent. It wasn't exactly the same smell as the limestone caverns of southern Italy, but it was close enough that it brought back a painful memory of his passed wife. He had once found a rock inside one of those Italian caverns that had been naturally worn into the shape of a heart by thousands of years of erosion and water, and he had given the precious stone to his dear Kate on Christmas morning—the day she was killed. A tear escaped his eye, even so many years later.

But now he had Iris. Did he love her as much as he had loved Kate? It was hard to tell. The love was not the same. But yes, he did love her. But if there was no way out of this mountain, he may never see her again either.

He sniffed at the air again. There was something unusual about the scent here. It wasn't just organic rock. There was something else. Something familiar. Something he recognized.

What is that?

He turned his head around in all directions, trying to pinpoint the direction of the smell. It seemed to be coming from everywhere though.

"Christian," he whispered again.

Again, no answer. Cameron began feeling around the front of his coat with his uninjured arm. He always kept a lighter with him when in the snow. Always.

Once upon a time, back in a previous life it seemed, part of his special forces training had included two weeks of phase-three mountain exercises. And one of the things that had been taught in regard to snow travel was to *always* carry a lighter with you. One of the truths about avalanches is that they will tumble and bury you faster than you can say somersault; but another truth is that most people who die in an avalanche do not do so from the impact. Death came from suffocation and hypothermia. Avalanches trapped their victims. And because bodies are denser than snow, they sink.

The general rule was to immediately dig a hole around your head for air. Then, begin to dig your way out. The problem however was that many victims would become so disoriented from the spin and tumbling of the avalanche that by the time they came to a stop, completely underneath the snow, they no longer knew which way was up, and would sometimes die because they would actually dig in the wrong direction, burying themselves further and further into the debris.

That is where the lighter came into play. Cameron was taught that once you got a hole dug for air, you then lit a lighter. *A flame always burns up.*

Fortunately, Colonel Skull had never been put into a position to have to test it—yet. But he was certainly glad that he had followed his instructor's advice. He found the BIC in one of his inside pockets and pulled it out. The first few flicks of his thumb over the striker wheel only produced sparks which burned his eyes in the darkness. Finally, one of them caught and a small flame rose up, casting an orange flickering glow over the hollow cavity in the mountain.

Cameron was taken by the sight. But before he could consider it, he looked down at the body of Christian below him. He hadn't even realized it, but he had landed on top of the man after the fall. Christians eyes were frozen open, and one of Cameron's ice axes was sticking out of his chest.

Cameron's heart ached. Worse yet, the cushioning of Christians body is probably what had saved him. He had been trying to save Christian, and now Christian had lost his life to save him. And in his current condition, there was no way he was going to be able to scout a way out and carry Christians body at the same time. He was going to have to leave him.

He wiped his face. His hand was cold, and he wondered if Christian's hands were even colder. His other hand was not cold though. The lighter became hot to the touch and he had to let it go out for a moment to cool down. In the dark again, he patted himself down, feeling for anything he could remove to cover Christians face with. His remaining gear and clothing were essential though, now more than ever. He felt for Christians face and let his fingers slide gently down it, lightly closing the man's eyes.

Rest peacefully, my friend.

His hand kept moving down Christian's face, over his throat and onto his chest. Cameron's fingers felt the smooth, cold stainless-steel of his axe and his fingers slowly closed around the handle. He turned his head and pulled. The ice axe made a scrapping noise as it dragged along the ribs in Christian's chest. A nauseating sound.

He struck the lighter again and stood, going back to the search for the source of the smell. The inside of the mountain was a huge open cavern of shiny, translucent blue ice. Stalactites and stalagmites pierced the floor and ceiling. A few drops of water dripped from one of the larger stalactites, and suddenly Cameron heard it loud as could be. It rang through the cavern like a bell keeping rhythm to a metronome, and he realized that his ears had been plugged earlier from the rapid change in elevation as he fell.

Smoke came from his mouth like a dragon as he swung his head back and forth. Several more tunnels branched out from the cave. Unfortunately, none of them looked like they had a light at the end. Swinging his head back to the right however, he did notice now that the odor was a bit stronger in that direction.

What is that?

Carefully he took a few steps over the uneven slippery terrain. His entire body was hurt, but his shoulder most of all, and he was scared of falling and having to catch himself. A few steps further and his foot did slip, but only a few inches, and he was able to grab one of the smaller stalagmites next to him with his good arm.

Slowly he made his way through the cavern. With each step the smell grew even stronger. He stopped and took in a long draw of it with his nose, and suddenly it dawned on him what it was. *It's machinery,* he realized. No doubt about it. Rust and oil.

He took in another breath, but a sound in the distance behind him took him off the scent. A sliding sound followed by a thump. Then another identical sound a few seconds after.

"What..." he said out loud to himself.

Then a new sound came from where the thump had been. The light of his flame did not reach back that far, but he knew right away what it was now. The new sound was a low groaning.

The escaped creatures were falling down the hole.

"Are you kidding me?"

He turned and headed away from the things behind him, and towards the smell of old metal. It was coming from the mouth of one of the small tunnels that connected to this chamber. It would be a tight squeeze, but even with his injured shoulder, he could make it through.

Cameron took another look over his shoulder. So far there was no sign of the creatures catching up to him, but he could hear bodies falling and tripping over themselves as they tried to navigate the jagged floor of the cave. A loud, angry cry came from one of them.

He paused only another second, then turned and ducked into the mouth of the tunnel.

CHAPTER 13

60° N, 0° Longitude

"You should call your brother," Francesco said. "See how he and Kendall are doing. It's probably around dinner time for them right now. But do *not* say anything about her d..." He stopped. "About Professor Skull right now."

Iris shook her head. That wasn't a phone call she wanted to make right now. She knew herself well enough to know that she wouldn't be able to hide her concern. "I'm sure they're fine," she said. "I need a little more time. I'll call them tomorrow."

"You're right. I'm sorry," Frank said. "You should try to get some sleep."

Sleep sounded wonderful. She stood from the couch and caught the look in Francesco's eyes. Before he could say anything, she said, "I appreciate the offer. But I'm okay. I've never been one who could sleep on couches very well."

Frank nodded and walked her to the door. She opened it and turned around to face him again. "What do you think that email is about?" she asked.

"Just go get some sleep, Iris. We can think about that in the morning. Do you want me to walk you home?"

She shook her head. "I have a class to teach in the morning," she said, as lightheartedly as she could manage.

"Get out of here." Frank smiled and gave her a friendly nudge out the door.

It was about the distance of a typical neighborhood block from Frank's cottage to hers. There was no sidewalk though, so Iris kept her eyes focused on the ground in front of her as she went. It was a beautiful night. The coolness of the air didn't bother her. She had grown up near Gothenburg Sweden and was used to low winter temperatures. In fact, she enjoyed it. It invigorated her.

It was hard to get Cameron out of her mind though. *Maybe Frank is right though*, she thought. But even if Frank wasn't right, she needed to convince herself right now that he was. *They haven't found a body. Maybe it wasn't even a person. Maybe it was an animal or something.*

She redirected her thoughts to the email as she approached her front door and considered calling Director Kestner to get his thoughts on it as well.

She unlocked the door and went inside. Her cottage was quaint. The front door that she closed behind her was a light wood, with a rounded top and glass windows at eye level. Once inside, she entered the living room—cream colored walls with a few generic, but pretty, landscape oil paintings on them, and a wood paneled ceiling. A small round coffee table sat in the center of the room with a comfortable couch facing the small fireplace.

To one end of the home was her kitchen. It was also modest and welcoming. A basic rectangle shape with her refrigerator, oven and stove on one side, an island in the middle, and sink with a window over it on the other—a small vase full of flowers that she had picked sat on the sill. She went for the refrigerator and took out a bottle of water, then headed to her bedroom at the opposite end of the cottage.

She sat on the edge of the bed and took off her shoes, then looked at the clock and hoped it was within hospital hours so she could call James. It was only 3 a.m. though, and Oslo was only ahead by an hour, so talking to the director would have to wait.

Kauai however was almost completely on the other side of the world. *I wonder what time it is there?*

She picked up her phone and did a quick Google search for the time difference. Unlike Francesco's cottage, hers was closer to campus, and the cell repeaters reached her fairly well.

As it turned out, it was almost exactly 4 in the afternoon there. *Still within normal business hours.*

She opened the email again and reread it. Down at the bottom, included in the signature, was CSS Awapuhi's department number and her direct extension.

Iris entered the number and held the phone to her ear.

—

Lea Awapuhi sat behind her desk, thinking

about cutting out early for the day. After all, it had been a very long day. For the last three days actually, since the man—Kekoa, he said his name was—had emerged from the jungle, she had practically been married to the office. Coming in early and staying till way after the sun went down.

She gathered up some of her things and tucked them under her arm when the phone rang. "Hello. This is Sergeant Awapuhi. How can I help you?"

"Oh, hi. My name is Iris Wilhelmsson. I was actually looking for *CSS* Awapuhi," Iris said, confused. "Is she available?"

It took Lea a second to understand the mix-up as well. "This is her," she answered. "Sorry, you must have seen the signature at the bottom of my email. I haven't got around to changing it yet, but as of this week I have moved on from Crime Scene Specialist to Detective Sergeant."

"Congratulations on your promotion," Iris said.

"Thank you. Can I assume that your call means that your team has decided to consider our request for assistance?"

"Well, first I was hoping to get a little more information," Iris said. "When I talk to the director about this, he's going to want a few more details."

Lea sat back down for a moment. "You two haven't discussed it yet?"

"Not yet," Iris admitted. She did not feel comfortable telling anyone about Kestner's medical condition though, so she avoided the next truth a little bit. "He is handling other personal matters at the moment. I should be in contact with him sometime early this afternoon. Our time."

Lea stood from the desk again. "Miss Wilhelmsson, would you mind if I called you back from my cell in a little bit? I was just about to leave for the…"

"That's fine," Iris interrupted. "You can reach me back at this number. Just dial 011 first, the U.S. exit code, then my country code 46, then my number."

"Got it," Lea said back. "Give me a half hour or so, okay. Talk to you soon." She hung up the phone and left the building.

It was about 10 miles from the station to her house. Lea lived in a small one bedroom, one bath home at the very edge of the Wailua homesteads, near the base of the sleeping giant—Nounou Mountain. Her property was a secluded quarter acre, full of tropical fruit trees and native flowers. Sometimes she felt lonely there, without even neighbors visible through the foliage, but deep down she knew that she would never leave or trade the life for anything.

She had married once, when she was very young. But her husband felt his masculinity challenged when she took a job in law enforcement, and they divorced shortly after. Now, only a year away from 40, she felt too old for that sort of commitment, and preferred to keep her focus on her job. Although, she was attractive and never failed to gather attention on the seldom occasions when she would go out with her girlfriends.

She pulled her white Ford Explorer onto the dirt driveway and stopped just in front of the screened patio that spanned the front of the house. It was not cold outside, but judging by the dark clouds building up, there was rain on its way, and she looked forward to sitting on that patio later with a blanket and a tall glass of wine, listening to it. There was a fresh bottle of Pinot Grigio in her fridge that she could almost taste already.

Before walking into the house though, she stopped and stared up at miles and miles of lush green forest beyond. Somewhere deep in that rainforest is where Kekoa had spent the last year and a half. What had happened to him out there? What were all the scars? He had given a statement, but it couldn't be true. Could it?

The roll of thunder sounded off somewhere in the distance and snapped her out of her trance. She walked up a few steps and into her home.

"Kai Kai," she called, and a long-haired grey and white cat lifted her head from the pillow of the couch, and then went back to sleep. Lea shrugged.

Sitting down on the sofa next to Kai Kai, she took out her cell and dialed Iris. It rang twice and she picked up. "Hi, Iris. It's Sergeant Awapuhi. Can you talk?"

"Yes," Iris said. "I called earlier because I was hoping you could explain a little further to me what sort of expectancies your department has for us."

"Well," Lea said. "First we need to investigate the statement that Kekoa gave in more depth. And until you have signed the NDA, I can only tell you bits and pieces."

"Understood," Iris said back. "But anything you could provide right now would be helpful in our decision of whether or not this is something that Alpha-Meridian wants to take on."

Lea held the phone to her ear with her shoulder and dug a few papers out of one of her folders. "The reason we are requesting your help, is because we are not properly equipped for deep jungle excursions. And yes, of course there are other avenues we could take for something that simple, but the man who emerged from the rainforest and gave us the statement has indicated some very unusual phenomenon's, as well as the possible existence of a rare artifact that was supposedly found there."

"The artifact is no longer there?" Iris asked. She already suspected that Sergeant Awapuhi was not going to tell her what exactly the artifact was right now, so she didn't even ask.

"Well, we have no way to be sure," Lea answered. "But that's not all. The artifact described has a lot of historical and religious ties to it."

Now it was beginning to make sense why they had requested the help of Meridian. Iris remained silent though, waiting for Lea to continue talking.

Lea finished thumbing through some of her paperwork and pulled out a copy of the medical reports. "The only solid evidence we have right now to back up his story is the medical exam that was performed on him."

"The medical exam?" Iris asked. *What does a medical exam have to with it?* she wondered.

"Yes. He was severely wounded during his time in the rainforest. Normally, old injuries wouldn't concern us too much. But in this particular situation, the scars on his body do seem to indicate a highly unusual type of injury."

"I'm confused," Iris admitted. "What..."

Sergeant Awapuhi interrupted her. "I apologize," she said. "I can definitely see how this would not make any sense to you right now. Unfortunately, until you have agreed to assist us, I can't tell you the whole story." She waited a second before continuing. A tiny voice inside her head told her that it was okay to say it. *You reached out to her.* The voice said. *You want her help. She needs to know something at least.*

Lea hesitated, then took a breath. "Kekoa has wounds on him that suggest both incision and burn. The lacerations on his body have been thoroughly examined and are believed to have been made by something of razor sharpness."

The artifact, Iris thought.

"Definitely not from anything that could be found naturally in the rainforest," Lea continued. She held up one of the photographs of the man's body.

The photo was a picture of him, shirtless, showing his body from the bottom of his chin down to the line of his waist. His chest and stomach were lined with raised scar tissue. "The wounds," she continued, "also appear to have been instantly cauterized." She looked again at the strange formation of the scars. "There is scar tissue not only on the outside of his skin, but on the inside of him as well."

CHAPTER 14

41° N, 15° E.

Two specific animals, with traits unlike any other, were the starting point for Bastian Santé's version of gene editing. The Tardigrade and the Turritopsis Dohrnii—the immortal jellyfish.

For Bastian Santé's purposes, the indestructible characteristics and capabilities of the Tardigrade were absolutely essential. No human could even come close to doing what he needed them to do without them.

Tardigrades, or Water Bears as they're commonly known, can withstand almost anything imaginable. If the world ever faced a global extinction event, Water Bears would probably emerge from the rubble, unscathed.

Found all over the planet, microscopic Water Bears can survive dehydration, starvation and levels exceeding 4000 Grays of helium ion radiation. They are found living under layers of ice high in the Himalayas, and in boiling undersea volcanoes. Basically, capable of creating their own outer fortress of cells, Tardigrades are virtually invincible.

But the specific DNA protein in a Tardigrade that Bastian harvested was known as DSUP—the acronym for *Damage Suppressor*. DSUP is extremely unique in its ability to suppress DNA damage in both single-strand and double-strand breaks. It is what

Justin Hyde

allows the Water Bears their exceptional ability to tolerate stress and harsh environments.

At the University of Tokyo, researchers and molecular biologists had already begun experiments of sequencing the genome of the Water Bears into mammals—including human kidney cells, in an attempt to transfer the animal's resistance.

In Bastian's lab, the tiny creatures were kept in small, moss filled petri dishes. Next to them, in a small saltwater aquarium, were the Turritopsis Dohrnii. The jellyfish were collected from the Mediterranean Sea, six months ago.

Three of the little blob-like fish pulsed up and down through the calm glowing water of the tank. They swam about in a slow carefree manner, as though they were fully aware of their immortality. Sometimes Father Santé would provoke the animals by starving them for several days, or by releasing small turtles into the tank. The infant turtles would nibble at the jellyfish, triggering them after the attacks to revert back to an earlier stage of life, before the injury—a process which they could perform indefinitely.

Ultimately, with the invincibility of the Tardigrade and the immortality of the jellyfish, Father Santé was sure that one of his creations would be capable of serving his purpose. And so far, none of his experiments had died. At least not from the procedures. Their deaths all came from the first touch after. It was the touch that killed them, and it was Bastian Santé's custom genetic code that brought them back. As told in scripture.

And many of those who sleep in the dust of the earth shall awake, some to everlasting life, and some to shame and everlasting contempt. — Daniel 12:2

But none of them had been successful yet. Not for what he needed them for.

A sudden clang of metal dropping stirred the jellyfish into a fast, startled dash, but they quickly calmed again and went back to their rhythmic swim. The naked girl had mindlessly come through the door of the lab. She bumped another table, and this time an entire rack of distillation condensers and a boiling flask tipped over and smashed onto the ground, sending shards of sharp glass across the floor.

She stepped on them with bare feet. Broken bits of glass pierced into the soft bottoms of her feet, but she continued on, sweeping through the room in search of something, but not knowing what.

The Damage Suppressor protein in Bastian's monsters worked extraordinarily well in protecting them from things like shortwave UV radiation and extreme temperatures, but was having an almost reverse side effect on the durability of their skin. They could handle being frozen, extreme gamma ray exposure, and were even somewhat fireproof, but would cut or bruise easily upon impact or abrasion.

After the delivery of the CRISPR array, the epidermis of their skin slowly became soft and weak. A result of some underlying mutation. The DSUP protein was concentrating on the individual cells, but was so far unable to chain them together, as it did in the Tardigrades. Something that Bastian was very unhappy about. One of the last hang-ups in his trials.

Fortunately, the enzymes of the Turritopsis jellyfish were performing accordingly. Bastian's creations were showing signs of regeneration even faster than planned. Injuries, and even death, was reversed within hours, sometimes minutes, along with a numbing of their nociceptors. They felt no pain. However, the jellyfish enzymes were also not without some problems. They were rendering the brain functionality almost useless, bringing the neurons back too far—to an almost primordial embryo stage of life. And, seemed to be triggering extreme levels of aggression.

Her foot kicked the edge of the downed rack and it scraped across the floor with the high-pitched scratching sound of metal on tile. The noise stirred something on the other side of the laboratory wall. A chorus of moans followed by light pounding on the wall. She turned her body towards the sound as if it was calling to her.

She bumped into the doorless wall of the room and stood there, listening. The sounds beyond were familiar to her. They excited her. But how to get to them?

Slowly she turned and started walking back to the door from which she entered. She left the lab behind, but could no longer hear the calls. The castle was silent at this hour. Forgetting her purpose, she felt alone again, and anxious—and angry. She turned to her left, in the opposite direction of the room with the sounds, and towards the door of the castles lower floor apartment. Her body was still stiff, and each movement was slow and cumbersome.

Inside the room, the night watchman lay on a cot. Not in a deep sleep, but soundly enough to not hear the door creak open. Bloody footsteps followed the girl as she entered the room and approached the man. He stirred, but the movement did not concern or worry her. She came to the side of him. Again, he moved, this time rolling onto his back. The girl looked down at him. She didn't know why she was there, or why she was now reaching for him, but it had to happen. His pure existence reignited the rage in her. She would take away what was inside of him.

The watchman felt her presence. He opened his eyes and looked straight into the deathly face. She opened her mouth and let out a hissing, growling scream, and grabbed the man before he even had a chance to move.

—

Tony and his brother Sergio had driven all night trying to get back to Castello di Monte Sant'Angelo before the sun came up. It was never going to happen though. The best they could hope for was to reach the castle by 9.

Not only was father Santé going to be plenty upset, it was also going to make things a lot more difficult getting the girl into the castle without being seen.

"What time is it," Tony asked.

Sergio took a hand off the wheel and rubbed his eyes, then looked at the clock on the dash of the car. Tony was too lazy to even open his eyes from the passenger seat and look for himself. "It's almost four," he told him.

The little girl in the backseat remained absolutely silent. The last time she had cried, tony had reached back with a knife and held it to her cheek. But nothing could stop the tears from flowing or the tremble of fright in her lip.

Whatever they had planned on doing with her—whatever was going to happen to her—was all going to start in 5 hours...

CHAPTER 15

45° N, 7° E.
Elevation – 4,500 ft.

The Glacier Express had rerouted and crossed the southern border of Switzerland into Italy. After several hours of travel by both rail and bus, the passengers aboard were finally able to rest in the small mountain town of Staffa, just a little before sunup. The unscheduled detour was not logistically efficient, but without waiting for clear tracks from several other trains already in route, it was the quickest way to offload the frightened passengers. However, crossing an international border was going to make the legal paperwork and battle over jurisdictions a complete disaster later. A small price to pay though for avoiding the lawsuits that would certainly come from claims of not considering the passengers wellbeing first, had they chosen another option.

Matteo and his family were given a room at the Casa Alpina Don Guanella hotel, but unfortunately didn't have much in the way of luggage to check in with. Their trip through the Alps had been meant to be more of a one-night sightseeing tour rather than a one-way ticket to a destination.

After checking into their room, the family went downstairs and gathered around a small table in the hotel's restaurant. After their experience, even the eldest son Ben didn't object when his father asked them to take each other's hands and bow their heads.

"Heavenly Father," Matteo began. "We pray that in this dark time of confusion you will be our light. May you comfort those of us who are scared and bring peace to those who are suffering. Let us mourn this tragedy, but let our hearts also be filled with your love, so that we may share it with others."

"And help papa find a new job," young Adrian added. His head was still down, and his eyes still closed.

Matteo didn't let the comment distract him. "Amen," he said, then raised his head and looked at his youngest son. He was sympathetic to his boy, and felt sad for him. He knew how hard it had been for all of them when he had lost his job a year ago and was forced to move his family away from their home. Now, having lost another job, his young son Adrian was full of anxiety about the thought of having to move yet again. Unlike his older brother, Adrian was shy, and had trouble making friends. Matteo didn't let go of his hand when Emily and Ben stood up from the table. "I know this is hard for you," he said to him.

Adrian didn't say anything back right away. His father squeezed his hand. "I miss our old home," he finally told him.

Matteo knew that Adrian wasn't talking about their house now, or the home he had grown up in when he was very young, in northern Switzerland, but rather the home that they had made for themselves six years ago in Mount Gargano, Italy. Truth was, Matteo missed it too. They all did.

"I know," Matteo said gently. "But it was God's will. And so is this." He waited for Adrian to look up at him. "It will be okay. I promise. No matter what happens or where we go, at least we have each other."

Emily and Ben stood off to the side, giving father and son their moment. Although, both of them shared Adrian's feelings.

"Maybe you could try talking to the bishop again," Emily suggested. "He can speak to the brotherhood." Matteo shook his head in the background, but she continued. "It isn't right what happened. No one really believes that you took the sacred pebbles from the cave."

"But the minister does," he said back. "The pebbles went missing the morning of his arrival."

"But you didn't take them!" Ben said angrily.

"Matteo," Emily said softly. "You should try. What else will we do?"

Matteo thought back to that morning. *What could have happened to them?* He wondered. He had been the priest of the Basilica Santuario San Michelle Arcangelo for nearly six years. He loved his work and his congregation, and always felt that it was truly his place in the world to be there. *How I miss it...*

The day of the minister's visit was also the

first day that Father Bastian Santé had arrived. The timing of that now seemed very coincidental. Father Santé hadn't even introduced himself to Matteo. He just observed—silently and alone. Even at the time, Matteo had thought it odd.

Two days later, after accusations of a holy theft, Matteo was expelled from the church. It tore at his heart. But like always, he simply put his faith in God to provide and take care of him and his family. But the path God had chosen was not as easy or as rewarding as any of them had hoped. They ended up leaving Italy and returning to his hometown of Grindelwald, where he worked as a groundskeeper and assistant chaplain at Saint Bernard's English Church, while Emily took a part time data-entry position with a local land surveyor.

Unfortunately, three weeks ago, a new head chaplain was confirmed at Saint Bernard's, who brought with him his own assistant chaplain from his previous church. And while both of them were always very nice to Matteo, his responsibilities at the church quickly dissolved until he was no longer working as a chaplain at any level. And once the heavy snow started falling, even his groundskeeper work was no longer needed again until the spring melt.

Now he was unsure what to do. He did yearn for his church in the cave. Not a day passed when he did not think of it.

Will I ever be back?

He looked into the faces of his family

gathered around him. They would follow him anywhere and he would do anything for them. His wife, Emily, looked down at him with love, and the continued promise to spend her life for better or worse with him, as long as he always strived to fulfill his purpose to God and Gods children. Ben, his strong and rebellious older son, looked at him with defiance. Not a challenge to defy his father, but a challenge for his father to stand up and defy those who pushed him down.

He then turned to Adrian, still sitting across the table from him. The boy looked at him with sorrow. But it was not in pity for himself. It was a sadness for his father—his role model and his hero, who he was watching suffer at the hands of deception. Being punished, and punishing himself, for nothing other than being a good man.

Matteo's soul grew strong with determination. He knew now what he had to do.

CHAPTER 16

The tunnel Cameron was in kept getting consistently smaller as he continued through it. He made himself remain calm but couldn't truly convince himself that there was nothing to worry about. He wasn't generally claustrophobic, but with each inch that the tunnel shrank, he felt himself get a little more concerned.

Eventually he was forced to bend at the waist and the knees so far that if it got any smaller, he would have to go prone and crawl. And to make matters even worse, it was starting to angle down again. Not drastically yet, but he wasn't sure his body could withstand another fall.

On the plus side however, the smell of machinery was getting stronger. Whatever was causing it, was getting closer.

Cameron stretched his arm out a little further to let the glow of the lighter reach as far as he could make it. It didn't produce a beam of light like a flashlight though unfortunately, and so the narrow tunnel was only illuminated in a bubble around the flame.

After another step, he froze—unsure if he had heard a sound behind him. He let the lighter go out and remained still while he listened for signs that the creatures had entered behind him. Icy rock on rock grinding and soft groans came from way back in the distance. The things were still there, of course, but it did not sound as though they were in the tunnel with him yet.

Maybe they won't have the sense to know how to crouch, he hoped.

Turning around again, he flicked the lighter and continued deeper into the mountain. Finally, he could see the orb of light around his small flame break over an edge and disperse into a much larger area. Once catching up to the light, the tunnel opened up and the temperature dropped several more degrees—the scent of metal, rust and oil and grease, struck him hard in the nose.

The sight was incredible.

Cameron kneeled down on his perch, giving his aching legs a moment of rest, as he looked over the massive cavern in front of him. His tiny tunnel had let out high at the top of a huge manmade tunnel that seemed to reach out endlessly in both directions.

Below him, stretched across steel tracks and wooden ties, was the lost remains of a German Kriegsloks armored war locomotive. The KDL class steam train had once been part of the Deutsche Reichsbahn rail system of Nazi Germany.

This is it, Cameron realized. *It is actually here. I found it.*

From what he could see with the little light he had, he suspected he was somewhere towards the rear of the train. There was a visible private coach car in front of him, which typically would not be carried near the engine.

He investigated the drop it would take for him to reach the floor of the tunnel from his ledge. It must have been twenty feet down, and Colonel Skull would have traded his left eye for a rope. But since that trade was not up for grabs, he considered the least damaging alternative he could think of instead. He let the lighter flame burn out, then stuffed it back into his coat pocket and turned around—his back now facing the train. In complete darkness, he unclipped the two ice axes from his belt, then knelt and swung one leg over the edge, feeling for a foothold somewhere along the dirt wall below him. There wasn't one, but the walls were soft, and with a few easy kicks he was able to dent in the dirt enough to get a grip with his toes.

Carefully he repeated the motion with his other foot, and then dug the tips of the axes into the wall, one after another, until he estimated a safe jumping distance. Six feet or so from the bottom, he let go and landed hard on the frozen ground. One of the axes did not pull from the wall though and remained dangling above him.

He left it and dropped the other axe to the ground, then pulled out the lighter again and started walking towards the massive relic. There were actually two private coaches on the back of the train. Cameron walked up to the forward one. As he approached, the orange of his flame caught a few bits of exposed metal beneath the patina of a brass Parteiadler hung from the coach's door. The light reflected back at him as if to purposely get his attention.

Cameron stopped a few feet short of the emblem. The eagle, with its wings spread, standing atop a swastika, iced his blood and gave him chills.

He avoided it, trying hard to ignore and forget about it, and walked to the short set of steps leading up to the door of the car. It was unlocked, but resisted opening after all these forgotten years, and made a peeling, breaking sound as he tugged it open.

Another faint sound followed it and Cameron turned his head back towards the small cave opening that he had just come from. The things were there. He could hear their awful groans getting closer.

Quickly he hoped up into the train. It was like stepping into a time capsule to another world. A hand carved wooden table, large enough to seat 6 people, was in the center of the room—a meeting place for whoever was aboard. Papers were scattered over the table, along with a metal shortwave receiver and a few bottles of unfinished aged brandy. To the right, against the wall, was a large, wood-burning stove with a round stovepipe pushing out through the ceiling above it. Colonel Skull grabbed an iron poker from the wood stove and wrapped a piece of old cloth around the top of it. Then he took one of the liquor bottles and poured its contents over the fabric. It went up in a roaring flame at the first touch from the lighter, illuminating the entire room.

Looking around again, he noticed that the chair nearest him had a dust covered officer's coat hung over the back. But that is not what caught his full attention. The chair at the opposite end of the table had a man sitting in it. His uniform hung loosely over his pale bones—the hat on his head tipped forward, covering the hollow cavities of his eyes. One of his hands was on the table, still holding a Walther PPK pistol.

Colonel skull rounded the table and grabbed it. He had lost the Swiss assault rifle somewhere during his fall through the mountain and was relieved to have a gun back in his hands. He set the torch down and worked the safety lever of the gun a few times, then ejected a couple rounds from the magazine before reloading it and tucking it into his waistband.

There were a lot of other small, miscellaneous things scattered about the room that at any other time and circumstance Cameron would have loved to investigate, but he didn't want to be caught in here if the creatures caught up to him. He picked up the torch and peeked briefly into the back room of the car. It was the living quarters for whomever claimed title to this coach. There was a wooden armoire and a small bed with a little round table next to it. On the table was an oil lamp and a framed picture of a uniformed man, probably the man at the table, with his wife and two young girls.

It made Cameron think of Kendall, and he turned with determination and headed out of the train. His torch cast a much larger glow outside than the lighter did in the big open space of the tunnel, and Cameron ran immediately up to the next car. It was a boxcar. A cargo hold. The large sliding door on the side of it was already open, and he peeked inside. It was empty. But, like the shine from the brass swastika, there was another glimmer that caught his attention in the back corner of this car. He jumped up and eased closer to it with curiosity. As he neared, it became clear that the shine was coming from a single coin resting along the bottom edge of the back wall.

Cameron knelt and picked it up slowly, rubbing the dust off between his fingers. He held it up in the light in front of his face and inspected it with awe. The gold gleamed as he turned it. On one side was a relief of the eagle and swastika—the words Deutsches Reich, and the year—1937, underneath it. On the other side was the Fuhrer.

In the dirt on the wooden floor around him, Cameron now noticed footprints and the tracings of large rectangles where crates of these coins, and probably many more crates of gold bars, were once stored for transport. But why weren't they here now? Where could they have gone? Whose footprints were those?

A crash from outside the boxcar startled him and he looked up. It was the sound of one of the creatures falling into the train tunnel.

Crap.

He slid the coin into this pocket and ran back to the large open door of the car. He peeked around the edge of the wall and saw one of the things

129

picking itself up from the ground, in the same spot that he had landed a few minutes ago.

The injured man, or creature, would see the light from his torch for sure, so Cameron jumped from the boxcar and started jogging towards the forward end of the train, to gain some ground on it. Somewhere there had to be a way out of here.

He ran past two more boxcars and then a huge grey colored railcar that was different than anything he had never seen before. It was long and cylindrical on the top, perhaps some type of custom tanker car. Past that was the coal car and then the engine of the beast. The DRB class 52 steam locomotive was an 80-ton monster. Its massive drive wheels came up to Cameron's shoulders.

He passed the front of it. 40 feet beyond the front of the train, Skull stopped—devastated. He suddenly felt sick to his stomach. There was no way out.

He lifted the torch higher. It was already starting to lose its brightness, and in another few minutes, without adding another rag or something to fuel it, it would burn out. But it still cast enough light to confirm that the way out was completely blocked.

There has to be a way...

Another sound of a body falling into the tunnel came from far behind him. It caught his attention and he turned just in time to see the first fallen creature coming at him. One of its arms was hung limply at its side, clearly badly broken and flailing loosely; but the other was outstretched, reaching for him. Its mouth opened and it hissed at him.

Skull jumped back quickly and drew the Walther pistol with his free hand—again hesitating to pull the trigger though. But the remains of the man coming at him didn't even seem to recognize the gun as a threat and kept coming with aggression. Cameron kept his eyes wide open and fired. The round blasted through the creature's head and it stood for only a second longer before falling heavily to the ground.

The sound was deafening, and Cameron, still holding the gun, pressed his wrist tight against his ear. After a few seconds, the ringing in his ears finally stopped and he lowered the weapon and looked back again at the impassible wall of dirt at the mouth of the tunnel. It was a hopeless sight. But Colonel Skull never accepted hopelessness. He walked closer to the wall. It had once been an opening—the exit of the railway tunnel. How thick could the rubble from the cave-in be that sealed it shut now? Certainly it was too thick to dig through by hand. Right?

Then he noticed something on the ground in front of him. Tracks.

Not just the railroad tracks, but the imprint of belt tracks. *From a tank,* he thought. Maybe—a snow tank.

The ripsaw.

The tracks in the dirt ended at the wall of rock just to the side of the railroad tracks. Or, more accurately, they went under it.

"That's how they got the gold out," he whispered to himself.

Someone must have made this discovery before him and excavated the southern side of the mountain till finding the tunnel, then removed the Nazi gold and triggered a new cave-in to reseal it after. That meant that the wall of rubble and debris was probably not that thick after all. It was purposely put there, but only for concealment. A natural cave-in, or the original cave-in from the Russian bomb detonation, could be tens, if not hundreds of feet thick. But there was a good chance this was only a few feet. Still too much to dig through by hand unfortunately, especially with a dying light and a cave full of dangerous creatures behind him. But maybe not too thick that there wasn't something he could use to break through it.

He turned around again and headed back to see if he could find something inspiring on the train. But instead, to the absolute contrary, the first thing he saw was another large swastika painted right on the nose of the big steam engine.

Since it was doubtful that he would find anything useful in either the coal car or the empty boxcars, he picked up his pace, anticipating a run all the way back to the coaches at the rear. A spark fell from the flame in his hand and he quickened his steps to a fast jog. If his estimations were correct, he had only three or four minutes of light left before his torch was completely burnt out. And he did not want to imagine that situation.

Then suddenly one of the creatures stepped out from the back of the tanker car and appeared right in front of him. Cameron stopped fast, and again raised the pistol, when a second creature appeared out of the blackness beyond. Then another, and another.

"Oh shit."

He now realized that he had not counted the rounds in the gun and was unsure of how many shots he had remaining.

The first of the creatures lunged at him and Cameron fired. Again, the shot was on target and the thing dropped dead to the floor. Quickly he adjusted his aim and pulled the trigger two more times, ending two more of them. Focusing now on the fourth creature, he started to see the outline of several more emerging from the darkness beyond.

They all slowly came towards him, and he noticed how the sights of the pistol were now swaying up and down to the rhythm of his hard breathing. *Get ahold of yourself.*

He locked sights on the figure before him and squeezed the trigger. The gun made a faint click sound and Skull felt his stomach sink. *Empty.*

Without lowering the weapon, he glanced into the face of the person before him. It was the woman with the slash on her back. Her hair was dirty and tangled and fell over the front of both her shoulders, covering the purple-green skin of her breasts. Her right hand was still bloody from ripping the guards throat out, and she stopped walking and stared at Cameron, letting the other creatures behind her come forward and pass.

Cameron dropped the gun. His hands were wet with sweat and he wouldn't have been able to fire it accurately now even if had bullets left in it. The woman was toying with him. He could feel it. But he replaced his fear with anger and jumped up onto the tank car to his right.

"Can you sons-a-bitches climb?" he asked.

The first few of them bumped into the wheels of the train car below him and reached their hands up trying to grab at him.

Cameron climbed higher onto the rear platform and then on top of a stack of barrels. So far, the things down below were not following him up, but were growing in number below, trapping him.

Lost for what to do, he began searching everything around him. He looked down at the barrels he was sitting on. Painted on the side of one of them was the marking: K5 TREIBMITTEL.

Propellant?

He recognized the German word. After dating one of the most renowned translators in the world off and on for almost nine years now, he couldn't help but pick up on a few things. The barrel below him was actually a canister. It was then that Colonel Skull fully understood what he was sitting on. *Powder.*

The tank car was not a tanker at all. It was a gun. *A super tank!* A massive 80-foot-long, 200-ton German railway artillery cannon. The K5 shot 250-

pound, 280-millimeter rocket assisted projectiles, capable of shooting from Berlin to Poland. And Cameron Skull was sitting on a stack of them.

CHAPTER 17

**Latitude 22° N, Longitude 159° W
5:44 p.m. Hawaii-Aleutian Standard Time**

Kekoa lived in a small house overlooking Hanalei Bay on the northern coast of Kauai. On Sundays he attended Waioli Huiia, a Christian church which honored the traditional legacy and customs of the Hawaiian people. Several times a week, those who were spiritual in town, would gather there and perform Hula.

Kekoa was one of the Kanes, a male dancer representing the warriors of the islands past, and would often perform hula Kahiko, rather than the less traditional and more westernized Hula'auana.

His dance honored the ancient Hawaiian gods and goddesses. It used bamboo rhythm sticks and gourd drums. Not like the hulas performed for tourists at the resort luaus of Maui, which often fancied ukuleles and other more modern drum and string instruments.

For Kekoa, and all the other dancers, the dance told a story—often an ancient and sacred one. And to perform it correctly, he needed to be in the right spirit of mind and body. The land and the ocean were his training grounds. He would prepare, physically, by climbing the coconut trees, and by carrying heavy stones while running waist deep in the ocean over the sandy bottom of the reef. But his strength had been no match for the man in the jungle. The man with the sword.

Spiritually, Kekoa would meditate and pray at a spot at the edge of the rainforest. On a ledge directly above his home, overlooking the bay. As he was doing now. He sat cross legged on the rock with his eyes closed while the rain poured down over him.

The moon was bright tonight, when it found a break between storm clouds, and the temperature was warm. The cool touch of the rain, and the sound of the droplets pounding over the broad leaves of the Fan palms and running down the thin branches of the Koa trees was calming.

He opened his eyes and looked out over the moonlit cresting waves of the pacific—a flash of lightning sparked in the distance. Lifting his right hand to his shirtless chest, he felt along one of the raised scars that now littered his body. The doctors had described the wounds as "abnormal" and "irregular," but to Kekoa they were more than that. They were supernatural.

Standing from his perch, Kekoa started his walk back down the hill to his home. The ground was muddy, but he was accustomed to the terrain in all conditions, and had no trouble descending the 150 feet to the bottom. Reaching the backside of his house, he paused when a pair of headlights turned and pointed towards him.

The white SUV parked, and the driver's door opened. A slender dark-haired woman stepped out. "Kekoa," she called, as she pulled an umbrella out from the backseat. "Is that you? It's officer Awapuhi."

"Yes," he answered.

Kekoa approached her, and she couldn't help but suck in a gasp of air at seeing his bare chest. But she wasn't sure if her initial shock was from the sight of the scars on his body, or from the way the water glistened over the tight muscles showing beneath his tan Polynesian skin.

"I was hoping maybe we could talk," Lea said. She had tried unwinding back at home, but became restless—unable to relax, her mind not willing to slow down. And so she had decided to drive north and see if Kekoa would be open to share his story again. She waited for him to respond but he did not. "I know you already gave your statement. Probably more than once. But I..."

"Let's go inside and get out of the rain," he said, interrupting her. The suggestion was more for her sake than his own.

Lea smiled in thanks, then followed him up some steps and into the small house. "I had a little trouble finding the place," she admitted.

He had built the home himself, with his bare hands, 10 years ago. Wanting to live close, but not actually in town. It was modern, to some degree, but built on stilts to keep it off the forest floor. It had a wooden front porch which was once coated with green paint, but hadn't been refinished in many years and was now peeling and splintering.

Kekoa did not get many visitors, and now he

felt some embarrassment over his homes condition. The inside was showing similar signs of age. But it wasn't messy, and the furniture was comfortable, so after she folded her umbrella and leaned it against the wall outside the front door, he offered her a seat on the couch.

She accepted. The windows in the home were inexpensive and single paned, and so did a poor job of keeping out the sounds from outside, and Lea felt herself having to raise her voice slightly to compete with the rain. "I hope you don't mind me stopping by," she said. He shook his head and she continued. "Your story. It's…"

Again, he interrupted her. "You don't believe me."

"It's not that," she said.

"Then what?"

Maybe he was partially right? A part of her didn't believe him. Couldn't. How could it be true? "Can you tell me again what you all were doing that far out in the rainforest?" she asked.

He nodded. "Makehewa, boss man, hired us to take him there. He say he search for something in the garden, but did not tell us what. Just ask us to bring him to center of island."

Lea had hoped that he would have voluntarily continued and told her the whole story over again, but she didn't want to push him to the point of resistance when he stopped. He had shown signs of irritation at all the questions a few days ago when some of the other officers had overwhelmed him at the hospital. She changed the subject. "You have a very charming home," she said as she looked around the room.

There wasn't much in the way of decorations, but Kekoa did have a few things of interest. There was a small hand-carved replica of a canoe with sail. And hung on one wall was a black-and-white picture of a young boy and an older lady wearing a smile and a Plumeria flower in her hair. Lea suspected it was Kekoa as a child, and his mother. "Is that your mother," she asked. "She is a very pretty lady."

"Thank you," he said. "She was wahine nani." He pulled a shirt over his head, to Lea's disappointment, and sat down in a chair across from her. He knew that wasn't the reason she had come. "I the only one who survived," he told her.

Lea's tone changed to serious and concerned, and she leaned forward. "Kekoa. You said that the man was looking for something in the garden."

He tipped his head in agreement.

"But that could mean anywhere in Kauai though. This is the Garden Island."

"Why do you think that is?" he asked. "Why are we called that?"

That caught her off guard and she didn't have an answer right away. Hawaii was undoubtedly beautiful, especially the island of Kauai. But many words described beauty more so than garden. The only time garden was ever used to represent extreme beauty was when in reference to the biblical garden in the book of Genesis.

He continued. "Makehewa searching for something in the Garden of God."

You mean, the Garden of Eden," she said, already knowing the answer.

Again, he tipped his head.

"But this is Hawaii. There aren't even any ties to Christianity here at all. None. We're not even on the right side of the world! It doesn't make any sense to think that the Garden of Eden could have been here."

Kekoa shrugged. Truth was truth, and he believed what he saw. He had been the only one of the men in the rainforest that day who even believed in God, and he was familiar with the story of creation. He was also the only one who had survived...

CHAPTER 18

60° N, 0° Longitude
November 19, 2019
4:59 a.m. – Greenwich Mean Time
Alpha-Meridian

Ethan Price opened the door at the end of the hallway. The man was built like a truck, and had he been any wider in the shoulders he probably would've had to turn sideways to get through. Originally adopted by a family from New Zealand when he was 5, he grew up in the States, and started competing in the World Lumberjack Competitions in Hayward Wisconsin, before joining on with Nightcorp in 2008—usually placing in the Single Buck event, and always dominating the Standing Block Chop. He may have been the only clean-shaven man on the field, but Ethan was deadly with an axe.

From there, he started toying with the idea of entering one of the Worlds Strongman Competitions, but never actually got around to it. Now, at 34-years-old, and having moved to this new part of the world, to a territory in the north subarctic archipelago of Scotland, he had his sights set on the Scottish Highland games. He even kept a cut section of log behind his cottage so that he could practice for the caber toss on his own time.

This morning he was entering the dorms extra early to wake the students for their first day of field training. Eventually, field training would become full day outings, and then even multi-day experiences in Meridians backlot. But not all of the backlot was complete yet, and to start the students off slow, the first few weeks was only half-day entry level stuff.

Ethan oversaw this for the time being, even though he wasn't as limber as maybe he should have been for some of the courses. But he was still trying to find his place with A-M. With Nightcorp, Ethan was the muscle. He also handled the majority of the demolition work. But neither of those two things were prominently needed now unfortunately. Turns out, in a school for Hazardous Relic *Recovery*, Blowing-things-up-101 hadn't been embraced as an elective class quite yet.

One by one he opened doors and turned on lights. "Everybody up!" he shouted. "Outside in five minutes."

No one argued or complained. People tended not to with Ethan. However, in the back of his mind he kept thinking about the new kid who Director Kestner was pushing through the recruitment process to try and expedite into the program. From what everyone knew of the new guy, he was supposed to be a loose cannon, and no one could quite understand why the director thought so highly of someone with anger issues. They all figured there must be a back story that they were unaware of, but Francesco had given Ethan the heads up of the possible new student, yesterday.

"Outside in five minutes!" he hollered again. "We don't want to drag this out and have you be late for your class with Iris this afternoon, do we?"

He knew that would get them up and moving. Iris could be scary when she was crossed. She could curse you in a dozen different languages, and she would almost certainly double their workload for being late. But on top of that, the class of seven students included five men. Five of whom had a crush on their blonde teacher. From the way some of them acted around her you would have thought they were high schoolers, when in fact the majority of them were probably in their late 20's.

After making his way to the end of the hall and back again, Ethan went outside and stood in the cold while he waited for the students. It didn't take more than a minute or two for them to start trickling out one by one.

He checked the time on his watch as the last of the seven came out the door. The man cut it close, but technically wasn't late. They had been instructed on what to wear the night before, and all seven sported the gear nicely.

"Okay," Ethan said. "Follow me."

It was almost exactly a quarter of a mile from the dorms to the front entrance of the backlot. In the end, Meridians property line would be fenced, but that stage of the construction was still a few months away, and so the back half of the 100 acres was still wide open. Not anything that Ethan or any of the other staff were concerned with though. And definitely not a reason to hold off on field training exercises, since the Shetland Islands were pretty desolate to begin with, and this particular island and area surrounding Alpha-Meridian was about as barren as the Sahara Desert. There was a small farm with a breeding stock of Shetland ponies a few miles away, and maybe a few wild geese running around, but that was about it.

After walking the first couple hundred feet, Ethan looked off to his right and could see the living room light on in Iris's cottage. What was she doing awake so early?

From inside, Iris could see the group too. She watched them for a moment through her window. But it was a few hours still before the sun came up, so she couldn't see enough of them to tell who was who. Except Ethan. She knew exactly where he was. He towered over the group like the Incredible Hulk.

Sleep had been her enemy that night. She fought with it, and it fought back. She was too worried about Cameron. Francesco's talk had helped her for a while, and the email provided some distraction, but in the end, her fear of losing him had been more powerful than sleep and all other thoughts combined.

It was going to be an even tougher day now though, without sleep. She turned from the window and walked into her kitchen. Sitting on the counter by the coffee pot was her favorite mug. Cameron's daughter had made it for her several years ago for her birthday, and she cherished it. On the side was the store-bought printing that said HAPPY BIRTHDAY, but underneath that, Kendall had taken some permanent markers and written, "You're the best! Love Kendall," and drawn three colored balloons which were now sadly fading away. Permanent marker or not, Iris tried to take exceptional care to be very gentle when washing the outside of the mug.

While she waited for the coffee to brew, standing in the kitchen still in her pajamas, she took out her phone and opened up her emails again. Not surprising, there were quite a few new unread messages, but she filtered out all but the ones sent to her A-M email address. In that inbox there was only one.

It was another message from Sergeant Awapuhi. This time the email was describing much more detail from the man's statement about what happened to him in the jungle. Evidently, the sergeant had decided to forgo the non-disclosure agreement that she had earlier been so adamant about getting from Alpha-Meridian before allowing their involvement.

The contents of the email were confusing though. At least to Iris they were. Francesco was much, much more knowledgeable in these kinds of areas than she was. And whatever he didn't already know, he thoroughly enjoyed looking up and learning. His research abilities were incomparable and irreplaceable at Meridian.

She was going to have to wake him up.

CHAPTER 19

For the second time now tonight, Iris found herself banging on Franks door. "Frank," she yelled at him again. "I'm sorry to wake you, but can you let me in?"

Francesco opened the door, sleepy eyed, in a pair of shorts and a t-shirt. "Are you okay?" he asked.

"I'm okay," she said back. Then suddenly, seeing him, she had a moment of guilt. "I'm sorry. I shouldn't have woken you. This can wait till morning." She started to turn around.

Frank stopped her. "It is morning," he said. "And I'm up now. Come on in."

A little embarrassed, Iris walked past him and into the house.

"What's up?" he asked, closing the door behind her.

She didn't say anything right away but turned and looked at him.

Reading her thoughts, Frank said, "Don't worry about it. Truth be told, I didn't sleep that well either. I guess this whole mess with Professor Skull being MIA has got me a little more worried than I like to admit sometimes."

She managed a slight smile. Not that she wanted Frank to share in her sleeplessness, but that old saying, *Misery loves company*, did have some truth to it. She was comforted by the affirmation that someone else was scared with her. That wasn't the reason she had pounded on his door again though. "I got another email from the police sergeant in Kauai," she said, getting to the point.

Frank led her into the kitchen. There was already a pot of coffee brewing and Iris smiled again, and suddenly recognized the strong aroma of rich Costa Rican dark roast in the air. Frank had good taste, and apparently had already been up and pacing, same as her, before she came over. He opened the refrigerator door and took out a half carton of milk and set it on the counter. "I take mine black," he said. "But I do have this, and maybe some sugar in the pantry." He pointed to the door behind her.

She was grateful for the cup. Never having finished hers before leaving her cottage. The mug Kendall had made her still sat half full, and cold now, on the counter.

"What did the email say?" he asked.

Again, getting right to the point, Iris answered. "She says that the man in the jungle claims he was attacked by someone with a sword. And that that's what he says caused his injuries." She took a sip from her coffee.

Francesco wasn't following. "Wait," he said. "Can you start from the beginning? I remember you reading me the last email, but honestly I was pretty distracted by what might have happened to Professor Skull and didn't catch all of it."

Iris realized that Frank probably hadn't even given it another thought since she was last here.

"The story is," she said. "That three days ago a man walked out of the rainforest with dozens of old wounds on his body. He was a local from one of the small towns on the island, but went missing a little over a year ago, along with several other men, during a hunting party into the jungle."

"Okay," Frank said, joining in. "And he claims that a man with a sword attacked him."

Iris nodded. "Attacked him and killed everyone else he was with. But then the email lost me a little bit." She took another careful sip from the hot cup of coffee in her hands, then set the cup down. "She started making references to the Garden of Eden and fire angels or something like that. It wasn't really clear to me."

"Can I read it?"

She shook her head, feeling a bit absentminded for a moment. "I left my phone on the kitchen counter, accidentally."

Instead of asking her to go back and get it, Francesco took a sip from his own cup and dismissed her embarrassment with a wave of his hand. "No worries," he said. "What else did she say?"

"Well. It sounded like the man was suggesting that his hunting party had been searching for the Garden of Eden, right there in the rainforest."

The brow over Franks left eye went up. Cleary, he thought it was just as ridiculous as she did. "In Hawaii?" It was a rhetorical question.

"I know," she said in agreement. "But there was also mention of an ancient relic. The sword, in fact. The man claimed that the sword he was attacked with was found out there in the jungle. Whether anyone wants to call it the Garden of Eden, or just the Kauai rainforest, doesn't really matter. But that's why they reached out to Alpha-Meridian."

Having a sudden thought, Frank's tone changed a bit and he sounded even a bit defensive. "Actually, Hawaii *IS* probably the most beautiful place on earth," he said.

"Come on, Frank. There's a big difference between Hawaii and the Garden of Eden."

Now both his eyebrows went up. "Is there?" he asked, mostly to himself, suddenly not so sure. His mind began racing. That was one of the things that made Frank so valuable and unique. He always considered everything.   "I want to check something," he said. And without waiting for a response, he left Iris standing in the kitchen alone.

She took no offense. She understood Frank and his behaviors and followed him into the other room. "What are you doing?" she asked.

He already had his laptop out and powering on. "I want to see where the Garden of Eden is."

"You're going to need to explain that to me a little further, Frank." She sat down next to him on the couch. "Unless I'm mistaken, and I'm pretty sure I'm not, no one knows where the Garden of Eden is."

He opened up a web browser and started typing. He was in his zone now. Research was what he loved the most.   "I just want to see what Google has to say about it real quick, before I get into the real digging," he said. "I know we won't find the answers here, but it's usually a good starting point for the basics."

He ran a hand through his hair as he scanned over the lists of websites that popped up, and Iris let him be. His craft required concentration. After a few minutes and a few clicks, he seemed content with enough new information for his mind to chew on for a little bit, and he pushed the computer aside and leaned back.

"Well, you're right," he said. "It's probably not in Hawaii."

"Probably?" she asked, emphasizing the word.

"I never trust that thing entirely," he said, pointing at the screen. He sat up and leaned his elbows on his knees. "But a betting man would put his money on the Middle East. Maybe somewhere in Iraq or around the Persian Gulf. Back in what used to be Mesopotamia." He pulled the computer back towards him and looked at something again. "The bible is pretty clear about its location actually. According to Genesis, the Garden of Eden fed four rivers." He traced the screen with a finger as he read them off. "The Pishon, the Gihon, the Tigris, and the Euphrates." He turned to Iris. "Even today, the Tigris and Euphrates rivers still run through Iraq."

CHAPTER 20

45° N, 7° E.
Elevation – unknown.

Somewhere inside the center of a mountain, Cameron Skull squinted at the faded German text on the side of the munitions charge. There were two separate stacks of the canisters on the rear platform of the K5, but it was unclear what each of the two stacks were for. There was also a long cable tethered to the back of the mighty cannon, which Cameron suspected was the firing line, and a wooden rod two inches in diameter with a flat plate attached to one end. He had an idea what that might be for as well. He had used a smaller version of something similar when he was a kid.

Cameron's childhood was not particularly great though. Born in 1980 and growing up in a bad area of Chicago, his father was an abusive alcoholic who would beat both him and his mother on occasion. One day, just before he turned sixteen, Cameron had come home from school to find his father in a drunken rage—again.

It had been only in the last year that Cameron had started standing up to his father, and it just made Joseph Skull even more angry and violent. His desperate attempt to not lose his dominance in the family.

That day, Joseph Skull had tried grabbing

Cameron's mother by the arm, but she shook him loose and ran out of the kitchen.

"Get back here, you stupid bitch!" he yelled.

Joseph had fallen to his knees on the tile floor when Cameron's mother dodged his attack. One of his hands held him up, saving him from landing completely on his face, while the other hand clutched onto a kitchen knife. Neither his father nor his mother had noticed Cameron's presence yet.

An anger rose inside Cameron at the sight, but he walked slowly into the kitchen where his father still had not risen to his feet. Walking straight up to him, Cameron pulled back and punched his father in the face, harder than he'd ever hit anything before in his life. Joseph Skull flew back—a splatter of blood spraying from his nose over the white cabinet doors.

Young Cameron then turned to go look for his mother. He made it to the door of the kitchen when a sharp pain sliced through his arm. He turned quick. His father had picked the knife back up and slashed at Cameron from the ground—cutting a three-inch opening into his left forearm. Blood poured from the open wound.

Joseph swung the knife again, but this time Cameron jumped back and avoided it. He tried kicking the knife out of his father's hand but missed, and was about to try again when his mother appeared at his side. She had heard the commotion and returned.

"Joseph!" she screamed.

Joseph turned his eyes away from Cameron. A drunken hatred burned beneath his pupils at the sight of her standing there. He swung again. Cameron tried pushing his mother to safety, but the blade caught her in the belly. Her mouth opened and she grabbed her stomach with both hands. Tears instantly filled her eyes and started pouring down her face.

From there Cameron blacked out. He did not have any memory of what had happened after that moment. But his mother had told the police later that Cameron had jumped onto Joseph, wrestling the knife from him, before turning it and stabbing it into his father's upper abdomen.

No one had died that day though— fortunately, and unfortunately. Joseph Skull served three and a half years of a six-year sentence for felony assault at Stateville Correctional Center outside of Chicago, then was never seen or spoken to again.

But not everything about his childhood was bad. Cameron had a few very close friends, and a very kind and loving mother. He also had a few role models who he looked up to dearly. One of those role models was one of his earliest employers.

After finishing his sophomore year of high school, Cameron had taken a summer job as a deckhand aboard a salvage ship in Lake Michigan. A job which, at the time he did not know, would lead to a lifetime love of adventure and exploration.

His ship, the *Blue Odyssey*, was captained by

a man named Walter Tin, who took Cameron under his wing immediately. Captain Tin always saw exceptional heart in Cameron. And after finding out about Cameron's father and home life, he sort of assumed the role of mentor and father figure for the impressionable teen—working him hard, but rewarding him with experience.

By Cameron's second summer with the Captain, he had made Seaman on the *Blue Odyssey*, and couldn't wait to send off in search once again for the legendary *Le Griffon*. The 45-ton, 7 cannon *Le Griffon* was sunk somewhere in the Great Lakes in 1679, carrying 6 men and a load of furs. The gentle story of her sinking was that she was taken down in a storm. But the more exciting stories told tales of Indians sailing out and boarding her—stealing the furs, killing the crew and setting fire to the ship, sinking her to the depths of the cold deep waters. Captain Tin always believed the second story. Or at least he said he did. And that was the story he told. Cameron believed it too. That's what made it all so exciting.

They never found the wreck though unfortunately, but the voyages were rewarding nonetheless. On calm days at sea, Captain Tin would bring out his pistols and old black powder rifles and teach Cameron to shoot off the side of the ship. They would toss out rubber buoys on a line and Cameron would be told to hit them as they floated in the current. The constant movement of the targets as they raised and lowered in the surf increased the difficulty, but improved his skill.

Finally, one day, as they came back to port in Chicago, Captain Tin handed Cameron the Remington Model 1863 that he had only let him shoot a few times before. The rifle was originally issued to a Union soldier of the Zouave regiment of Chicago during the civil war.

"It's seen enough of this sea air," Captain Tin had told him.

Cameron knew the guns value and did not want to accept it. "I can't take that," he said.

"Take it," the captain instructed. "You're pretty good with her. Just take good care of the old girl, okay."

Somehow, at that moment, Cameron knew he would never see Captain Tin again. Walter Tin knew it too. "You might have to get a new ramrod though. That one got a little bend in it, remember?" the captain said. "Maybe you can make one yourself if you can't find a replacement."

Cameron nodded to him, trying to hold back his emotion. The nod also served as an unspoken promise to his captain that he would always remember him and take good care of the rifle.

Now, creeping up on 40-years-old, and sitting on top of a Nazi K5 railway gun, Cameron recognized the wooden rod on the platform next to him. Just like a massive version of his civil war muzzleloader, the K5 used a very large ramrod to seat the rounds in the chamber. And the two canisters must be those rounds. They were each exactly the same diameter, and nearly the same length, but not the same outer material. And then Cameron spotted the difference and knew exactly what they were. One stack was the 283-millimeter ballistic tipped rounds of the gun, and the other stack was the high explosive boosters that got loaded behind them.

He grabbed hold of the rear breechblock hatch of the cannon and swung it open. It was heavy and the steel was cold. He had to set the torch down on the metal platform beside him and use both hands to open it.

Judging which of the two canisters was the rocket projectile cartridge. He grabbed it and stuffed it into the firing chamber. It slid easily into the space a few feet, before meeting some resistance. Cameron then grabbed for one of the explosive booster cartridges. He lifted it and was about to insert it behind the rocket when a terrible roar vibrated and echoed through the train cavern.

Oh crap...

He recognized the sound. It was the other creature from the top of the mountain. The rabid, hyper-aggressive creature who had grabbed him once, and also nearly tore the guard to shreds before the woman ripped his throat out.

Its angry roar became a panting growl, accompanied by the scratching sound of its long nails digging into the icy rock as it ran towards him on all fours.

Shit, Cameron. Hurry up, he told himself. He fumbled with the explosive charge but still managed to get it seated in the chamber, then turned and reached for the ramrod to press both cartridges into place. But beyond the dozen or so creatures that still reached for him from the ground along the side of the K5, Cameron could see the dark form of the animal-like creature charging at him in the distance. At the speed it was going, Cameron knew he only had a few seconds left before it reached him.

He stood and braced his weight against his back foot, then held the ramrod up in a batter's stance. His heart pounded as the thing neared, and Skull prepared to swing.

Five feet from the train, the creature reached the blockade of its brethren and scrambled up and over them—clawing and tearing its way over their backs and across the tops of their heads. It stood and leaped the last foot onto the K5 platform, and Cameron swung the ramrod. The creature flinched and Cameron's bat caught it in the shoulder instead of the head. It let out a bone chilling cry and he tried bringing the bat back around and hitting it again. But the thing turned and looked at him, and Cameron knew he was in trouble. The flame of the torch blazed across the creature's corpselike eyes, and for a split-second Cameron thought he saw the trace of a human soul still alive somewhere deep in that stare. But then it opened its mouth and bared its pink, blood stained teeth—a trail of saliva formed over its bottom lip—and all trace of the humanity disappeared.

Cameron kept his eyes locked on it. He

couldn't tell any more if the fire in its eyes was from the reflection of his flame, or from an actual fire burning within it. But before he could think any more about it, he got his answer. His torch burnt out, and all went dark.

—

The next thing he knew, Cameron was on his back in the frozen dirt somewhere next to a wheel of the train car. His eyes closed from the impact of the landing, but when he opened them nothing changed. He was still surrounded by darkness—and the sounds.

The pack of creatures on the other side of the K5 stirred in gruesome excitement. They began shuffling and moaning as they attempted to find passage through the steel barrier of the train. Except for one of them. The hyper-aggressive creature that was unlike any of the others jumped down and landed on him. It stunk of rot and Cameron had a momentary flashback of a fight that he had once had with another creature, almost like this one, inside the Church of Bones in the Czech Republic.

One deathly creature was enough for his lifetime though, and Colonel Skull had no intentions of letting this become a habit. As terrifying as this thing was on top of him, it wasn't all that strong, and he was able to keep it at arms distance. The things nails tore and slashed at him but couldn't break through the thick skin of his winter gear.

Cameron's only real fear was its jaws. The clawing was merely a side effect of it trying to pull itself close enough to get its teeth into him; and he did not want to try and push its head away, for fear of not being able to see and accidentally sticking one of his bare hands right into the creatures mouth.

He pressed up harder on its chest with one hand and felt around the ground beside him with the other. Like all railroad tracks, this one too was covered with small ballast stones—thousands of golf ball sized rocks used to hold the wooden cross ties in place. They would do him little good though. Much too small to cause any real damage, even if he grabbed a whole handful of them.

He stretched his arm out further. Maybe, hopefully, somewhere among the stones, there would be one large one with enough weight to have some crushing force behind it. He only needed one. But the thing on top of him seemed to never tire. It came at him with just as much energy and aggression as it had in its cell up above. Eventually, Cameron's arm would become too fatigued to keep it off him.

On the verge of having to change tactics and try to flip the creature over, Cameron's fingertips suddenly felt the edge of a long square piece of metal. One end the steel was mushroomed out, and on the other end it had been ground into a point. *One of the railroad spikes.*

He summoned the last bit of his energy and just managed to get his body over enough to wrap his fingers tightly around the rusty rail spike. It was heavy in his hand and he flipped it over so that the point was facing down, then thrust it into the side of the creature's head.

The thing collapsed, instantly losing whatever life it had and dropping dead again onto him. Cameron wasted no time in rolling its body off to the side and getting to his feet. The other creatures were not as fast or agile as this one had been, but they were still here, and they were still dangerous.

Quickly feeling his coat for the lighter again, he found it and pulled it out, sparking the little flame back to life. It was meager compared to the torch, but still cast enough of a glow for Cameron to see with.

To his left, two of the other creatures had found a way to this side of the train and were slowly coming towards him. The rest still wandered on the other side.

He ignored the pair and jumped back onto the K5, picking up the ramrod again with one hand and shoving it into the open rear of the cannons barrel. The two cartridges seated in place and he swung the breechblock door shut behind them.

Below, on both sides of him, dead hands reached up. Were they still trying to grab him though? Or were they now begging for mercy from what was about to happen?

Cameron kept the flame of the lighter burning and picked up the firing cable with his other hand. He took another look around him, then knelt on the platform behind the big gun—taking as much shelter as he could from it.

"You ready, fellas?" he asked out loud.

He dropped the lighter and put the hand over one ear as tight as he could. Then pulled the cord.

BOOM!

The blast was incredible. The entire mountain shook like an earthquake. The round flew over the tops of the coal car and engine and exploded against the sealed rock wall of the tunnel, creating a deafening boom of sound and a shockwave that nearly blew Cameron off the train. Thousands of tiny pieces of debris peppered the inside of the tunnel, ripping apart anything in their path.

Cameron felt the weight of the massive Kriegsloks war locomotive lean over like it was about to topple, and he held tight to the platform. The train teetered momentarily, then slowly righted itself and crashed back down onto the tracks in the midst of the thick smoke cloud left behind. A dozen or more bodies lay spread out over the ground surrounding it now.

Slowly, Cameron peeked out from behind his cover and eased his grip on the platform rail. The dust began settling, and the light of the morning sunrise poured in from the mouth of tunnel. He could feel its warmth and he smiled.

Jumping down from the K5, Cameron walked tall, past the front of the German train engine and out of the mountain. He looked up at the sky and smiled again. Thinking only two thoughts.

Kendall and Iris.

—

From deep inside the cave, a figure stepped out from behind one of the boxcars. She took a step forward and stopped before entering the light—watching the man as he walked away into the small valley that lay between the mountain peaks of the Alps. New trails of fresh blood dripped down her face and body from the splinters of wood that had blown off the boxcar and ripped into her. She ignored them. They were healing. And they did not hurt her.

CHAPTER 21

59° N, 10° Longitude
7:58 a.m. – Greenwich Mean Time

Francesco had abandoned his Google search after several minutes. He always suspected that most articles of information on the web were written by a small handful of people and based off of other articles that they had also probably read on the web. Essentially creating a big loop of reworded gibberish. Whether that was true or not he didn't honestly know. But what he did know was that ancient handwritten texts were rarely wrong or misleading. Hundreds of years ago people did not dedicate hours, sometimes years, scribing nonsense and false information.

Again, Iris took no offense when Frank got up to leave. Although it concerned her a little bit that he was taking A-M's plane. The school only had the one aircraft, and even though she couldn't fly it, with Frank taking it, she would be stranded. What if she got word from Cameron and he was in trouble, or hurt, and she needed to get to him quick? She could only hope.

The flight Frank took from the islands into Norway was around 400 miles and took a little less than two hours in the dual engine plane—the Learjet 45 could cruise at just over 500 miles per hour. Franks destination had been scouted a couple weeks ago, when Director Kestner had first started having his medical issues. Frank had gone to the hospital with him and spent two additional days in Oslo while James underwent his initial tests. And being the research fanatic that he was, he had of course gravitated to the local libraries.

After parking the jet at Oslo International Airport, Frank went out and called a taxi to take him to Old Aker Church, the oldest building in all of Oslo. Ultimately, he wanted to go to the Oslo Public Library, Deichmanske bibliotek, but it didn't open till nine, and his cab ride from the airport was only about a half hour. He had also considered stopping by the hospital, but decided to postpone that visit till later in the day. The director would ask a lot of questions, and Frank didn't have a lot of answers.

Pulling up to the curb, the cab dropped him off outside the church property, and he handed the driver a U.S. hundred-dollar bill to cover the fare. He wasn't exactly sure of the conversion rate, and deep down suspected that he had just gotten taken for two rides, but he thanked the driver anyways and started walking through the Old Aker Cemetery.

Many of the tall headstones around him dated back to the middle ages, as did the church itself, and Frank found it fascinating. He took his time walking up to the front entrance of the thousand-year-old Norwegian church, gazing at the way the morning sun cast stretched out shadows in the shapes of crosses and headstones over the snow-covered ground, and marveling at the architecture of the small cathedral above. Its single tower poked into the sky like an arrow. But, like the library, the church was not yet open to visitors this early in the morning, but Frank enjoyed the quiet and peacefulness here as opposed to waiting in town.

On his last trip he had been able to enter. The inside of Old Aker Church was even more impressive than the outside. It was built of dark grey stone, cemented together like the walls of a medieval castle. Arches and large pillars lined both sides of the interior and the pulpit, with flat circular chandeliers hung from the tall ceilings. Over the centuries, the church had fallen prey to thieves and vandals, storms and fires—but it had survived them all.

The worst destruction it had seen had come in 1703, when a lightning bolt set fire to the original bell tower and destroyed much of the church's possessions. A dreadful event for the preservation of history. What little that did survive though was cared for by the parish priest and his sons for nearly a hundred years. Until the construction of the Oslo Deichman Library in 1784—less than one mile away.

The Oslo Public Library originally opened with a collection of almost ten-thousand books and hundreds of manuscripts—the remaining books and ancient scripts from Old Aker Church among them.

Frank paused a few steps from the front door of the church. It was cold outside, and he thought about how glad he was that Meridian had upgraded to the Learjet a few months ago. Prior to that, they had been using a small 4-seater Cessna that he would have had to wrap with cowl and spinner covers to keep the oil from freezing.

He pulled his phone out of his pocket and checked the time. It was about a quarter till nine now, and the walk to the library would take about ten minutes, so he turned around and headed back out towards the street.

If he remembered correctly, the library was just south of the church, so he made a left onto Akersveien. Familiarity struck him as he saw Vor Frue Hospital coming up on the left, and he knew he was going the right way.

Hopefully James isn't looking out a window right now, he thought.

Passing the hospital, quickly, he made another left just before the roundabout and came to the library. The building had been moved and upgraded and renovated many times over the years and had no resemblance of its original form. Compared to the neo-gothic construction of the old Trinity Church next door, the library was fairly modern.

The front entrance had a wide stone staircase and a series of decorative large white round columns in front of it. They reminded Frank a little of the Lincoln Memorial in Washington D.C. as he passed between them.

He entered the building and retraced his steps from his last trip to the classification desk. Like most libraries, the Oslo public library used the Dewey Decimal System for categorizing books. Narrowing his search by religious subject matter and estimated publication dates, Frank was able to locate the section of the library most likely to contain the medieval texts and manuscripts that he was looking for. Aside from a 4th century Latin bible, the library kept all of its books and papers available to the public.

Once reaching the row of shelves, he began searching the class number stickers on the spines of the books till he found the sequence associated with his search results. Once finding them, he gently pulled several and began scanning their contents for pertinent information. The books and papers were hundreds of years old, and Frank was a bit surprised that they were left out to be handled. But then he realized that several of them were reprints, and several others were bound in protective binders. Only a few seemed to be the true originals.

Gathering up an armful, he brought them over to one of the desks and began doing what he did best. Reading.

—

Iris was in her classroom prepping for the afternoon class later, but also teaching herself a little bit as well. She may have been fluent in eleven languages, but Hawaiian was not one of them. And with the current circumstances in Kauai, she suspected that an understanding of the native language might be of some value.

She wasn't completely unfamiliar with Polynesian languages though. Hawaiian was sort of similar to Māori or Tongan; and on a hopeful trip to Easter Island one time, which in the end she never wound up taking, she had studied a bit of Rapa Nui, which was also in the same family of Austronesian dialects.

Unlike Francesco though, Iris didn't mind learning things from a computer. Before Alpha-Meridian, she had taught some online classes herself, and even made a little bit of money from some algorithms she wrote and patented as "useful processes" once selling them to a few of the big-name players in the language learning software business. But most mainstream online software, such as Rosetta Stone and Fluenz, did not offer a Hawaiian course. So, she was unsure of some of the correct pronunciation as she read over the text translation files that she was now looking at.

She stood to stretch her back a little and give her eyes a break when her cell rang.

"Hey Francesco," she said, answering it. "How was the flight? Did you stop by the hospital?"

"Buongiorno," Francesco said back. "No, I'm going to hold off a while on seeing the director. But I found some really interesting information at the Oslo Library."

"Let's hear it, Frank. I got another email from Sergeant Awapuhi a little while ago asking if Meridian would be willing to send me out there for a few days to lend a hand with things while they continue their investigations. But I think eventually they are going to request us to send a team into the rainforest."

"I think we should," Frank said.

"Should what? Send a team into the rainforest?"

"Into the Garden of Eden," he said confidently.

CHAPTER 22

60° N, 0° Longitude

"Come on, Frank. You can't be serious," Iris said. Although, she could tell by the tone in his voice that he was indeed very serious.

"Have you ever been to Hawaii?" he asked her.

"Yes, but..."

"When you were there," Frank continued. "Did you not tell yourself at least a dozen times that it was paradise?"

"Of course I did," she admitted. "But... but I didn't mean that kind of paradise."

"Are you sure about that?" he asked. But Frank did not want to keep her under interrogation to prove his point, so he kept talking before letting too much awkward time pass. "You're not alone," he said. "Probably everyone who has ever been to Hawaii has considered it paradise. It's so obvious, as a matter of fact, that that's practically the very first thought you think when getting off the plane."

Iris still didn't respond. Frank was right though, obviously, but it felt a little like his point was a bit childish.

"And what is the Garden of Eden?" He didn't wait for her to respond when he answered his own question. "It is paradise."

Iris walked over to the window in her

classroom and looked outside at the morning sky. She knew Francesco would not be making this claim unless he truly believed it and had enough evidence to back it. "What else?" she asked.

Franks voice became less aggressive now that he knew he had her serious attention. "The islands of Hawaii were completely isolated from the rest of the world for thousands of years," he began. "For centuries, not even Polynesians inhabited the islands, and then, after they settled there, it was another thousand years before James Cook arrived with the first Europeans."

In the background Iris could hear pages being turned and books sliding over tabletops. No mouse clicks, like she would have been doing.

Frank continued. "And out of all the islands, Kauai is the oldest of them all. It was the original Hawaiian paradise. And still generally considered to be the most beautiful."

Iris remembered just how truly beautiful it was. Many years ago, she had honeymooned in Maui with her ex-husband—Jake's brother. It wasn't the best of memories, because of the company she had been with, but the island paradise was truly magnificent. Some of the trails and waterfalls were beyond breathtaking.

"Its nickname," Frank continued, "is the *Garden* island." He paused. "I probably don't need to explain to a language specialist why other synonyms for beautiful could be considered more appropriate titles."

She chuckled. "No. I get it."

"And the name of the mountain, Waialeale, means *Overflowing Water*," Frank added.

"Overflowing water?" she repeated. "Why is that relevant?"

Francesco shifted gears a little bit. "Remember when I told you that the bible clearly states that the Garden of Eden was located at the source of four rivers, two of which still run through the Middle East today?"

"Yes," Iris said.

"Well, the Middle East cannot possibly be the location of the Garden. The problem," he said, before she could ask why. "Is that the entire land mass of Iraq, and that whole region, is on top of sedimentary strata. The ground, hundreds of feet below the desert, is littered with fossils. Think about it," he said. "Everyone knows that the Middle East is the oil capitol of the world. There are literally billions of gallons of oil underneath Iraq and Saudi Arabia."

"And oil comes from dinosaurs," Iris said, thinking out loud.

"Exactly!" Frank said with excitement. "How could the Garden of Eden be sitting on top of dinosaurs? Or anything dead for that matter? Including humans. Did you know that they have even found Homo Sapien finger bones that are almost a hundred-thousand years old there?" He stopped, then added, "The Garden of Eden predates dinosaurs, and all off mankind, except for Adam and Eve. It predates *sin*! If the Garden of Eden was there,

Justin Hyde

there should be nothing underneath it."

"But things change," Iris said. "The earth is constantly changing. Rock forms over old rock all the time, on a geological scale anyways. Couldn't the fossils be on top of the Garden of Eden, not under it?"

"No," Frank said. "If that were true then the Tigris and Euphrates rivers would also be underneath. But they aren't. They are on the surface, still to this day."

Iris walked back over to the computer at her desk and sat back down. She leaned back a bit in her chair and felt a pinch of excitement grow in her chest. "That is an interesting point," she admitted. "But why are the two rivers of the bible there then?"

Francesco wasn't finished. "Technically," he said. "One of them isn't. The Tigris river, in Genesis, is actually called the Hiddekel. But for some reason no one disputes it as being the Tigris today. But even if we ignore that. You can't ignore the fact that only two rivers exist there, where according to the bible, there should be four. No matter how you try to dissect a map, you cannot find four rivers anywhere in the Middle East that satisfy the location."

Iris was becoming anxious and started fidgeting with a pen.

"According to Moses, who wrote the book of Genesis" Frank continued. "The Garden of Eden was the source of these rivers. So, somewhere, they all have to connect. But the Tigris and Euphrates rivers flow in the wrong direction for this. The only place

174

they actually connect is right where they enter the Persian Gulf. They should connect upriver and flow apart. But they start apart and then flow into each other downriver. It's backwards."

"Okay," Iris conceded. "I'm with you that the Garden of Eden is not in Iraq then. But how does this prove that it's in Hawaii? Just the claim that the island is beautiful isn't enough."

"Not just beautiful," Frank corrected. "It is paradise."

"That still isn't enough," she said back.

Frank nodded as if she could see him. "I know. But let me ask you something."

"Okay."

"Do you know why Native Americans are called Indians?"

"Don't be condescending, Frank. Yes. I do know why."

He lectured the elementary school lesson anyways. "Because when Christopher Columbus landed in the new world, he had thought that he had landed in India. And he was so sure of it that he insisted that the people were Indians.

"I know, Frank," she said, a bit annoyed.

"The same is true for the Tigris and Euphrates," he said.

"What do you mean?"

"There are tons of examples in the world of people giving names to places and things because of mistaken identity. In this case, it was Noah who named the two rivers in Iraq." He flipped a few of the old pages of one of the books in front of him. "I found records of this in one of the books from the church. After the great flood, Noah's ark landed near the top of Mount Ararat, in Turkey. Which is directly north of Iraq.

Again, Iris stood up and walked anxiously around the room as Francesco continued. She was becoming more and more interested, and had a deep appreciation for Franks abilities to catch the details.

"When the ark came to rest, it makes sense that Noah could have seen a river that looked familiar to him before the flood, and so he gave it the same name, if not actually mistaking it for the same river altogether. Just like Columbus and the Indians."

"Still not seeing the connection with Hawaii though," Iris told him.

"Hawaii," Frank said in response. "Is almost exactly on the other side of the world from the Middle East. If you spin a globe around its vertical axis and draw a line straight through the widest part of the northern hemisphere, you can basically connect them. They are about as far away from each other as physically possible." He paused a second to make sure she didn't have any questions. "Why do you think God chose that point for Noah's landing? Because," he answered himself. "God took Noah and all the creatures as far as humanly possible away from the Garden of Eden, where the flood began."

"Where the flood began?"

"Yes," Frank said. "The flood began in Hawaii. Actually, it began in *Kauai*. That is where Adam and

Eve sinned for the first time. And so, it is where God started the cleansing of the world. And he took Noah as far away as he could away from it. He wanted to get Noah as far away from sin as he could, before starting over."

"What about the four rivers?" Iris asked.

"The four rivers," Frank answered, "spread out in four directions across the globe from the Garden of Eden, just like it says in Genesis, but were consumed by the great flood. They are now at the bottom of the Pacific Ocean."

On the other end of the line, Frank could hear Iris breathing, but she wasn't saying anything. "Think about it," he continued. "The Hawaiian Islands are the most remote islands in the entire world. They are more than two-thousand miles from the nearest continent. There is literally *nothing* surrounding them—except *water*." Again, he paused. "Not only that. But Kauai, even to this day, is the wettest place on earth. It is still not uncommon for it to get over forty inches of rain in a single day. Remember the name of the mountain?"

"Overflowing water," she said, slowly realizing the truth.

"Yes," Frank said back slowly. "A paradise of overflowing water."

Justin Hyde

CHAPTER 23

41° N, 15° E.
9:36 a.m.

Further down along the hillside from the cave of
Saint Michael, the castle of Monte Sant'Angelo
overlooked a wide canyon and endless miles of low-
brush wilderness beyond. Tony and Sergio parked
their car along the one narrow road that traced the
hilltop, just below the castle.

Tony was extra angry this morning, from the
little bit of uncomfortable sleep he had gotten. Once
parking the car, he got out and squinted his eyes to
try and keep out the morning sun. The rest of the
small parking lot was deserted, as was the road.

"Let's go," he said. He was speaking to both
his brother, and to little Becca in the backseat. The
girl quivered with fear and she began to cry. She
pulled herself into a tight ball against the opposite
door of the car, putting as much distance as she
could between her and the evil man.

Sergio stood behind the door, preventing her
from opening it and running away. But that was all
he did. He couldn't bring himself to have any more
involvement beyond just standing there.

"I said, let's go," Tony repeated. He opened
the rear door of the car and reached across the seat,
grabbing Becca by the ankle.

She screamed and fought to pull her leg back.

"No!" she cried with tears in her eyes. "Stop! Let me go! Please!" She tried holding onto the other door, but Tony was strong enough to pull her away from it. "I want to go home! Daddy! Where's my daddy? Help me! Somebody, help me!"

Sergio plugged his ears, but her cries bleed through his fingers. Finally, he looked up as his brother pulled the girl to his chest and held his hand tight over her mouth. "If you don't shut up," Tony said, threatening her. "I will toss you over the edge of this cliff right now and then leave your broken body to feed the wolves."

Becca's face was bright red and soaked from tears—but it was beyond her control to stop them from flowing down her face anymore. Her nose ran and her chest pumped with heavy rapid breaths. She looked up at Tony, terrified. His hand over her mouth smelled like a toilet, and she knew that there was nothing she could do.

Tony saw the look of surrender in her face and eased his hand from her mouth. "That's a good girl," he said. "Now, for the last time, let's go." He looked up at his brother and signaled him to follow as well.

For a second, Sergio had an impulse to grab Tony and throw HIM over the cliff. And had he been within arm's reach, he might have done so. But Tony was on the other side of the car, and Sergio's surge of adrenaline died quickly.

They walked to the hidden rear entrance of the castle. The small door was concealed by brush in the side of the hill just outside the castle walls. It was only about 3 feet tall at its highest point, and even little Becca was going to have to duck slightly to get through it. It was not part of the original design of the castle, but rather a feature that Bastian Santé had added a few months ago, for just such purposes as what they were now using it for.

Once inside, they sealed the door behind them, also sealing out all traces of the bright morning sun, and followed the tight space of the dark winding passageway that led underneath the thin courtyard of the castle, and then straight into the original underground dungeon. This design was thought out and served Bastian well. The castle dungeon had cells with strong iron bars, and could serve as another point of defense, should his secret entrance ever be discovered from the outside. It also prevented anyone, or any*thing*, from being able to escape the castle through that passage without also first getting past the bars.

Bastian Santé was the only one with the key.

Once reaching the dungeon, Tony grabbed the bars, but they did not open. The room around them was cold and damp, and smelled of mold and decay. "Santé," he called at a loud whisper. "Open the gate."

Disturbing sounds of shuffling and moaning came from somewhere deeper in the dungeon. But there was no answer from Bastian Santé.

"Father Santé," Tony said again, this time louder than the first.

Again, no response.

Becca looked behind her at the small passageway they had entered the prison from. She wanted to run. A voice inside her told her to turn and flee. Maybe she could make it out without being caught again. After all, she was smaller, and probably faster than both of the men, and could navigate through the tunnel much quicker than they could. A twinkle of hope rose inside her as she tried to summon the courage to act.

Then a *swoosh* and a *clang* sound came from the opening, and her hope died instantly. A solid sheet of thick metal slid down over the entrance like a guillotine slicing through her chance at freedom.

"What the hell?" Tony and Sergio turned around to investigate.

"What's going on?" Sergio asked fearfully. "What is that?"

Tony ran over and kneeled by the sealed passage. He punched the hard metal and it responded with a dull thud, but did not bend. Standing, he turned to the main bars of the dungeon cell. "Bastian," he yelled loudly. "Sblocca questa porta del cazzo!" he screamed. *Unlock this fucking door!*

Father Santé slowly appeared. His footsteps tapped off the stone steps as he walked down them and passed underneath the archway leading into the dungeon. Neither of the two brothers said anything as he approached the cell, and he ignored them equally.

"Hello," he said calmly to Becca. "I hope that these two have not been too harsh with you."

Becca sniffled, but felt an unexpected soothing from his tone. Perhaps this man was not bad like the other two. She looked up at him with watery eyes. "Will you help me?" she asked. Her lip trembled.

Santé bent down to look at her at her level. He had come because he wanted to see her. "I know you are frightened. And I am sorry for that." He reached a hand out and wrapped his fingers around one of the bars. "You are a great gift to this world. Do not forget that." He stood and turned, then began walking away from the prisoners. "It will all be over soon," he said quietly over his shoulder.

CHAPTER 24

The captors had become the captives.

Less than ten minutes after Father Santé left the dungeon, two other men dressed in black monks' robes entered. Their hoods were pulled over their heads, but the lower half of their faces were still visible. They walked up to the cell where Becca and the two men were locked. One carried a lantern, which he held to his side, and the other carried Bastian's set of keys.

As they neared, Sergio thought he saw a strange tint to their skin beneath the cloaks. At first it was like a shadow, but then he saw that both their faces were dark in complexion. Like they had been bruised.

Tony did not yell at them, but spoke with a quiet, desperate anger in his voice. "You better open this damn door. *Right now*."

Neither of the two monks spoke back to him, but the one with the keys inserted one of them into the lock of the bars and turned it. It creaked as the bolt disengaged.

As the door started to swing open, Tony secretly pulled his pointed dagger from its sheath and held it tucked in his palm with the blade flat against his wrist and lower forearm. Whatever games were being played, whatever tricks Bastian Santé thought he was going to pull, Tony was not going to be a part of. The door of iron bars swung fully open and he spun the knife around and stabbed it into the monk's side—twisting it, then pulling it out again, allowing the man to fall.

Right away blood started flowing from the hole in his side, but the monk did not fall. He did not even flinch. He had been gifted with the first phase of Bastian's CRISPR formula. His body had been changed, but only by a fraction of what was delivered to the rest of the people Bastian experimented with. All of the monks in the castle had been given a tiny In Vitro dose of DSUP from the tardigrade, mixed with a modified version of Alzheimer's.

In Bastian's other creations—the zombie-like creatures who had been put through his tests—the numbing of their pain receptors had been due to a side effect from the immortal jellyfish enzymes. But Bastian did not want his small army of castle monks to lose the brain functionality that was also the result of the turritopsis gene. So, he had developed an alternate way to achieve almost the same result. The Alzheimer's disease had been tweaked to specifically target memory loss only associated with the nervous system. So technically the monks could still feel pain, but their brain could not process a memory fast enough to make them aware of it. Essentially, they forgot about it before they even knew about it.

The monk turned to Tony and looked at him from under the hood of his robe. The man's indifference made Tony cringe. He took the blade and stabbed the monk again, in nearly the same place as before. But again, the monk did not move.

All eyes were focused on them. Becca was terrified and hid partially behind Sergio's large leg—for lack of a better place. Sergio remained still. He didn't show it, but he was also afraid. Was this monk possessed? Was he some sort of demon? "Diavolo," he whispered.

With the attention still on Tony, no one paid attention to the second monk creeping up behind him. The cloaked figure now held a blade of his own and silently inserted it into the small of Tony's back. Tony's body arched in pain and he dropped his knife and reached his hands around, trying to cover and hold the wound. He took a step forward then fell to his knees, and then onto his side.

Sergio reacted. But instead of charging to his brother's aid, he put a hand in front of Becca to shield her. "Stay behind me," he said to her.

The monk who had been stabbed stepped towards them, but paused at the open cell door. He looked momentarily at Becca, then up at Sergio before closing the door and relocking them inside. Then he turned. Tony was still on the floor, writhing with pain, and each of the monks grabbed one of his arms and began dragging him down the dungeon corridor and up the steps. Tony tried to fight, but his efforts only caused him more pain, and a dark trail of blood followed them as they disappeared out of sight.

Sergio turned to Becca who again had tears in her eyes. He looked down at her and almost felt a tear form in his eye as well. It was his fault that she was in this situation. He should have backed out last night like he had wanted to. Before they even took her. But he didn't. And now they were both here. Prisoners. Whatever was going to happen to her, was now also going to happen to him. And deep inside he knew that he deserved it.

"I'm sorry," he said with shame.

Becca held her arms over her chest and sniffled. "I want to go home," she cried. But speaking the words only made it worse, and she began crying harder.

—

The two monks lifted Tony onto a stainless-steel table. He grunted and cried out as they stretched his arms open and pushed him down flat. One of the men held him still while the other fastened leather straps around each wrist and then around both ankles. Once finished, they stepped to the side of the room and stood there, patiently.

Tony tugged on the restraints, but they were strong, and he knew the effort was useless. Below him he could feel a puddle of his own blood forming under his back. It was warm compared to the cold steel of the table. He grunted and gave one last hard pull on the leather wrist straps. "What is this?" he asked. "What's going on?"

The familiar voice of Father Santé answered him from just outside the room. "This is the end of your life."

Tony raised his head as much as he could to try and look for the voice. "You lying piece of shit!" he said furiously. "Get me off this fucking table!" He pulled again, but again his restraints held.

Slowly Bastian walked into the room through the open door by Tony's feet. He held a syringe in his hands and played with the needle of it as he walked to the side of the table. "Try to calm down," he said. "Getting excited is not going to help you." He raised the syringe and flicked the needle. "This is only the end of the life that you are accustomed to." He looked down at Tony stretched out across the table. "Your body will live."

"What are you talking about," Tony asked. All the toughness in his voice had faded.

Bastian answered. "In Vivo Veritas," he said, accentuating the second V in Vivo. He placed a hand on Tony's arm and held up the needle, but looked him in the eyes before inserting it. "In the *living*, lies the truth." He smiled at Tony and then stuck the tip of the needle into the vein in his right arm.

"You might be thinking that this is an anesthesia," Bastian said as he slowly pushed the plunger on the back of the syringe. "But I don't want to mislead you. This is actually an aggravated form of immunodeficiency. It will neutralize your B and T cells causing a failure of your immune system." He pulled the needle out of Tony's arm and set it down on another table behind him, then picked up something else and turned and looked at him again.

The room was quiet now except for Tony's heavy breathing and the drip of blood from the wound in his back as it slowly spilled over the edge of the table and formed a small puddle on the floor next to him.

"We don't want your body trying to fight off my bacteria now do we?" Bastian asked rhetorically. The CRISPR gene-restructuring needed a noncombative environment to perform at its optimal level. "Not that I expect this to work," he continued. "You are far to filthy and sinful. I have already tried with many others just like you, and none of you ever work."

Santé held up a scalpel to the light. The ultra-sharp blade reflected light into Tony's eyes and his body began to hyperventilate.

"I was hoping to start with the boy this morning," Bastian said. He leaned down close to Tony's face and saw the fear in him. "And then with that nice little girl that you brought me." He stood. "But I can't have you acting out against my men the way you did."

"Please stop," Tony said. He sounded like a scared child now. "I don't want the money anymore. Just let me go," he begged. "I won't say anything to anyone. I swear it!"

Father Santé used the scalpel to cut open the front of Tony's shirt. He ignored the man's pleading. "When you act out that way, you upset my creations. They get all worked up and hard to handle." He folded the shirt open, then set the sharp edge of the scalpel onto the top of Tony's bare chest. "You will soon be one of them. And you will see." Again, he looked Tony in the face. "But don't worry. I have a nice place up in the mountains for you to live. You'll love it." He smiled. "It gets a bit too crowded to keep you all down here. And lucky for you, you will probably change before the next truck leaves this afternoon."

"Please stop," Tony begged again. His face was turning red with fear.

"Unless," Bastian said, giving Tony a split second of hope. "You somehow succeed, and the sword doesn't kill you!" His eyes went grim and he shook his head. "But unfortunately, I do not think that will happen."

He pressed down on the scalpel and traced it down the front of Tony's chest, opening him like the top of a box. "But let's see," he said.

CHAPTER 25

Latitude 22° N, Longitude 159° W
9:50 p.m. Hawaii-Aleutian Standard Time

Kekoa only believed in one God—the Father in Heaven, and his son, the savior, Jesus Christ. But he also kept a strong connection with some of the Hawaiian traditions. He did not worship the sea as a god, the way some of the other islanders did, but he respected it for the power and glory that God gave it. He believed that the ocean was a gift from God to his people, but not that it was a god itself.

Likewise, he believed in the story of creation, but he saw no difference between the story of the bible and the story passed down by his people. Both stories, to him, were the same—all began with darkness. To his ancestors, it was the god Kane who created the universe out of nothing. To Kekoa, he was just God. Then there was Kanaloa, Ku and Lono. And Kekoa believed in them as well. Except he knew them as the Father, the Son and the Holy Spirit. Both stories also had the lesser gods, which were deities to some, and angels to others. Finally, there was man and woman. Both, the ancient Hawaiians, and Christianity, believed in the same thing. That one male and one female were created from the darkness to spread life to the world.

So, it was not surprising for Kekoa when he found out that all of creation had begun here in

Kauai. He had known that all his life, even before becoming a Christian. Hawaiians have always known it.

He sat in his living room, not at all tired, carving on a small piece of whale bone with a pocketknife. Blowing off some of the dust, he held it up to the light and looked it over. Trying to carve fire was not easy.

Over the years Kekoa had carved many things, and from many different materials. The canoe he kept on a shelf in the living room he had carved from a piece of mango wood. The tiki on his front porch from a piece of tropical ash. And the decorative ring that he never wore, from a piece of conch shell.

He leaned over again and carefully worked the blade of the knife over a curve in the bone sculpture, scraping away a little more material, trying to give life to one of the flames. But it was the hilt of the tiny sword that he was really going to struggle with later. He had never actually seen it. Makehewa had never let it go.

He wiped off a little more dust and inspected his work. The blade of the small sword was becoming visible beneath portions of the white bone fire. It was straight, but the flames that danced over it gave the illusion of it having curves. It's length and width, and the way the steel tapered out towards the bottom, were just as he remembered, and even the fuller that ran up the middle was the correct depth. The guard above the handle was also right. It was thin and flared out and back at each end, like the flights of an arrow.

Then there was the pommel—the endpiece just blow the grip. Kekoa would never forget it, even though he had only seen flashes of it as the sword was swung through the air that day, slicing through him and the rest of the men. The pommel was egg shaped on the outside, but with two cutouts passing through it. Looking at it from one direction showed the cutout of a cross—the arms of the cross filling up the widest points of the oblong oval. When the cross was right side up, the sword pointed to heaven.

Looking from another direction, from the side, the pommel's cutout was in the shape of a U. Both, the cross and the U intersected each other in the middle. Kekoa had started with that, and carving it had required a lot of patience and a steady hand, just as the flames now required.

In the past few days, whenever the police detectives or Sergeant Awapuhi had asked him to describe the weapon to them, he had struggled. His English was good, but not good enough to find all the right adjectives to properly explain it. And in Hawaiian, the adjectives just did not exist.

Several hours ago, before Lea had left, he had tried his best to describe the sword to her one more time. And to some degree he had been able. But tomorrow morning, when his small replica was finished, he would just bring it to her and let her see it for herself. That was the best way.

—

Back at her house in Wailua, Lea reached for her cell and dialed Iris.

"Sergeant Awapuhi," Iris said, answering the call. "What time is it there? Shouldn't you be asleep?"

"It's about ten, I think," Lea said. "But I don't think I'm going to be getting much sleep tonight. There's too much going on."

"Like what? Did you find out something else?" Iris asked, suspecting that the purpose of the call was for more than just a casual chat.

"I did. I spoke with Kekoa again. The man who survived the attack," she said, clarifying. "During our conversation he was persistent that the original story he gave was correct."

"What was his story?" Iris asked.

Lea had forgotten that no one at Alpha-Meridian had been given the complete details yet. They knew some, but not enough. And all they knew about the artifact was that it was supposedly found and taken from the rainforest. But they did not know that the sword that the group was attacked with was itself the artifact. "When he first gave us the statement a few days ago," Lea said. "Most of us thought maybe there was some misinterpretation. But his English is pretty good. In fact, I think he has been bilingual his whole life."

Iris listened intently as Sergeant Awapuhi continued.

"You remember in my last email that I told you the hunting party was in search of the Garden of Eden?"

"Yes," Iris answered. "And actually, while we're on that subject, can I tell *you* something?"

Lea paused her own story to allow her. "Sure," she said. "Go ahead."

"Well," Iris started. "This might be a little hard to believe. But..."

She told Lea all the details that Frank had discovered and gone over with her. She remembered them well. In the end, after almost 10 minutes of conversation and questions, Sergeant Awapuhi was convinced that the conclusion was correct. "Wow," she said. "I never would have thought that that could actually have been true. But it is true. Your friend is right."

"He usually is," Iris said with pride.

"How could no one have realized this before?" Lea asked softly.

"Honestly, I don't think anyone was trying that hard," Iris answered. "I think people have been content thinking that it might have been in Iraq."

"And how could no one have found it here before now? Even just stumbling across it. This island isn't that big," Lea said. "People have been all over it, exploring for hundreds of years."

"People like Kekoa?"

Lea paused to think. "Yes," she finally said, remembering that even Kekoa, a native Kauaian, well familiar with the jungle, had told her that certain parts of the rainforest were rarely traveled, if ever. He had also said, in his own words, that the wall they had found surrounding the Garden of Eden had a celestial aura to it, and that it seemed to be alive, and moved as it pleased.

The other end of the line had gone quiet. "Are you still there?" Iris asked.

"Yes, sorry," Lea said. "I was just thinking. Anyways, back to the reason I called. I actually wanted to fill you in on the artifact from the jungle. I want to see what your thoughts are on it, and see if you think maybe it would be worth it for you to come out here with your team and investigate for yourselves, since you know much more about ancient relics than we do."

"It's not the relics in particular that we specialize in," Iris corrected. "We are dedicated to their recovery and preservation; whatever they happen to be. But if we can be of help, and there is enough evidence to suggest that the artifact is there and of enough importance, then I'm sure the director will be more than happy to support our involvement." Now it was her turn to pause. "What exactly is *the artifact*, Sergeant?"

"I guess this won't sound too crazy anymore, now that we know that this really is the Garden of Eden." She took in a breath that Iris could hear on the other end of the line. "The *sword* is the artifact. It is the sword of Uriel. One of the seven archangels of God."

Iris sat back. *I better text Frank,* she thought.

CHAPTER 26

60° N, 0° Longitude

Frank landed the Learjet back at the small airstrip behind Meridian and pulled it into the dome-shaped steel Quonset hut near the school's backlot. He went through his usual checklist: *Cross flow valve, closed. Check. Thrust reversers, off. Check. Panel switches, off. Check.* Once satisfied that everything was as it should be, he hoped out of the plane and placed a couple chocks behind the wheels, then walked from the hanger around to the front entrance of Meridians main building.

His stomach growled, ready for lunch, but he bypassed the cafeteria and then his own office and headed for Iris's classroom, suspecting that that's where she would be. Upon reaching the room he found that his intuition was right. "Knock knock," he said from the doorway.

Iris looked up from her computer screen to the clock on the wall. "Wow, you're back already?"

"Yeah," he said, walking into the room. "And look who I brought with me."

James Kestner appeared behind Francesco in the doorway.

"Director!" she said. "They released you?"

Frank moved aside and James stepped passed him and into the room. He looked thinner than usual from the lean diet the hospital had kept him on, and for once his collared shirt didn't look ready to rip any time he moved. "I wasn't in prison, you know," he said chuckling. "And it's a good thing I called Frank here when I did. I think our little Italian was going to try and skip town without me." He turned his head and gave Francesco a friendly evil stare.

Frank cowered. He exaggerated the motion to put some humor into it, but the hint of red on his face gave away the fact that he really was a little embarrassed at being caught. "I thought you were still going to be there at least a couple more days."

"That should have been even more reason to stop by!" James said loudly, throwing his arms out to the sides.

"Yeah, but I..."

"I'm just giving you a hard time, Frank." He turned to Iris. "In all seriousness though, the timing was pretty lucky, with Frank still being in town and all. They discharged me this morning."

Iris had already stood from her desk and she walked up and gave the director a warm quick hug. "That's great to hear. Did they find out what's going on with you?"

"Yeah. It turns out I have an arrhythmia. The chest pains I've been getting, and the shortness of breath, are actually from my heart, not my lungs. They aren't sure what caused it," he said, when he saw Iris looking at the tip of a cigar sticking out of his shirt pocket. "But," he added, "Could be stress related." He winked at her.

"Oh please," she mumbled sarcastically as

she turned and walked back towards her desk.

The director and Frank followed her. James said, "Frank filled me in a little on what's been going on around here." His voice got a little softer. "I'm sorry about Cameron. We'll figure out what happened, one way or another. But no one is giving up on him."

Iris stopped at her desk but didn't sit. Her back was still to them. She didn't speak but nodded her head once.

There was a silence in the room following that, and to try and ease everyone's sudden sorrow, Frank changed the subject. "James doesn't think we should send you to Hawaii," he said.

She turned. "How come?"

The director sat down in one of the student's chairs in the front row before answering. Class wasn't scheduled to start for another hour. "It doesn't sound like the sword is there anymore," he said matter-of-factly. "My understanding is that the team that found it removed it from the rainforest."

"Not exactly," Iris said. "It was just one man who removed it. He used it against the others, killing all but one of them with it."

"But it's still gone," James pointed out. "I can't send you halfway around the world just to help the police with their investigation. If the artifact had been left, or never found at all, I could justify it. I'd probably even send Ethan with you. But without it, the members of this academy can't get involved."

It was a fair point, Iris knew. She had sort of

even expected this. After all, Alpha-Meridian was not just some team of crime detectives available for hire.

"He does have another idea though," Frank added.

Iris leaned against her desk and looked at the director. "What is it?"

Director Kestner ran a hand over the top of his smooth black scalp and leaned back in the chair. It squeaked in protest beneath him. "Think about this," he said. "Why would someone search for the Garden of Eden, looking for a sword? It doesn't make much sense. There are thousands of people who have searched for the location of the garden over the centuries, and I'd bet that not one of them was after a sword."

"They're all after the tree of life," Frank said.

Kestner stood back up. "Exactly. In the Garden of Eden there is the tree of life and the forbidden tree of the knowledge of good and evil. According to the bible, man's fate was sealed the moment Adam and Eve ate from the tree of knowledge. But depending on what you believe, the tree of life may still be the key to immortality. That is what all these religious explorers and archeologists search for, typically." He walked over to a globe in the far corner of the room by the window and spun it. "But even if the tree of life did not guarantee immortality anymore, which it may not, after Adam and Eve, it would still be one of the greatest archeological and religious discoveries of all time."

The globe slowly stopped spinning and James

adjusted its position a little until finding the Shetland Islands. He placed his finger over them. "This is us," he indicated.

Iris wanted to make a sarcastic remark about him stating the obvious, but thought better of it. "Yes, it is," she confirmed, a little confused at the direction this was going.

Frank joined them by the globe. "James has an interesting thought," he said, jumping back into the conversation. "If the archangel Uriel abandoned the garden, but left his sword behind for whatever reason, how would anyone have ever known that, or even thought to suspect it?"

"I don't know," she admitted. "That's a good question though I guess."

Francesco continued. "The man who led the hunting party in search of it obviously had reason to believe that it was there. You said yourself that Kekoa was certain that the sword was the objective."

"Maybe he found an ancient script, or a lost book somewhere that had a record of angels leaving, or maybe even being called away?"

"Or," James said. "Maybe he found another weapon already, somewhere else." He looked down at the globe again. "If someone were to have found a biblical weapon left behind somewhere, and then wanted to find another one, they would naturally look where the bible tells them to." Again, he spun the globe, this time putting his finger over the Hawaiian Islands. "In Genesis, God clearly says that there is a flaming sword in the Garden of Eden."

"Makes sense," she said. "But where does that leave us now?"

"Well," again he turned the globe. "My only guess would be that whoever took the sword might be looking for more of them."

"There are seven archangels," Frank said. "And I don't even know how many other angels."

"Wait, so that's what this is?" Iris asked. "Someone is trying to collect the weapons of the angels?"

"Sounds crazy. But yes, it seems so."

"But why? I mean, why kill people over it? Why not just request permits and organize legal expeditions? You would still be the most famous archaeologist of our time. Not to mention make tons of money. It would easily pay for itself a thousand times over, in the end."

"None of that matters to someone who isn't interested in money or fame though," James said.

Iris was confused. "Then what?" But she knew the answer right away. "Power," she whispered.

"Power," Kestner repeated. "And what could be more powerful than men armed with the weapons of God?"

What would that kind of power be capable of in the wrong hands? The thought scared her. "What can we do?" she asked.

Francesco leaned in and pointed to a spot on the globe just a little south of Alpha-Meridian. "We go here. To the island of Skellig Michael."

"Why there?"

It was Director Kestner's turn to speak again. "The grand prize," he said. "If you were interested in angels, then Saint Michael would be your holy grail— so to speak. He is the leader of the archangels and the one in command of God's army. It was the archangel Michael who defeated Satan and cast him from heaven. Ultimately, this person will go after the sword of Saint Michael. If he hasn't already done so."

Outside the window Iris heard faint voices. It sounded like Ethan was leading the students back from their first morning of field training. They would need to shower and change before coming to her class, but she still had some prep work that needed to get done first and her mind wandered for a minute. "What is that place? How do you know Saint Michael's sword is there?"

"We don't know for certain that the sword was left there," Francesco admitted. "But we do know from the records kept in a twelfth century Irish manuscript that I found, that Saint Michael *did* at least leave his shield there." He pulled a piece of paper out from his pocket and handed it to Iris. She unfolded it and began reading. "That's the name of that manuscript," Frank told her.

She looked down at the words. "It's Latin," she told them. Libellus de fundacione ecclesie consecrati petri. She had to think about the translation for a moment. "I think it means, 'Peter's petition for the foundation of a new church,' but I'm not a hundred percent sure on that."

"You would know better than I would," Frank said. "Even finding bits of translated pieces of it was very difficult for me. But I was able to find enough. The manuscript recounts the events of Saint Patrick's battle with the serpents and demons who invaded Ireland. It says that Saint Patrick was able to fight of the creatures to the farthest southern corner of Ireland on his own, but could not drive them out completely. So, he called to heaven and Saint Michael came down with an army of angels to destroy the beasts forever."

"The point though," James interrupted. "Is that this document proves that angels did in fact leave things behind. We know for sure that Michael left his shield on Skellig Island, so it's a reasonable assumption to think that his sword may be there too."

"Makes sense," Iris agreed. She looked at the globe in front of them again. The Island of Skellig Michael was not that far away from them. They could probably be there in just a few hours in the jet.

Frank continued. "It also says that Michael returned to the island every year after that and would fill their jars with enough wine for every monk who lived there. And ever since, Ireland has considered Michael their great protector. Sometime around the year 600, the monks on Skellig Michael built a church to the archangel that still stands today among the ruins and ancient stone huts. That's where we should start looking."

Iris's eyes were wide as she thought over this

new information. *So, it's true. The angels really did leave weapons behind.* "How did you learn all this?" she asked.

Frank's face got a little red again. "It's Luke Skywalker's hideaway in the last two Star Wars movies."

The director rolled his eyes.

"I'm a big Star Wars fan, okay!" Frank barked at him. "Anyways," he said, redirecting his words back to Iris. "After the movies came out, I became really interested in the location. I just thought it was so cool. So, I did a little research on it on my own."

"Of course you did, Frank."

"Nothing even close to this in-depth," he said. "But enough to give me the insight to look deeper now. I spent the entire flight back from Norway reading about it while James flew the plane. And I think this is it."

"If we're not too late," James said.

Iris looked at him. "Then we should go. I'll text Ethan right now and let him know to tell the students that class will be canceled today."

"There is no landing strip on the island," Frank added. "I checked that too. We'll have to fly into Kerry and then charter a boat in the Portmagee marina."

"You two go," Kestner said. "I'll stay back and work on things from here."

Francesco and Iris both nodded then turned to leave when Iris's phone rang. She stopped and looked at the caller ID but didn't answer it.

Frank noticed she wasn't moving anymore. "Iris, you okay?"

She looked up at him. Then fainted.

CHAPTER 27

45° N, 7° E.

"Iris," Cameron said again into his satellite phone. "Iris, are you there? Hello." A scraping sound came through the line and then the broken-up voices of James Kestner and Francesco Ferrari in the background. "James, Frank," Cameron said loudly.

Frank picked up the dropped phone. "Professor. Is that you?"

"Frank what happened to Iris? Is she okay?"

"Yeah she's okay," Frank said. "She saw your name on her caller ID and fainted. But only for a second. James just got her up and into a chair. God I'm glad to hear from you! Where the hell have you been?"

"I'm going to go get you some water," James said to Iris in the background.

"Are *you* okay?" Frank asked. "We've all been really worried here. We thought maybe you..."

Cameron was sitting with his back against a rock at the base of one of the mountains. His body was beaten from head to toe, and he felt like he could fall asleep and probably stay asleep for a year. But he was also badly dehydrated. As Frank spoke, he felt around for the lighter in his coat pocket again. He needed to melt some snow and replenish himself. Eating snow, he knew, would only make his dehydration worse. Another lesson from his past.

Snow was mostly made of air, and required eating about 10 times as much of it as its equivalent in liquid water. But the real reason was that the body had to use up its own energy to heat and melt it— making dehydration even worse. Much better to melt it somewhere else.

He pulled the lighter from his pocket. "I'm okay, Frank. A few minor injuries, but I'll live."

"Where are you?"

Cameron looked around. That was a good question. "I must be somewhere on the southern side the mountain," he said. He had walked a quarter mile or so before sitting, but back in the distance to his right, he could still just barely see the outline of the blasted hole in the mountain. And to his left was a small tree covered valley between two rows of more mountains on each side. "I can't see anything recognizable or any major landmarks from where I am though."

"You made it over the peak then," Frank said. "We weren't sure. We got a call from the Swiss police commander saying that he thought maybe you had fallen. And then when we lost contact with you... Why hasn't your sat phone been working?"

That made Cameron realize that Frank and Iris probably thought he was still somewhere at the top of the mountain. "I did fall, Frank. Sort of. But I am not the man the police are talking about. Someone else fell. There's a prison at the top of the mountain. The prison is full of... of, zombies or something. I don't really know. But they..."

"Colonel!" Frank said loudly. "What the hell are you talking about? Slow down! A prison? You fell? *ZOMBIES?*"

"Let me talk to him!" Iris said.

Frank handed her the phone. "Cameron! You're alive! Are you hurt? I've been so scared."

Her voice was like an angel speaking to him. "I'm alright," he said calmly. "I'm going to find my way out of here and be back before you know it."

"We thought you were dead." There was a deep sadness in her voice.

"But I'm not," he said reassuringly. "Things definitely took a turn though."

"Where are you? Francesco and I were just about to get on the plane and fly out to Ireland, but we are coming to pick you up instead."

Ireland? "There's no way you could get a plane in here," Cameron said. "I'm not even sure this is accessible by helicopter." He looked around some more. *Actually. Maybe it is accessible by helicopter*, he thought. But Meridian didn't have one. So it didn't matter. "Why are you going to Ireland?"

"There has to be some way for us to come get you," she said, ignoring his last question.

"There's not. Trust me," he said, looking around again at the dense wilderness surrounding him. "This is by foot or snowmobile only. I'll find a way out of here though. If I'm right about my location, I think I'm somewhere southeast of the Matterhorn. Maybe getting close to the Italian border. I know there's a couple remote towns scattered around down there. I'll see if I can get to one of them and then arrange transportation from there if they don't have a landing strip or at least a helipad. I know there's at least one town south of me somewhere that's within driving distance of Zermatt. I overheard a few people talking about it the other night when I was there. Before I headed out yesterday morning. Lucky enough," he added lightly. "The town has a sanctuary. The group was pretty talkative about it. Must be a sign from above that I'll be okay, huh?" He managed a small laugh, mostly to try and give her some comfort.

"How's the battery holding up in your sat phone?" she asked. "I do not want to lose our line of communication again."

Cameron pulled the Iridium away from his ear and checked the status indicator on its screen. "It's pretty good. I've had it powered off a lot." He cringed at his own words.

"Don't do that!" she yelled at him.

Knew that was coming. "I wouldn't have gotten a signal inside the mountain even with the satellite phone though. But I'll explain later." With a little bit of a struggle he managed to get himself to his feet while still holding the phone to his ear. He looked off into the valley and the scattered trees ahead of him. There was a chill to the air this morning, but his clothing was plenty warm, as was the early afternoon sun when it peeked through some of the lingering clouds, and suddenly he had to squint and wished for a pair of sunglasses to protect his eyes from the harsh reflection of it off the snow—his were still in his bag at the top of the mountain. "Why are you and Frank going to Ireland?" he asked again.

"That's a long story too," she said. "And might be a bit hard to believe at first, honestly. I'll have to give you most of the details some other time. But in short, Alpha-Meridian has gotten semi-involved with a situation going on in Hawaii. They had an artifact removed from the rainforest on Kauai, and it has some pretty heavy religious ties to it. Specifically, to Uriel, and to Saint Michael, two of the archangels. Frank and I are headed for an Island off the southern coast of Ireland to investigate what's left of a sixth century Gaelic Monastery there that was dedicated to Michael over a thousand years ago."

Cameron stared off into the distance for a moment—thinking. "Interesting," he finally said. "The sanctuary I just told you about is also dedicated to Michael."

"Michael the archangel?"

"I'm pretty sure. I don't exactly remember everything those guys were saying about it since I wasn't paying that close attention. But I do think I remember hearing that it was some type of monastery. And I definitely remember them talking about Michael."

"That's strangely coincidental," she said.

"What is?" Frank's voice said from somewhere behind her.

Iris turned and shushed Frank with a finger. "Can you remember if they said anything else about it?" she asked Cameron.

"No. That's all I really picked up on, unfortunately."

"I'll have Francesco look into it," Iris said.

"Look into what?" Frank asked.

"Good idea," Cameron said, drawing back Iris's attention. "Listen, I better get going. It's early, but so is sunset around here, and I want to take advantage of the light as much as I can."

"Cameron, wait."

"Yeah?"

She hesitated. "Nothing. Never mind."

Professor Skull knew what she was thinking. But for some reason neither of them could say it still. Even after all these years. The occasional times that they had actually did say it, it was casual. Kind of the same way they would have told a friend that they loved a movie. It was still sincere and from the heart but lacked the passion that they both desperately wanted to express. *Stupid*, he thought. "I'll call you again in a few hours, okay," he said, still holding back his true feelings.

"Okay," she agreed. "Promise me you won't get yourself into any more shit between now and then though."

"Haha. Okay, I promise I'll try not to."

She knew that was the best she was going to get. Cameron would never promise something that was out of his control.

"Hey Iris, hang on a second."

"Yes?"

"You didn't tell Kendall anything did you? She doesn't think I'm..."

"No," Iris said quickly. "No one has said anything to her. Last time I talked to Jake he said that she hated him dropping her off at school every day, but other than that was having a good time."

Cameron smiled. "Can you call over there again soon and let her know that you talked to me and that I'll give her a call myself in a day or so?"

"Of course," she said.

"Thanks babe. I'll call you in a few hours, okay," he promised again, then hung up the phone.

CHAPTER 28

45° N, 7° E.

Cameron held the lighter in his mouth while he lifted the bottom of his coat and clipped the satellite phone back onto his belt. He looked around for something to melt some snow in. Not surprisingly though, he found nothing.

"Well, a man's got to do what a man's got to do," he said to himself as he reached down and picked up a handful of snow and tossed it into his mouth. In the end, it might not actually do anything for his thirst except worsen it, but it was momentarily refreshing, nonetheless. The cold stung his tongue and he ate it with his mouth open in the same way he would have eaten a hot coal. "At least it's not yellow," he said again, talking to himself with his mouth awkwardly open.

After a few seconds he was able to swallow. "Ahhh." Then he looked around again. The sun had moved enough now since he first left the tunnel for him to determine direction, and a little way off to the south it looked like there might be an opening through the trees. Maybe even a river or stream that he could follow.

He looked briefly behind him again at the tunnel before moving. It was a black hole in the side of a white wall until something fluttered over the darkness of it. Maybe a patch of snow that had been

Justin Hyde

barely hanging on had finally given up and fell. It fluttered again. At this distance whatever it was was blurry and Cameron squinted harder at it.

There it was again. Larger than before. And this time the fuzzy image didn't disappear, but instead seemed to grow a little larger. It leaned to the side then straightened again.

"What the hell is…" A clump rose in his throat and he coughed. *Are you kidding me?* With each passing second the image became more and more recognizable, although still a good 200 yards away. It was clear now that it was a person. One of the creatures.

A second form appeared just behind the first. Two of the things were emerging. Maybe more. *How can this be happening?* Even with all that he'd seen so far, the reality of these things was still unbelievable.

He turned around to run—definitely not wanting a rematch with them. *I have to get into those trees,* he realized. They were not too far away. Maybe 50 yards. And in full strength Cameron could run that distance in 10 seconds, easy.

Starting at a jog he began quickly picking up speed as his body got used to the motion of his legs and the swing of his one good arm. The shoulder on his left was still injured, and he kept that arm held across his chest. But the run was difficult through the fallen snow and he stumbled twice, barley catching his balance before falling.

Suddenly a pair of birds flew from the tops of

one of the trees directly in front of him. They took off in a fast, almost frightened flee, instead of a graceful rise into the air. He was approaching quick and must have startled them from a distance. But their commotion did not slow him down and he continued to run until making it within 10 feet of the nearest pine. Then he stopped fast and threw both arms up in surprise as the pointed front end of the Ripsaw super-tank broke over a thin sapling and nearly ran him over just as easily.

The electric powered snow tank was a silent hunter and Cameron had not heard even the faintest sound from it until it was right on him, breaking down the tiny trees on the outskirts of the forest. The driver saw him and stopped the treads on the ripsaw just as Cameron dove sideways for safety. He landed in a dirty clump of stick and debris covered snow, but rolled over into a prone position quickly and turned to face the side of the tank. It stood still and silent like a big metal beast stalking its prey— except for the caged sled attached to the rear of it.

Cameron tried to remain hidden in the snow as best as he could while he watched the creatures stirring inside the cage. The flat-bottomed sled, surrounded by bent and bloody metal bars, creaked. The creatures inside seemed confused and angry. At first, he counted four of them, but then a small fifth one appeared. They bumped into each other as they tried to each find their place along the bars. One after another, dead hands began reaching out from the cage, mostly in his direction, and Cameron wondered if they had seen him or if they somehow sensed him there?

Can they smell me?

Their hoarse, raspy groans and noises created an eerie soundtrack to the otherwise silence of the isolated valley. One of them—a particularly disgusting one—opened its mouth and yelled out loudly. It was the remains of a man, as best as Cameron could tell, but looked as though it had been underwater for years. It was hairless and wrinkled; its skin a dark shade of purple. Rotten green teeth were exposed under constantly pulled back lips. The sight of it made Cameron's own skin crawl.

Then there were two others who were only slightly better off it seemed. But then there were the last two who looked almost normal, and Professor Skull had a small feeling of compassion for them. Aside from the unblinking hollow look in their eyes and their stiff body language, he might have almost thought that they were just people.

He looked to the front of the tank again. The side windows of the futuristic looking attack vehicle were all tinted, and Cameron couldn't see how many people were inside. But then one of the wing doors of the cabin opened. It swung upwards and a small woman crawled out of the opening. She pulled herself out and stood atop the long all-terrain tread of the beast. It was the same woman who Cameron had seen drive off in the tank last night at the top of the mountain.

She was wearing the same all white parka

and snow gear that she had been wearing the night before. But at this close distance her facial features were much more discernable. She was petite, with messy brown hair and tough eyes. Her complexion was almost as white as her jacket and Cameron suddenly recalled that she didn't speak English, at least not as her first language. Last night she had spoken in what sounded to him like French. And judging by her features now, he guessed that he was probably right. She had a "French" look about her.

She also had a gun—a small pistol held to her side. Skull couldn't tell what kind it was, and he really didn't care. He didn't have one at all.

She looked around for only a second before spotting him trying to hide in the snow. She said nothing, but pointed the pistol at him and pulled the trigger. The shot purposely hit the ground a foot from his head. The message was clear.

Cameron stood up, raised his right arm, and tried lifting his left as best as he could. "My shoulder is dislocated," he called out, hoping that she could at least understand his tone enough to understand his predicament.

She ignored him and hoped down off the tank in one smooth motion, like a jaguar coming off a branch. Her legs sunk into the snow almost to her knees—the big tread of the tank behind her almost as tall as her head now. She waded through the snow in his direction, keeping the pistol and her eyes pointed at him the whole time.

"Qui es tu?" she asked in heavy French.

Justin Hyde

"My name is Cameron Skull."

To his left, Cameron thought he heard something. He listened closer and realized it was the faint sounds of the creatures from the tunnel slowly catching up to him. He turned and repositioned himself in a non-threatening way, but so that he was facing them. So far, the girl in white had not noticed them coming. She was too focused on Cameron and must have mistaken their sounds for the sounds of her own creatures locked up in the sled. She mirrored Cameron's motion as he turned, putting her back to the things approaching. One of them began to reach an arm out and Cameron hoped that it wouldn't make any more noise.

"Faire demi-tour et marcher jusqu'á la cage."

He had no idea what she just said, but if "*marcher*" and "*cage*" meant what he thought they might mean then she was about to be very disappointed. There was no way he was marching into that cage with those things.

She waved the barrel of the gun in the direction she wanted him to go.

Come on, Cameron thought, staring at the creature approaching. *I know you want me. Come get me.*

The first creature in the pack that was moving in on them was the woman. The relentless female with the long open cut up her back that had been after Cameron since the prison. She moved silently now, just as she had when reaching for the guard's throat.

218

Just a little closer...

The girl in white must have noticed Cameron staring over her shoulder. She spun around and ducked just in time to avoid the grasp of the dead woman. She pulled the trigger on her pistol and two rounds drilled into the woman's gut making her lean over and fall. Behind her, two more of the things tripped over the fallen woman but grabbed desperately for the girl in white at the same time.

Cameron took full advantage of the distraction and took off in a run. He rounded the back of the tank and hoped over the hitch joining it to the sled. The shock had worn off the girl in white and she shot both other creatures in the head, then turned and fired another two rounds towards Cameron, but both shots missed. One of them ricocheted off the back of the tank and the other missed the tank completely and hit one of the creatures inside the sleds cage. The remaining four were unphased by the threat.

The girl in white started after him, but Cameron, under attack, was fast, and he scrambled quickly up the opposite side of the snow tank—climbing the thick rubber tread until reaching the top. His shoulder screamed and didn't cooperate well, but he hardly noticed with so much adrenaline pumping through him. He rolled over the top of the tank's cockpit just as the woman reached the rear, then flung himself feet first under the open wing door and into the driver's seat. With no sound from the engine he couldn't tell if the steel beast was on or not, but it was configured similar to a car, with steering wheel and gauges, although it was much more tactical and cramped—*it's like a like a jet fighter*, Cameron thought—and he pushed down on the throttle and the machine raised up from the torque of the motor and took off.

A few feet ahead and just to the left, the dead woman was rising to her feet again—fresh blood pouring from her belly. The two other creatures who had taken bullets to the head were still down though, not moving. But past all of them was one more of the dead men. It was in bad shape from the earlier explosion in the tunnel. Half the skin on its face had been scraped off from flying debris, and its right leg was dangling and dragging through the snow behind it as it very slowly tried to catch up to the rest of them.

Professor Skull turned the wheel hard and the tank plowed into the creature and lifted up as the treads easily ran over it. The sled behind the Ripsaw did not handle the impact as well though and bounced up as it hit the zombie speed bump. The creatures inside flew into the air, crashing into the roof of the cage, then landing back down in a pile on top of each other. They roared and screamed but could do nothing else as they were towed away.

Cameron looked in the small side mirror outside the driver's window of the tank as he sped off. In the foggy reflection he could see the woman in white lift her arm and fire the last shot of her pistol into the head of the dead woman. Killing her again.

CHAPTER 29

41° N, 15° E.

"Bring it to me," Bastian Santé said to one of the monks.

Tony was still lying on the table, hours later. He had been given an extreme dosage of Bastian's CRISPR formula—a level that had never been toyed with before in any of the other creations. But Tony was filthy and rotten already. His mind was perverted, and his soul was wicked. Those types of people never worked in the end.

That is why Father Santé had decided to start experimenting with children. They were clean. And in a few more hours, once he was completely done with the man in front of him, he would go get the boy.

He was convinced now, after so many failures, that the problem must lie in the person, and not in his genome recipe. *To be among the gods, one must be godlike.* But just in case he was wrong, he had decided to infest Tony's body with outrageous amounts of the altered protein enzymes. So much so that it should remove all doubt, one way or another. Theoretically now, Tony was so pumped full that his body should have mutated to a point where he would basically never die.

But whether or not that was really true, Bastian was about to find out.

From the end of the room, one of the monks wheeled in a steel cart and brought it alongside Tony's table, then stepped back nervously, staring at the object lying on it.

There were several factors that contributed to the outer appearance and the level of destruction associated with each of Bastian's creatures. How badly their bodies reacted and how extreme the wounds on them depended on a lot of things: the ratio of tardigrade vs jellyfish enzymes, the amount of the dosage, the placement of the dosage and how the blade was introduced and delivered to them, were just a few.

Then there were also aftereffects. Once everything was done, the creatures tended to be careless and would often injure themselves even further by sometimes attacking each other, or simply by falling or bumping into things. Eventually they would heal, some faster than others, but it gave most of them a very gruesome appearance. Just last night, one of the creatures—a female—had gotten out somehow and attacked one of the guards. She had wandered through the lower floor laboratory of the castle, unnoticed in the dark of night, before attacking the man and then walking straight into a fireplace that was burning at the bottom of one of the castles watchtowers. The warmth and the glow of the flames must have attracted her.

She had been nude, and her body was more than moderately fireproof. But somehow she must have spilt one of the methanol containers on her while she was in the lab. The liquid chemical was kept as a base product for Bastian's formaldehyde—another small additive of his formula. And it was highly flammable.

She had set herself on fire and then continued to wander the halls like a human torch. The flames blinded her, and she occasionally bumped into other things as she slowly set one thing after another aflame in the castle. Had the walls of the medieval structure not been made of stone, she would have burned the entire place to the ground.

Bastian had heard the commotion of the other guards and several of the scientists and monks once they were woken and realized what was going on. The guards had avoided the woman, as did the scientists, afraid of being set on fire themselves, but the monks were different. Like her, they too had a level of protection, and quickly smothered her with a fire blanket.

She had survived, of course, and was now locked in the overcrowded containment room, but she was a horrific sight. Her body had withstood the flames, but it had changed the pigment of her skin to a grey speckled black color, and the whites of her eyes were now a bright solid red from ruptured blood cells. The cartilage in her nose and ears had not melted away, but distorted and reshaped into abstract formations on her face. She had also ingested some of the burning chemical and it filled her parotid and sublingual glands with ash, restricting her from being able to produce saliva. So her cries and moans were deep, dry and terrifying.

Situations like this were not uncommon with the creatures. Half of them showed signs of damage from something external. And the other half Bastian had simply gotten tired of stitching up after his surgical implantations, and just left them open to bleed out. One of the other men in the containment room had been given the Cas9 protein through his genitals. And when the results did not work properly on him either, his reanimated body had stood—but the incision had then opened wider from the weight of his internal organs, and his bladder and half his small intestine had spilled out. He drug them around below him now when he walked, like a dog whose owner had let go of its leash.

Bastian reached down with his gloved hand and gently picked up the object from the top of the metal cart. Its temperature raised and lowered back and forth beneath his grasp and it hummed like the low frequency of a tuning fork.

Tony turned his head towards it, but his mind was already going blank. He was still alive, for now, but all feelings were gone inside him except for an unexplainable anger. Strangely, he felt no fear from the object or from the man wielding it. But as Father Santé brought it closer and closer to him, Tony's body began to pulse, and his skin began to pop.

Bastian brought it even closer. Tony's body flexed away from it like the opposing pole of a magnet. Tied to the table though, his body could not escape. It came closer. The skin on Tony's arm ripped

Justin Hyde

open. Then his ear drums burst, and his heart and lungs dilated.

Closer.

He cried out in rage.

Then the object touched him, and it was all over.

Another failed experiment.

CHAPTER 30

45° N, 7° E.

Ahead of him, Cameron could see the blown open train tunnel getting closer again as he drove the Ripsaw away from the girl in white. Driving into the tunnel would be a pointless maneuver though and would only leave him trapped in there once again.

He angled the tank to the right and could feel the weight of the sled behind him as it pulled through the deep snow. The restless movements of the creatures inside constantly shifted the payload around and made it difficult to get a good feel for how the vehicle and trailer handled. But worse, there was no way out of this canyon except to turn around. He was able to spot the treacherous narrow trail that the Ripsaw had carved out in the backside of the mountain—the secret trail that led to the mountaintop prison, where the tank had just been headed—but from there he would be just as trapped as he would be inside of the mountain. This was a one-way road, and if the girl in white had another magazine to reload her gun with, it wouldn't take long for her to get within shooting range of him again. He needed to get out of this valley and away from here fast.

"Alright. Let's see how well this thing corners. Hold on!" he said out loud, maybe to himself, or maybe to the creatures back in the sled.

He spun the steering wheel hard and the tank's computer translated the turning motion to the treads. The left tread reversed direction and the right tread sped up, flexing and bending under the sudden force, digging in and launching a wave of snow into the air. The sled behind him pulled hard and almost broke free, but the metal held, and it teetered on its edge then landed back down flat behind him. Even through the shatterproof polycarbonate windows, Cameron could hear the roars of the things as they were tossed around inside the cage.

He blew out a sigh of relief then slammed down on the throttle again. But buried under the snow in front of him now must have been a downed tree or a covered rock, and the tank hit it and bounced high into the air again then crashed back down like a whale breaching the sea. The sled followed and smashed the creatures against the bars along the top of the cage, even harder than before. Cameron felt the impact too this time. He hadn't buckled the five-point safety harness and he bounced from the seat and hit his head against the roof, sending a sharp pain down his neck and into his spine.

The jolt must have made him close his eyes for a second, because it wasn't the sight of the girl out of the front window that warned him. It was the ping of metal and the blast from the guns barrel that made him realize he was being shot at. Cameron looked up. The girl in white blended in with the background, but he could still see her brown hair and her hands wrapped around the black of the gun held in front of her. She did not fire again though, and Cameron suspected why. The tank was armored.

She must have hoped that Cameron didn't realize that though and was trying to scare him into stopping. Another threat, like when she fired at him in the snow a few minutes ago. The visual threat of a well-aimed shot through the windshield and into his forehead should have convinced him to pull over. But if she pulled the trigger too many times, it would give away the secret that the small pistol was useless against the steel beast. Fortunately for him, Professor Skull had figured it out with just the first shot, and he sped past the girl without even slowing.

She stood motionless and angry. She should have been thankful that at least the man in the tank had not run her over like he had with the creature; but being stranded alone in this valley after dark was almost a death sentence on its own. A much slower death sentence than being run over would have been. She turned and watched him drive away and disappear into the trees.

Cameron smiled—amused at the turn of events. He had tried to convince himself earlier that he wasn't worried about having to get out of the mountains on foot and with no gear. But the truth was, he had been very worried about it. He was no stranger to tough survival situations, but this would have been an extreme test, even for him. And truth be told, one that he may not have been able to survive. He had no idea how many miles or in what direction the nearest town might be, and it could have possibly taken days or weeks, depending on the weather and the terrain for him to find out.

But now with the Ripsaw super tank under his control, he felt much more secure. Even the battery level indicator on the dash showed more than half charged. What that meant range-wise, the professor had no idea, but regardless, it was comforting to know that he wasn't running on empty.

Up ahead the canyon began to narrow. Cameron also noticed that the sides of the cliffs were starting to show more bare patches of rock exposed beneath the thick snow, and the tree line was becoming more prominent—both indicators that he might be nearing the outer Alps.

Another draw up ahead worried him as he continued east. It was a steep rise that led up out of the tree line again and probably peaked sharply at the top. Cameron would normally have tried to avoid it, but there were still some sign of tracks in the snow signaling him to continue the course. He rose up the side and had to hold his breath as the tank reached the summit. From the angle, there was no visibility of the trail leading down the back of the peak, and Cameron gulped as the front of the Ripsaw teetered over the edge, then found ground again on the other side. The hitch joining the sled behind him high-centered and scrapped hard as it followed.

Facing downhill now, Cameron could see far off into the distance. The steep white snowcaps he had grown so used to seeing faded out a few miles away and were replaced with the gentler slopes of brown and green hills. Only small patches of white dotted the horizon—still a little too early in the year for the snow level to drop to these lower elevations. There was even a small lake, that from this distance, didn't appear to be frozen over yet. And past that, maybe another mile or two further out, Cameron could see the small rectangular shapes of buildings poking up in the base of a tiny valley.

—

I can't just ride into town pulling a cage full of friggin zombies, Cameron thought. He was already on the downhill slope of the grade though when the thought came to him. If he stopped now, the weight of the trailer would be pressing against the Ripsaw and he would never be able to unhook it. Especially with 5 pairs of hands reaching out trying to grab him—the creature that the woman in white had mistakenly shot was up and moving again.

He kept going and soon the ground below the treads was mostly dirt with the occasional boulder or patch of dirty ice. He noticed a body of water up ahead, along with a game trail, and decided to head for it. There was sure to be some level ground around the small lake that he could stop at.

"Look out!" a voice cried.

Two men were hiking up the hill and rounded a bend right in front of him. One of them pushed the other and they both rolled off the thin trail before

Cameron ran them over. Professor Skull hooked the wheel and brought the tank to a stop as fast as he could manage. He lifted open the wing door and pulled himself out quickly and began searching for signs of the two men. He spotted them a few feet away, lying in the cold dirt. "Are you okay?" he called down to them. It hadn't been a game trail after all. It was a hiking trail.

Both men got to their feet but didn't answer him. They were facing the side of the tank but staring at the cage full of corpses behind it.

"Do you speak English," Cameron asked.

One of the two men looked at him with fear in his eyes. "What are those?" he asked, answering Cameron's question by asking another.

Professor Skull walked across the top of the tread to the back of the Ripsaw and jumped down to the ground, then approached the pair. "Can you two step over here for a second?" He gestured to the front of the tank where they would be out of sight of the creatures. No real conversation was ever going to take place while they were understandably distracted by what Cameron had just brought in front of them.

They hesitated and took several more looks before agreeing and walking with him to the front. Both had scared looks in their eyes. But it wasn't just the things locked in the cage that they seemed afraid of. Cameron sensed that they might also be afraid of him. The two looked to be about the same age— both maybe in their early 20's. "You're Americans?"

Cameron asked.

The smaller of the two nodded. "Yes. We're from Georgia."

Cameron scratched his face and felt the length of the stubble on his cheek and suddenly realized that he must look like shit. He probably didn't look much better than those things he brought with him. No wonder the two were nervous around him. "What are you doing out here?" he asked the boy.

The kid misunderstood the question, thinking that Cameron had asked why he wasn't still back home. "We graduated in June and our parents paid for us to come to Europe for our graduation present," he said.

Cameron knew the boy wasn't talking about college graduation. These two kids were even younger than he had suspected. It was common for kids back in the States to travel Europe after high school. A relatively affordable and fun way for them to experience the world before being locked into the reality of adulthood. Especially if it offered a temporary relief from the humidity of the American South. His own daughter Kendall had even brought up the idea to him once, and she hadn't even started high school yet.

"My name is Cameron Skull," he said to them. "I am a professor at an archeological institution north of Scotland."

"Alpha-Meridian?" the other young man said excited.

Cameron looked to him. "Yes. Alpha-Meridian." The school was over a year old now, but Cameron was still adjusting to the switch from Nightcorp and was surprised that the kid had heard about it.

"Oh man," the kid said. "I want to go there so bad."

"What's your name?" Cameron asked.

"My name is Josh, and this is Samuel."

Naturally, biblical names from southern Baptist parents, Cameron thought. *Joshua and Samuel.*

"What are those things?" Samuel asked timidly, still upset by what he saw locked up behind the tank.

The professor decided not to lie to them but give them a very short version of the truth. "I don't know for sure," he admitted. "I was here in search of something and I stumbled across a few things that maybe I wasn't supposed to."

"You're one of the first. Aren't you?" Josh asked in awe. "You were part of Alpha-Meridian when they were still the secret military force, huh?"

Cameron paused and looked at him with a mix of amazement and confusion. "Nightcorp," he finally said, confirming. "How do you know so much about us?"

"I've always wanted to be an explorer," Josh said. "And I love adventure. Both of us do. That's why we're out here." He pointed to Samuel, then pointed to the stitched insignia on the collar of

Cameron's jacket. "That's the sign of the originals. I saw a picture of it when I was trying to get us information on applying to A-M."

They're brother's, Cameron realized. Fraternal twins. He almost told them that students at Meridian were only considered by referral, but decided not to crush their hopes just yet. Instead he nodded.

Cameron noticed that Samuel was not moving or speaking. He was still worried about the creatures locked in the cage. They were out of sight, but their endless moaning and shuffling could still be heard in between sentences. "They can't get out of there," Cameron said to him. He was still not willing to lie to the boy though. "You're not in any danger, right now."

"What happened to them?" the kid asked.

The question triggered Professor Skull into remembering that what he was dealing with was in fact—people. He had become so accustomed now into thinking of them as zombies or creatures that he had forgotten that they were once just like him. "I'm not sure," he admitted. "And I'm not sure how to help them yet. But I can't bring them into town. How long did it take you two to hike up this far?"

Josh turned and looked at his brother. "We've only been out about an hour I think?"

Samuel nodded in agreement.

These kids are here by themselves, Cameron thought. *Maybe...* "Where are you guys staying?" he asked.

Any fear that they had of the professor was now gone, and Josh answered him quickly. "We have a room at the Casa Alpina Don Guanella hotel."

CHAPTER 31

51° N, 10° W.
2:16 p.m. local time

It took some searching before Francesco was able to find a private charter that was willing to take him and Iris out to the island so late in the day. Sunset was around 4:00 p.m. and most of the commercial ferries made their departures in the morning so they could be back before nightfall.

Him and Iris had flown into Kerry then got dropped off by an Uber at the Portmagee marina about 30 minutes ago. After having little luck at the harbor, they had gone into town and found a willing captain sitting at a small restaurant bar called *The Moorings* who agreed to take them for a generous fee plus his bar tab.

"It's going to take almost an hour to get beyont to the island," Captain Duffy said in his thick Irish accent as he untied the bow line from a piling and tossed it onto the boat. He was a grizzled looking man. Captain Duffy was a retired lobster fisherman who had a scruffy white beard and weathered skin. He wore a white turtleneck shirt under a dark blue wool coat with a tear in one of the arms. There was a beat-up baseball cap on his head that leaned to one side with a faded compass on the front. Below the brim, his right eye didn't quite open all the way, like the tilted hat was pushing it closed. It gave him a suspicious look.

His vessel was an old beat-up Aquastar 38, and it made Frank's stomach a little uneasy just looking at it. The only waters Frank cared for were the backwoods rivers that him and Professor Skull used to trout fish before he left the States. "Do you know much about the island?" he asked the captain.

Duffy stepped off the dock and onto the boat then turned to help Iris aboard. "Sure, look it. I know lots about the island," he said as he took Iris's hand. She stepped aboard and Captain Duffy began pulling up the rubber fenders along the side of the boat. "I've been sailing these waters since before you were born, lad," he added.

Francesco was not exactly a young man and seriously doubted the accuracy of the captain's comment, but decided it wasn't worth questioning. He reached out for the boat with a cautious hand and grabbed the rail, then jumped onto the deck. In the distance the sky was beginning to darken with storm clouds and Frank silently prayed that the sea remained calm while he was out on it.

"Put your pack in the wheelhouse," Captain Duffy told him once Frank had got his balance back. "Gonna be a whale of a time with this rain a'comin."

Damn it... Frank thought.

Iris found a spot to sit in the open stern while Frank and the captain went into the small wheelhouse. Duffy grabbed hold of the cracked steering wheel and turned the key—the motor cranked but didn't start. He turned it off then back on again two more times before the engine sputtered to life. They hadn't even left the dock yet and Frank already felt like he was going to throw up.

"So, you know the story of Saint Michael leaving his shield here," Iris said loudly enough for them to hear her up front.

The captain steered the ship out of the marina and into the open waters of the Celtic Sea—ignoring any respect for maritime speed limits. "Ay," he said. "On the Great Skellig." Already the winds were picking up and Duffy looked to the sky at the black clouds blowing in as he spoke. "Michael blessed this spot after his battle, then let the wine flow a'plenty!" he said laughing.

"Has anyone ever claimed to have found the shield?" Frank asked from beside him.

The captain shook his head. "It's like hens' teeth. Some say that a monk gave it to Olaf."

Frank stared at the captain, obviously needing explanation.

"One of the monks from this island baptized King Olaf of Norway a thousand years ago," the captain said. "Some say that he also gave the shield to him." He turned and looked at Frank. "Me? I think Vikings stole it."

Frank and Iris both knew that this area was prone to Viking attacks for hundreds of years around the ninth century. Perhaps the captain was right. No Viking would have ever left a great shield behind.

Iris felt the first drop of rain land on her head. She was thankful that she had worn a jacket but wished she had worn a hat now as well. She stood and joined the two men inside the small covered wheelhouse. For a while they stood in silence, then up ahead, the island started coming into view. "There it is," she said, pointing over the boat's bow. The craft hit a swell in the surf and a spray of ocean splashed against the windshield.

"Don't act the maggot," the captain said. "That's Little Skellig. The Great Skellig is on the other side."

"Is there anything left on the island?" Frank asked.

Duffy turned to Frank but kept both hands on the wheel. "Besides the beehives?"

"Excuse me," Iris interrupted. She wasn't sure if maybe the captain's accent had made her misunderstand him. "Did you say, *the beehives*?"

"Ay. The beehives. The remains of the old monastery way at the top of the island. The buildings are round and made of stone. They look like big beehives." The boat hit another cresting wave. It rose then rolled forward and Frank had to sit. "Besides that," Captain Duffy continued. "There's the old stone church and the monk's graveyard. But that's about it. Lots of birds. But we won't see them in this weather."

Frank looked to Iris. He could tell that she was thinking the same thing as him. *If Saint Michael's sword is here, we're probably going to have to dig for it—and we don't have the time, or the shovels.* He decided to ask the question outright. "Captain

Duffy," he said. "What we are really looking for is Michael's sword. Do you think there's any chance it is here? Or even any chance that it used to be here?"

"Hang on," the captain said.

Frank thought his words were a request for momentary patience while he gave the question some thought. But the captain's words had actually been a suggestion. They hit another rough patch of sea and Frank was nearly thrown from his seat. His stomach knotted up and gave him a fright, but settled back down after a few seconds. Iris had still been standing, but luckily heeded the captain's warning and had braced herself quickly before the impact.

"This *is* Michael's sword," Duffy said. He pointed at the great island now visible in the distance. "That there be the pommel."

"The pommel?" Iris asked.

"The bottom of the sword," Duffy said. "The knob below the handle."

Rain began falling harder on them. "I don't understand what you're saying," Frank told him. "What does that mean when you say the island is the pommel of Michael's sword?"

"Christ on a bike, you don't know about Saint Michael's sword?" the captain asked a little confused. "Michael's sword goes all the way from here to the holy land."

Iris moved closer and put a hand on the wheel of the boat. A move that Frank would have never dared attempt. She had a very serious look on her face and a strong tone in her voice. "Captain Duffy. Neither of us knows what exactly that means. Can you please just explain what you are talking about?"

The man looked at her with some mild anger, but also with respect. He waited for her to remove her hand from the wheel, then nodded and reached into a cubby by his knees. He pulled out a stack of maps, then pulled back the throttle and brought the boat to a much slower speed. He tossed the maps onto the seat next to Frank and started unfolding one. "It'll be easier if I just show you what I'm talking about," he said.

Frank stood. He looked over the captain's left shoulder and Iris over his right. The map in his hands was covered in lines and curves and was confusing to look at. Duffy pointed to their location but then must have also realized how confusing a nautical chart could be to someone not accustomed to seeing them. "Stall the ball," he said. "Let me get a different one." He handed the map to Frank to fold then bent down to the few others scattered over the seat. "Here we go." He picked up a more traditional map of the north Atlantic then opened a panel on the dash of the boat and took out a black Sharpie marker. Pulling the cap off with his teeth, he drew a circle around Skellig Michael. "We are right here. At the back end of Saint Michael's sword."

Frank folded the nautical map, although not correctly, and kept it held in his hand. "Okay," he said, verbally acknowledging that he was so far following along.

Captain Duffy drew another circle. "There are seven monasteries of Saint Michael. They go from here to Israel—the holy land." He drew a third circle. And then a fourth. "All seven monasteries are perfectly in line with each other."

Frank and Iris watched intently as the captain drew the sixth and seventh circles. He then took the black marker and drew a straight line through them all. "This," he said, "is the sword of Saint Michael."

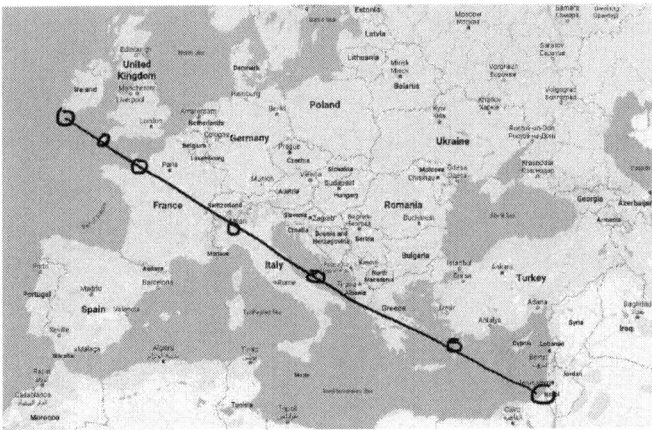

"Me hands are a quare shakier than they used to be," he added. "So, me line might be a little arseways. But if you pinpoint all seven of these for real you would see that they are perfectly straight with each other. The last one, the tip of the sword, is in Israel."

"That's incredible!" Frank said with astonishment.

"Are you serious? Is that for real?" Iris asked.

"Ay!" said Captain Duffy. "Go way outta that! I *am* serious. It's for real alright." He had an obvious offended reaction to Iris doubting him, even though her exclamation was more a figure of speech than actual disbelief. "And that's not even all of it," he added. "They are at twenty-four degrees. The line matches exactly to the sunset of the summer solstice."

Franks jaw hit the floor.

"Wait," Iris said. "So does this mean that there is no actual physical sword?" *What do we do now then?*

"Now I didn't say that," Duffy said. "Michael's sword is real alright. Both of them. He didn't kill off the demons here in Ireland with a bunch of monasteries, now did he?"

Frank hadn't spoken in a minute. How could he have missed this? Suddenly it all seemed so clear to him, but he was disappointed in himself for not seeing it sooner. And now they were on a boat in the middle of the Celtic Sea. "The sword is pointing us straight to it," he said quietly. "We should be in Israel."

Iris and the captain looked at him. "Oh, I don't know about that," Captain Duffy said.

Frank looked up at him. "What do you mean?"

"I've been beyont to Mount Carmel," he said. "It's a big holy looking building alright, but I don't think you'll find Michael's sword there?"

"Why not?" Iris asked.

"Well, there's too many people been there over the years to miss it for one thing. But also, a sword pointing to a sword? Just seems a might stupid to me."

I don't think it sounds stupid. Iris thought. *It sounds pretty logical to me.*

The captain's argument was so weak and simple though that Frank couldn't actually find the right way to dispute it. And amazingly, he could even make a little sense out of it. "Maybe he's got a point," he said.

Iris's eyebrows went up. "Is that a joke, Frank?"

"No joke," Frank said. "The tip of a sword is sort of like the head of the sword, right?" He stood up. The rain was coming down harder now. "Glory is never found in the head. Usually, the mind, or the head of something is misleading, or even dangerous. Like the head of a serpent." He paced a few steps while his own mind worked, then stopped, not wanting to walk out from under the cover of the wheelhouse. "But, the heart is true. The body is the answer." He looked straight into Iris's eyes. "Just like we take communion to remember and find salvation—in the *body* of Christ."

Iris realized something else too at that moment. She looked down at the map again and at the circles that Captain Duffy had drawn. "Look here," she said to Frank, pointing at one of the marks. "This monastery is way up in northern Italy. It's right by where Cameron is." She tapped her finger on it. "This is the one he was telling us about. And it's right in the center of them all."

CHAPTER 32

45° N, 7° E.
Elevation – 4,500 ft.

The evening was brisk and the streets were empty as Matteo walked back up Via Horlovono to his hotel. He had gone out to get some fresh air and clear his head, thinking that perhaps he would have come across a church or even a park during his outing. But apart from the stone and wood faced homes along the narrow street, all he had found was a few pubs and taverns.

He closed the front of his coat tighter around him. The last of the evening sun was just starting to fade away but he still had enough light left to find his way back without worry of getting lost. Tomorrow morning him and his family were going to walk to the bus station in Macugnaga and finally go back home.

Over the fence to his left now, Matteo saw a small and familiar grassy yard that he had passed just after leaving the hotel. He had only been gone an hour but was already looking forward to getting back inside and spending the evening with his wife and sons.

"It's just up ahead," a young man's voice said.

Matteo looked up surprised. It sounded like his older boy Ben's voice. And sure enough, up the hill in front of him were two boys who looked to be about the same age as his. They were headed towards him, coming down the hill with an older man.

"Right there," the smaller boy said, pointing a finger at the Casa Alpina Hotel.

"Adrian?" Matteo said. "Is that you?" They were still a little too far away for him to see them clearly.

The man walking with the two boys put his arms out in front of them and slowed them down. He whispered something to the two kids, but Matteo could not hear what he had said. He could tell now that it was not Ben and Adrian though, and felt a little embarrassed at having called out to them. The man with them was probably their father. Suddenly Matteo realized that he was the stranger, not them.

"Hi there," the man ahead called out.

Matteo raised a hand in greeting. "Hello," he said back.

The man and the two boys started walking again—and so, so did Matteo. All of them crossed paths at the front door of the hotel. "After you," the man said, holding the door open.

Matteo waited for the two boys to enter then tipped his head in thanks to the man holding the door and walked into the hotel lobby. He recognized the two young men now. He had seen them earlier. But he did not remember seeing the man with them. For a reason that he could not explain, he went and sat at one of the tables in the hotel restaurant right adjacent to the front desk instead of heading up to his room.

Cameron Skull walked up to the young girl at the counter. "Buona sera signore," she said to him.

Crap. She doesn't speak English. He thought about pulling out his in-ear translator, but the device was a receiver only. He would be able to understand her, but she still wouldn't be able to understand him. He turned to Josh and Samuel for advice. Josh shrugged and Samuel took out his iPhone and handed it to him. "I've got a translation app," he explained.

Matteo stood back up from the table and walked over to them. "Excuse me," he said politely. "I didn't mean to overhear you, but I can help translate if you'd like."

Cameron turned his head to look at him. Something about Matteo made him cautious, but something else about him made him comfortable. It was a strange mix of feelings. "Thanks," he said.

Matteo smiled. "Are you trying to get a room?"

"I am."

He turned to the hostess. "Ciao signorina. Ci sono camere disponibili?"

She tapped several keys on the computer before answering. "Si, ce ne sono rimasti due. Costano ottantanove dollari a notte."

"Grazie." Matteo turned back to Cameron. "She has two rooms left. They are eighty-nine dollars per night."

Cameron instinctively reached for his wallet then suddenly realized he didn't have it. He didn't even have an ID. He didn't have *anything*! Everything was in his pack—probably buried under 10 feet of snow by now at the top of a damn mountain. "Shit," he whispered. "I need to make a call." He stepped away from the desk and took the satellite phone off his belt. He dialed Frank and held the phone to his ear.

"Profess...," Frank said. His voice was choppy and there was a lot of noise in the background. "Where... gotten to the..."

"Frank," Cameron said. "I can hardly hear you. You're breaking up on me."

"One seco..."

Francesco's voice disappeared but Cameron could hear a lot of staticky commotion in the background. It sounded like maybe wind or rain.

"Professor Skull," Frank came back on and said. "Can you hear me any better? I stepped back into the wheelhouse."

The wheelhouse? "Yeah, that's better. What's going on? What's all that noise?"

"Iris and I are on our way back to the mainland from Skellig Island. It's raining like crazy out here. Throwing cobbler knives, as our captain puts it."

"What did you find out there?" Cameron asked.

Frank didn't hear his question. "Where are you?" he asked. "We can come get you after we get back to the plane."

Cameron looked at a welcome brochure on

the counter of the hotel. The young girl smiled at him. "I'm in a town called Staffa. I really doubt they have an airport here though."

The hostess must have picked up on the word airport and said from behind him, "L'aeroporto? Malpensa é a circa un'ora di distanza."

"Un'ora?" Cameron mumbled, repeating part of her statement. "I think I was just told that there's an airport about an hour away," he said to Frank."

"We can't be there in an hour though unfortunately."

"That's fine, Frank. Listen, I have no money and no ID on me though, so I'm going to have a hard time doing anything till we meet up."

"I can try to wire you some money right now," Frank said. "But we're not in the best spot for cell service honestly. I'm surprised your call even came through."

"Where exactly are you guys?" Cameron asked.

"We chartered a boat to take us out to Saint Michael's monastery on Skellig Island. We're on our way back right now."

Cameron walked a few steps away from Matteo and the two boys and looked out one of the front windows of the hotel. The weather here was much better than where Francesco and Iris were. The evening sky was clear outside, and a few stars were already beginning to outshine the sunset. He thought back to his last conversation with Iris, right after he had blown his way out of the mountain, and only vaguely remembered her mentioning that her and Frank were going to Ireland. "You actually found the monastery of Saint Michael huh? How? What was there?"

Matteo straightened up attentively. Now intentionally eavesdropping. Why had this man just spoken of Saint Michael's monastery?

Frank explained to Cameron what he and Iris had learned so far. "At the monastery you told us about," he said, wrapping up the recap. "The one close to you. It's called the Sacra di San Michele. The inn and sanctuary you heard those guys about was built in the tenth century by Benedictine monks in honor of Saint Michael. And it's right in the middle of Saint Michael's sword!"

"Saint Michael's sword?" Cameron said, again repeating what he heard.

"I'll explain it all better when we see you later," Frank finished. "The weather isn't getting any better here. I should see if I can wire you some money while I've still got a signal. What's the name of the place you're at?"

Cameron walked back over to the front desk and looked again at the welcome brochure. "The Casa Alpina Don Guanella hotel," he read.

"I'll try and remember that," Frank said, hopeful. The rain was coming down harder and he had to raise his voice a little louder. "Do you want to talk to Iris?"

He did, but he said no. "Tell her I'll talk to her in person in a few hours."

"Got it," Frank said. "I'll try calling you once we get to the plane."

"Sounds good, Frank. Thanks." He hung up the phone. Everyone in the lobby was staring at him now like he was a math problem that they couldn't figure out. Except for Samuel. He was looking at something on his iPhone.

"Sir," Matteo said, breaking the silence. "Please excuse me for being so forward, but did I hear you mention the sword of Saint Michael?"

It was getting warm inside the hotel lobby now with all his snow gear on. Cameron clipped the phone back onto his belt then took off his heavy jacket. "You did," he agreed. "You know something about that?"

"I am trying to get to a monastery on Saint Michael's sword as well." Matteo said. "I was once the priest of Basilica Santuario San Michele Arcangelo."

"That's quite a mouthful," Professor Skull said. Josh and Samuel were still standing uncomfortably near the front desk and he waved them over. "What happened?" he asked Matteo. "How come you aren't the priest there anymore?"

Matteo hung his head in embarrassment. "I was accused of theft," he said sadly. He lifted his head back up and looked sincerely at Cameron. "I was *falsely* accused." There was strength in his voice now. "I am taking my family back there. Monte Sant'Angelo is our home. The church is our home."

"What about the sword?" Cameron asked.

Matteo smiled slightly. "My church was built in the cave of the Archangel Michael. He blessed it as the most sacred of places. It is one of the seven monasteries devoted to him now, and it sits right at the heart of Saint Michael's sword."

"Okay," Cameron said in curious surrender. "I'm listening. Tell me more."

CHAPTER 33

22° N, 159° W
5:01 a.m. Hawaii-Aleutian Standard Time

Sergeant Awapuhi sensed something outside her home. She had just woken up from a restless night's sleep and walked into the living room in her pajamas when she thought she saw the movement outside her front window. Her property was secluded, and she was well attuned to the natural sways of the trees and flowers. What she had just seen was something else.

She ran back into her bedroom and swiped her finger over the biometric fingerprint scanner of the safe that was bolted to the nightstand next to her bed and picked up her department issued Glock 17. The safety on the firearm was already off and there was already one in the chamber.

Slowly she crept back towards the front room when there was a knock at the door. Her reflexes forced her body against the wall, and she listened for another second.

Knock knock.

She leaned her head around the corner of the wall and sighed a small breath of relief. Whoever it was that was creeping around her property hadn't meant to sneak up on her. She was just being paranoid. She lowered her weapon, but as a precaution anyways, kept it held down low behind her back as she went to answer the door.

"Kekoa," she said, surprised. "What are you doing here so early?"

The sun hadn't even started coming up yet but Kekoa did not consider it early. His daily routine involved waking up around 4:00 a.m. on any average morning and he just assumed that most other people did the same. "I'm sorry," he said.

"Oh, it's okay, you just startled me a little that's all. I'm not used to getting a lot of visitors, especially before the sun comes up." She gave him a small smile. Last night she had intruded on him at his home, and now he was returning the favor. "Is everything alright?" she asked. "Come on in." She led him into the living room then politely excused herself for a minute to go change into something besides her pajamas. When she returned, she was wearing a pair of tight jeans and a light blue tank-top.

She was very beautiful, and Kekoa had a hard time imagining her in a police officer's uniform. "I wanted to show you something," he said. He was still standing and held out the white bone carving that he had spent the night making.

Lea looked down at it in his hand. "What is that?"

"This is Makehewa's sword."

She reached to the wall and turned on the ceiling fan light above them. "That's incredible," she said. "How did you do that?" She gazed at the sculpture. It was about 8 inches long and one of the most detailed pieces that she had ever seen. The whale bone had been completely transformed into a blade—carved so smoothly that it looked polished and seemed to shine. It had white flames coming off it that she was almost convinced were actually moving. The whole thing was the natural white of the whale bone, except for some dark green around the handle that looked like maybe it had been wrapped in Koa leaves. The contrast in color also highlighted the unique intricate pommel of the sword. She looked up at him. "That must have taken all night."

He nodded.

Lea reached out to take it, thinking that he was trying to hand it to her, but Kekoa pulled his hand back quickly and she jumped a bit, not expecting that. "Oh, um." She didn't really know what to say in response. "I'll be careful with it, I promise."

Kekoa shook his head. "You cannot touch it. It's not safe."

"It's not safe?" she asked, confused.

He shook his head again. "No," he answered.

"I don't really understand," she admitted.

"The sword can kill by itself," he said. "Not everyone in the jungle died that day from being cut or stabbed." He took his small replicated sword and made slicing motions over his head and body with it, then shook his head. He then took it and touched it very gently against his arm and then his chest and nodded. "The sword cannot touch you. If it does. You die."

Justin Hyde

"Oh, because of the flames," Lea said, starting to understand. "You get burned."

Kekoa's face showed a look of consideration, then of doubt, but he didn't argue. "At first we did not fight," he said, thinking back. "When Makehewa came out from the garden with the sword, we were afraid. We did not want to fight the man with the fire sword. We had no reason to. But he attacked us. He killed two of my friends." Kekoa looked away for a second then remade eye contact. "I wanted to run away, but I did not. I ran to him and tried to stop him, but he swung fast and I was hurt. I fell to the ground. Could not move."

Lea listened intently. This was the most details of the event that Kekoa had given so far.

"The other three men," he continued. "Only one of them fight. Then... Makehewa cut him in two." He drew a line across his stomach indicating that it was not a figure of speech, but showing where his friend had literally been cut in half. Lea swallowed and Kekoa continued. "But the other two men kneeled. They begged, and they prayed to Kāne, but Makehewa touched them and laughed." He took the small sword and touched its blade very softly to his forehead. "Dead," he finished.

Sergeant Awapuhi suddenly realized she still held the Glock in her left hand and was squeezing dangerously on it. She quickly relaxed her grip and set the weapon onto a table, not wanting to touch it either now. "How can that be?" she asked. "How could *he* have held it then if just touching it can kill you?

Kekoa shrugged. "I don't know," he said. "Makehewa had gloves on. Maybe they protected him?"

She shook her head. "That doesn't make sense." Something didn't sound right, but the last time she had doubted Kekoa's story she had been proven wrong, and so she was hesitant to want to doubt him again. "It's hard to believe that something so powerful could be controlled by something so simple as a pair of gloves." She looked up and down Kekoa's body. "And how come you didn't die?" The question sounded cold and she regretted the tone that she had used, but hoped Kekoa didn't take it the wrong way.

He didn't say anything, just shook his head a little.

"Maybe it just looked like he didn't swing it at them?" she said. "Or stab them? You said that you had already been cut and were on the ground when this happened, so maybe from your angle..."

"No," Kekoa said forcefully. "You cannot touch! I don't know why Makehewa could. But you cannot touch the sword. I saw what happens."

"Then how come you survived?" she asked again with a bit of aggravation and sarcasm. "The sword touched you, obviously."

There was deep sincerity in Kekoa's voice when he answered her. "Because, God saved me."

CHAPTER 34

45° N, 7° E.
7:16 p.m.
Elevation – Descending.

The voice of air traffic control came into Frank's headset. "Lear four-five, turn left heading two-seven-zero to intercept the localizer, cleared MXP runway one-niner into Malpensa, maintain two-thousand-five-hundred feet until established."

"Are we starting to descend?" Iris asked Frank who was up front in the pilot's seat.

Francesco turned his head around. "Yeah. We're about eighty nautical miles from Malpensa airport. We should hopefully touch down in about twenty minutes." They had flown in at just under 30,000 feet the whole trip. Frank preferred to cruise the jet lower that most aircraft—never wanting to burn up the extra fuel it would take to climb to the higher elevations unless there were favorable winds up there or bad weather down low. Iris must have felt the nose of the aircraft drop a second ago when Frank idled the engines.

"Are you sure Cameron got there alright?"

Frank didn't turn around again but yelled over his shoulder. "He got the money I wired him and told me not to worry after that. You know how he is. He always figures it out somehow but doesn't explain it to anybody." Now Frank did turn around again. "I'm sure he'll be there. The thing I'm more concerned with is the people he's bringing with him."

Iris was worried about that part too. It was very unlike Cameron to do something like that— bring strangers into Alpha-Meridians business. *And onto the A-M plane,* she thought. On top of that, it wasn't even just one or two people. Professor Skull had told Frank to make room for *SIX* people. *He must have bumped his head pretty damn hard on that mountain somewhere.*

From the cockpit Iris could hear Frank talking to tower control on the ground. He was speaking to them in English though, which she thought was a little strange, but began putting her things back into her bag as he brought the plane down. A moment later Frank turned around again. "That was Director Kestner," he said.

"Oh, I thought you were talking to the airport. I was wondering why you weren't speaking to them in Italian."

"I do need to get back to them about our approach and get final runway instructions, but James just called me directly on the cabin-com because he said he couldn't reach you on your cell."

"She looked at the screen of the phone in her hand. No missed calls.

"I'm not sure why," Frank said. "Your phone and Wi-Fi should work fine in here. But either way, he told me to tell you to check your email."

Iris turned on the phone and opened her email. *Guess the Wi-Fi is fine.* There were several unopened messages, but she clicked on the most recent one.

To: IWilhelmsson@alphameridian.com
CC: JKestner@alphameridian.com
From: LAwapuhi@kpd.gov
November 20, 2019.

Subject: Don't touch the sword!

Miss Wilhelmsson,

I've been trying to reach you on your cell. I need to tell you that I met again with Kekoa early this morning, the man from the jungle, and was able to get some further information regarding what happened to him the night he was attacked. He seems very convinced that the sword he was attacked with contains some sort of supernatural power, and that it does not need to be used in offense or aggression against you in order to cause harm. According to him, just touching the sword, even just placing a fingertip on it, is enough to kill you.

I know this raises a lot of questions and I have probably asked him all of them already, but for the sake of time I am going to keep this email short and sweet. I believe that after our last conversation though, you and your team may be looking for the sword yourselves, or for the man who took it, and if that is true than I needed to pass on this information, for your own safety. If you find it, do _not_ touch it!

Don't forget, Kekoa was right about the Garden of Eden. He may be right about this too.

Please be careful.

—Lea Awapuhi

Frank lowered the landing gear of the plane and prepared to touch down. "Iris, is your seatbelt on?"

She double checked by feeling the strap over her lap. "Yes." She was about to start telling him about the email when she heard him talking to air traffic control through his headset again. This time he was speaking Italian—so definitely not to James Kestner.

"Lear four-five. Cleared to land runway one-niner," Frank said back to ATC in Italian.

Iris looked out the window. It was dark outside, and she watched as the lights of the miniature world became life-sized and the terminal buildings of the airport whizzed by. The plane touched down and the tires screeched against the blacktop, then a minute later they were stopped outside of Milano Malpensa Terminal 2, way in the back near gate D16.

Frank unclipped his seatbelt and ducked into the rear cabin of the jet with Iris. "Can you see if you

Justin Hyde

can reach Cameron and let him know we're here."
He swung opened the door and lowered the steps.
"I'm going to try and get us fueled up."

"Francesco, wait. My phone isn't working,"
she said. But it was too late. Frank was already out
and stepping onto the tarmac. "Ugh." She ran to the
door and yelled down. "Frank!" He stopped and
turned. "Hey," she said. "I thought it was only like
sixty miles to the monastery from here?"

"It is," he said in agreement. "And it's even
less than that to Turin airport. We aren't flying, but
we don't have enough fuel to get back to Meridian
from here. I just want to get fuel now, so we don't
have to do it later."

He turned around again, and again Iris tried
stopping him. "Hang on a second, Frank. My phone
isn't working, remember," she said.

"What do you need your phone for?"

Iris gasped and swung her head towards the
voice coming from the building to her right. Walking
out the door, followed by a small group of people,
Cameron smiled at her. "Expecting a call?" he asked
jokingly.

"Cameron!" she screamed. She dropped the
bag in her hand and ran down the steps. He braced
himself for impact as she crashed into him and
squeezed her arms tightly around his neck. She knew
he was alive, but this proved it wasn't a dream. This
was the first time she'd seen him since thinking that
he had fallen from a mountain and died, and it
brought tears of joy to her face.

When they finally let go of each other, the group that Cameron had brought with him was gathered around. Young Adrian was not shy and was staring straight at them.

Cameron kept one arm around Iris. "It's cold out here," he said, rubbing some warmth into her shoulder. He could tell that she was feeling a little uncomfortable with these strangers around them, so he didn't waste time making introductions—starting with Matteo. "Iris, this is Matteo. He is a priest from one of the churches of Saint Michael. We're going to give him and his family a lift home." Cameron swept a finger across the direction of Emily and the kids.

Francesco walked up from the side, pulled a pair of gloves off his hands and threw them to the ground. "Okay. They're fueling us up right now." Then he started laughing as he reached out a hand and pulled Cameron away from Iris and gave him a hug of his own. "You had us all worried, my friend. È bello vederti! Good to see you again!"

"Good to see you too, buddy."

"You look like crap," Frank said back with a smile on his face.

"Hey man! I..."

Iris interjected. "You leave him alone, Frank." She turned to Cameron. "You *could* use a shower though," she joked.

Cameron huffed out a breath of air. "And some sleep," he mumbled.

Emily whispered something to Matteo in the background and Cameron heard the sound, although didn't hear the words. "Everybody," Cameron said, regaining focus. "This is my girlfriend, Iris. And this wop over here is Francesco Ferrari. He leads all the research and development at Alpha-Meridian. He's ridiculously smart, so don't try and pull anything on him."

Frank was a generally humble man but straightened up his posture a bit with pride and gratitude from the professor's compliment. Cameron winked at him—making up slightly for the *wop* comment.

"We should head over to car rental," Frank said. "It's going to take two cars now that we have so many people." He lowered his voice so that hopefully only Cameron could hear. "I hope you know what you're doing, bringing all these people with you."

Iris had heard him too and leaned in. "I agree with Frank," she said quietly. "Who exactly are all these people? And why are they going with us?" She looked at the group. "Most of them are kids!" she added.

"We're not kids," Josh said a little defensively.

Iris was embarrassed that he had heard her but stood her ground. "I wasn't trying to offend you. But you're obviously young, and we can't..."

This time Cameron stepped in. "You're right," he said to Iris. "But we aren't adopting them or anything. We are just taking everyone as far as Monte Sant'Angelo. That's it. Then they're on their own."

"Professor," Frank said. "We aren't going to

Monte Sant'Angelo. Wherever that is. We're driving to Turin. To the Abby of Sacra di San Michele."

Matteo stepped a foot closer and raised his hand slightly. "May I ask why?"

All three members of Alpha-Meridian turned to him. "That's not a short story," Iris said.

"To tell you the truth," Cameron said to her. "I don't really know why either." He looked back over at Matteo and his family. "But if we're looking for something on Saint Michael's sword, this man may be able to help us."

Josh and Samuel looked uncomfortable. They were not part of A-M, nor were they part of Matteo's family. And they had been very surprised, even after all their pleading and badgering, when Cameron had agreed to bring them as well. He may not have said it out loud, but there was something about them that Cameron liked. Maybe it was their spirit for adventure or the fact that they reminded him of himself as a young man.

"Let's talk in the cars," Frank suggested. "It's cold out here. I can explain everything to you on the way."

"Wait a minute," Cameron said. "Just give me the short version before we go. Why are we going to that place? I'm not arguing it. Just trying to understand." Something in the back of his mind was nagging at him. It seemed too coincidental that he had run into Matteo, a former priest of one of the churches of Saint Michael. Coincidences like that were not something to be brushed aside.

Iris spoke loud enough for all of them to hear. "Cameron, remember when I told you that there was an artifact stolen from the rainforest in Kauai? And that it has ties to the Archangel Uriel?"

"Vaguely," he answered.

Josh and Samuel both perked up in excitement. This was cool!

"Basically," Iris said. "Someone has been collecting the weapons of the archangels. And whoever it is, is very dangerous. We believe that they will try to find the sword of Saint Michael next, and we are trying to stop them and find it before they do."

Matteo asked, "Why do you believe that it is at Sacra di San Michele?"

"You don't think it could be?" Cameron asked, coming to his girlfriend's defense a little.

Matteo shrugged. "I'm not saying it's not," he admitted. "I don't know. But Sacra di San Michele is along the road of pilgrimage which many Christians walk from the monastery of Saint Michael in France, to my church in Monte Sant'Angelo. I've been there many times. It is much younger than my church; by several hundred years actually. And it was built for Saint Michael, but never visited by him."

"What?" Frank asked. "Michael was never there?"

Matteo shook his head. "Not to my knowledge."

Franks heart sank in disappointment. *What is going on with me? I am missing everything. Am I really getting that old?*

"It's a beautiful building," Matteo continued. "Much prettier than my church actually. It sits way at the top of Mount Pirchiriano, and has been the inspiration for many books, such as *The Name of the Rose*, by Umberto Eco."

"But if Michael was never there..." Iris said.

"Then his sword certainly isn't there," Frank said, finishing her sentence with sorrow.

"Why did you think it was?" Matteo asked again.

Everyone listened as Iris answered. "Because it is right in the center of Saint Michael's sword. Right in the body of it. We believed that maybe the *body* was the answer. The clue that we were looking for."

"Like the *body* of Christ," Matteo said.

Francesco looked up. Those had been his words exactly.

"But what about the heart?" Matteo asked. "The heart of man is not in the center. It is just above. And that is where my church is."

CHAPTER 35

41° N, 15° E.

It worked.

Bastian looked down at the boy. He was still alive. *I knew it!* Santé thought. *A child was the key.* Someone who's soul was not corrupted. The boy was probably around 8 or 9 years old. Bastian had no idea, nor did he care or even know what his name was—but now called him a miracle.

He took the angel Phanuel's short-sword and touched it again to the boy's body. Just like the last time, nothing happened. The boy was unconscious from the procedure, perhaps from shock, but he was definitely still alive, and his body was having no reaction to the blade.

Father Santé was overwhelmed with delight. But the real test was still to come. Could the boy survive the touch of Michael's sword? Not even Bastian could touch that one. Not yet at least.

"Hand me the wire," he said to one of the two monks standing against the wall.

Bastian had injected the CRISPR formula straight into the left ventricle of the boy's heart. Now, he took the surgical wire and began lacing it around the two halves of the boy's breastbone and pulling it back together. The Cas9 protein mixture of DSUP and tardigrade enzymes would heal the boy probably within hours, if not minutes, but it would not pull separated bone back together.

He cut off the ends of the wire haphazardly then set the bloody tool and remaining wire onto a cart. "Come help me hold this," he instructed the monk.

The man took the hood off his head and walked over besides Father Santé and the boy. He grabbed the flaps of skin on the boy's open chest and pulled as Bastian took the skin stapler and clipped the two halves together. "Let's give him some time," Bastian said. "Then we will go to the cave."

CHAPTER 36

45° N, 7° E.
7:50 p.m.

"Wouldn't you already know it if Michael's sword was at your church?" Iris asked. "I thought you said you were the priest there."

"For many years," Matteo agreed. "But I have never looked for a sword there before."

"I wouldn't think it would be that easy to overlook," she said.

"You're right. If it were easy to find, then someone surely would have by now. Probably long before me." Matteo made good eye contact with her as he spoke, concluding that it was her who he really needed to convince right now. But he would not lie to her or make up stories just to make a point and get a ride home. If the truth did not satisfy anyone here then that was okay, he would simply find another way to get his family back to Monte Sant'Angelo. "Miss Iris," he said, not knowing her last name. "I am not telling you that Saint Michael's sword is there. It truly might not be. I don't pretend to know the answer. All I am saying is that the cave in which my church was built was chosen and blessed by Saint Michael himself. In his own words, the Archangel said: 'There will be no shedding of blood here. Where the rocks open wide, men's sins will be forgiven.'" Matteo repeated and emphasized the line. *"There will be no shedding of blood here."* He stopped to let them think about that for a moment. "Now," he continued. "Doesn't that sound to you like a place to lay down your sword?"

All were silent for a minute. Finally Cameron spoke up. "How big is this cave you're talking about?"

"It's very big," Matteo said. "The main grotto where we hold mass can hold hundreds of people. But there are also many side caverns and the crypts."

"The crypts?" Frank asked.

Before Matteo could answer, Cameron stepped forward. He had glanced over and noticed how cold Emily and Adrian looked just standing out in the night air. "I say we head to Matteo's church."

"This is all good enough for me," Frank said in agreement. "Iris?"

She nodded her head.

"I'll go make sure they're done fueling us up," Frank said. He turned and walked away.

Iris smiled at Cameron. Her admiration of him and his ways seemed to have no bounds. She then looked to the group of people he had brought with him. "Okay everyone, let's get on board. Hopefully Frank can get us in the air pretty quick."

Together, Cameron and Iris funneled all six extra passengers into the plane, maxing out the Learjet's seating arrangements. Fortunately, Josh and Samuel were the only ones who had any bags, otherwise they might have been pushing the limits of the jets weight restrictions too. Cameron took a seat

Justin Hyde

next to Iris, just across the narrow aisle at the front of the plane. Matteo and Emily sat across from them with their backs facing the cockpit.

A second later Frank came aboard and closed the door behind him. "Everybody good?" he asked as he took his own seat at the controls. A chorus of "yes's" rang through the fuselage. "Good," he said. "But I have one question." He turned his head around. "Where are we headed?"

Matteo turned his head as well. "With a plane this size we might be able to land at the small airstrip at Gargano Volo. If you want a bigger airport though I think we'll have to fly into Bari. But that's over an hour drive from Sant'Angelo."

Frank checked a map and looked up the IATA code, then put on his headset and requested departure clearance with ATC.

The air traffic controller responded. "Taxi to runway zero-six via Alpha-three right. Hold short at Bravo-four."

"Roger that," Frank responded.

"This is going to be a short flight," Matteo said to Cameron and Iris.

"That's too bad," Cameron said back. "I was really hoping to get a little shuteye."

Iris reached across the narrow aisle and squeezed his hand. "You should try to anyways."

If only, he thought. He squeezed her hand back. "I will."

From up in the cockpit the four of them could hear Frank on the radio. "Lear four-five, cleared for takeoff, runway zero-six." The twin turbofan engines screamed to life as Frank pushed forward on the thrust levers. Facing the back of the plane, Emily and Matteo each grabbed tight onto their armrests as the plane left the ground and they felt themselves being pulled out of their seats.

Once reaching cruising altitude, Frank pulled off his headset and spoke over his shoulder to Matteo in the back. "Hey, so can you tell me more about the crypts?"

Cameron opened his eyes back up and listened in.

"Of course," Matteo said. "The crypts beneath the bronze doors of the basilica were only just discovered in the 1950's, but date back to at least the sixth century. And some of the runic inscriptions weren't uncovered until even later. In the 1970's I believe. Things are still being discovered there all the time. There is also a mortuary cell with two large sarcophaguses in it."

"Who was buried in the sarcophaguses?" Iris asked.

"No one knows. One of them has never been opened."

"Wait, what?" Iris said, shocked. "*Never?* No one has any idea who's in it?"

Matteo shook his head. Everyone was thinking the same thing. *Michael.* "It is not the archangel though," he said quickly, extinguishing all their theories. "He is not dead."

Cameron would never admit it, but he

suddenly felt stupid for not remembering that right away.

Do angels even die? Iris wondered. Suddenly Matteo's comment sparked a memory of her email from Lea. "Sorry to change the subject," she said. "But I just remembered something." She took her phone out for reference. "I got another email from Sergeant Awapuhi with Kauai PD a little while ago. It was a warning. She said that if we do actually find the sword of Michael that we absolutely cannot touch it."

"Oh no," Matteo said. "Absolutely not. She is right." All eyes went to him. "Only another angel can touch the weapons of God."

"But," Iris started. "The man that found the sword of Uriel in the Garden of Eden was able to hold it. He used it against six men. Killed five of them."

Matteo cocked his head in curiosity. "Someone found the Garden of Eden?"

Crap, Iris thought. *I have to explain all this again.* "Yes," she said. "In Kauai of all places. It's really a long story though. I'd be happy to tell it to you—some other time. But right now we need to come up with a plan on how we are going to deal with this situation now. Not being able to touch the sword adds a little bit of complexity, don't you think."

Cameron leaned forward and rested his elbows on his knees then rubbed his eyes with both hands. He was exhausted and had the early signs of a headache developing. "Wait. Go back to the sword of Uriel for a minute. How was someone able to use it if you can't touch it?"

Iris looked to Matteo for the answer.

"Perhaps," he said softly. "The man is one of the Nephilim."

"The what?" Iris and Cameron both asked. Matteo's wife Emily looked at him curiously as well. In the rows behind them, Ben, Adrian, Josh and Samuel were still mostly concentrated on other things.

Matteo breathed in through his nose before speaking. "Genesis chapter six, verse four: 'The Nephilim were in the earth in those days, and also after that, when the sons of God came in unto the daughters of men, and they bare children to them.'" He paused, then paraphrased. "The Nephilim are the children of angels and mortals."

Frank was listening from the cockpit too and switched on the planes autopilot so he could walk back into the cabin with them. He remained standing just behind Matteo and Emily.

"They are also mentioned many times in the Book of Enoch and Jubilees," Matteo said. "And although the Book of Enoch never made it into the bible, Enoch himself did. Several times. Once in Genesis and a few more times in the New Testament. Enoch is an ancestor of Noah and is said to have been called away by God at a young age. Well... he was over three hundred years old actually, but during those times that was quite young. He is the only one who has ever entered heaven alive."

Samuel caught some of the conversation from the row back and was also listening in now. "Someone has actually been to heaven while they were still alive?" he whispered.

"Continue," Frank said, wanting more of the story.

"According to Enoch," Matteo said. "There were originally two-hundred angels sent to earth called *the Watchers*, who descended onto the summit of Mount Hermon, which some say is actually Mount Sinai—the same mountain where God gave Moses the Ten Commandments. Some of the Watchers became obsessed with human women though, and even married them and had children. Those children of angels and humans, and their descendants, are the Nephilim." Iris dropped her phone and Matteo looked at her. "But sometimes they are bad. And when God sent the Archangel Uriel to warn Noah of the great flood, he also warned him of the Nephilim."

"It was Uriel who warned Noah?" Iris asked. She continued thinking out loud. "So, Uriel was guarding the Garden of Eden and the four rivers, then warned Noah of the great flood coming. And then Noah built the arc and God took him as far away from there as he could." *That back's up Kekoa's story even more,* she realized.

"If that man was one of the Nephilim," Matteo added. "Then perhaps it would be possible for him to wield Uriel's sword."

Frank suddenly realized he had lost track of time and went back to his seat at the controls. He checked their coordinates then tried to locate the airfield somewhere in front of them. He was going to have to bring the plane down a little steeper than he would have liked now, and it was already going to be a tricky landing. The Learjet needed at least 3,000 feet of landing distance, and the short stretch of ground at the Gargano Volo airstrip was barely going to cut it. But he did not want to take them the extra 100 kilometers out of the way to the Bari airport. And to make it even worse, the small Gargano Volo airstrip did not have lights on the runway. "Seatbelts on, everybody," he said over the intercom. "This is going to be a fun landing."

CHAPTER 37

41° N, 7° E.
25 miles from Basilica Santuario San Michele Arcangelo
9:26 p.m.

From one of the rear seats of the plane, Ben took off his seatbelt and asked, "How are we going to get to Monte Sant'Angelo from here?"

No one had thought of that till now. Someone during the flight should have made a call to Director Kestner and asked him to try and send a car for them, but now who knew how long it would take if they tried that. They could end up sitting here all night waiting for someone.

Frank shut down the two jet engines and Iris looked at Cameron who was also undoing his seatbelt. He sensed her looking at him and turned to her, immediately recognizing the familiar look on her face. He rolled his eyes. "I'll take care of it."

Outside the plane, the airfield was deserted. The few small buildings were locked up tight and dark, and there were only a couple other small aircraft parked in a field beyond. However, parked just outside the smallest of the three buildings was a utility truck—an orange cabover with a flatbed with wooden sideboards on the back. Professor Skull grinned. *That'll work.*

Cabovers were ideal for hotwiring. In general,

cars and trucks could not be started without a key as easily as the movies made it seem. First of all, you had to get into the car. Second, fumbling around under the dash was more or less a waste of time. But on a cabover, all it took was a couple handle pulls and the entire engine compartment became accessible.

"Samuel, come with me," Cameron said. They walked over to the truck and Cameron tilted the front of it open. It was plenty dark outside and there was nothing else around except for open fields, so he had little worry of them getting caught. "Get your phone out and shine a light on this for me, will you?" he asked. Samuel did it without hesitation and Cameron took a small multi-tool out of his front pocket. He clipped off an 8-inch long piece of wire that went to the air conditioning pump—*That's not going to be needed*—and stripped the insulation off both ends.

Samuel watched from the side. His hands were shaking from excitement.

Red equals hot. Professor Skull stretched his piece of wire from the trucks battery to the coil to engage the starter. The truck fired up and he closed the cab back down. "Go get everybody," he said to Samuel.

Samuel ran back to the group and a minute later they were all piling onto the flatbed, although not without some complaints.

"We aren't going very far," Cameron assured them. He put a hand out and stopped Emily as she

Justin Hyde

was about to climb up. "Can you read a map?" he asked her.

She nodded yes.

"Good. You can ride up front and help with directions." He looked to Iris. "You drive."

"Ever the gentleman," she said smiling as she opened the driver's door and got behind the wheel.

Both women were glad to not be stuck out in the cold on the back of the truck. Cameron hoped up with the rest of the men in the back and tapped the top of the cab with his open palm. "Okay, let's hit the road."

—

Most of the town of Monte Sant'Angelo was asleep. They entered from the south then drove through the heart of the city until reaching the backroad of Via Estramurale. "This road will take us all the way to the basilica," Matteo told them. "It traces the north rim of the city."

Cameron looked out over the edge of the cliff past the city limits. There seemed to be nothing beyond but rolling hills. "Is the cave sealed?" he asked. "Will we be able to get in right now?"

Matteo shook his head to Cameron's second question. "No. I don't think we will be able to. The entrance is through the church now. It will most likely be locked for the night."

"But if we hurry someone might still be there," Matteo's younger son Adrian said. "It's

282

almost ten o'clock, but sometimes some of the Brotherhood stay late. Right, papa?"

It was true. Sometimes members of the ancient brotherhood would stay past hours to pray to the pontiff or to invoke the Archangel's help in protecting those on a spiritual journey. Matteo gave a look of agreement. "We should park behind the castle," he said. "There is a small lot where we can leave the truck. It will be better than driving to the front." He still did not trust the new priest here and did not want to announce his return just yet if the man happened to be around.

"The castle?" Cameron asked.

"Yes. There is a medieval castle next to the church that was abandoned centuries ago. It is largely rundown, but I did hear that the church recently leased it from the municipality of Monte Sant'Angelo. Although, I'm not sure why."

"Like, an actual big castle with walls and a moat and all that?" he asked again for more detail.

"The moat dried up many years ago. But yes, that kind of castle." Matteo looked through the back window of the truck and out the front windshield to the road ahead of them. He tapped on the glass to get Emily's attention. She turned around and he pointed forward and spoke loudly so she could hear him. "Keep going past the church. We'll park in the small lot below the castle."

Emily nodded. She was familiar with the spot. She had parked there occasionally in the past. Usually on holidays or Saint Michael's Day, when street parking would fill up quickly. It was just up ahead.

Iris pulled the truck in and everyone started getting out.

Before stepping down, Cameron looked up at the huge outer stone wall of the castle at the top of the hill next to them. It loomed over them like a giant shield in the darkness. "Why would a church want a castle?" he asked.

Matteo concentrated on not falling as he got off the back of the truck before answering him. He then helped all four of the teenagers down as well. "I have no idea. The priest who took my place is the one who arranged it."

"And how do they afford it?" Cameron added quietly.

Iris appeared at the back of the truck with them. "How do we get to the cave from here?"

Emily answered her. "It's just on the other side of those buildings over there," she said, pointing. But it's quicker if we go this way." She pointed in the other direction. To their right, the buildings stopped at the edge of a tree covered hill just below the castle wall. "There's a small path that goes up the hill over there."

Ben and Adrian both shook their heads in agreement and the group started walking up the path through the trees. It was a short distance and only took a few minutes to reach the next road. Directly in front of them now was the outer wall of the fortress. It soared into the sky and Frank, Iris and

Cameron all stretched their necks back to look up to the battlements at the top.

"What are those doors over there?" Josh asked.

Cameron followed his gaze and saw that there were indeed three or four small man-sized doors in the side of hill below the wall that looked like they went into the castle. Two of them were sealed with heavy metal fronts, but one other had no door on it at all and was a black void in the side of the hill. It had been hard to see against the dark of night and Skull might have missed it if Josh hadn't pointed it out.

"I'm not sure," Matteo admitted. "Castles are complex and mysterious structures. Maybe they weren't even part of the original design. Who knows?"

"They obviously go into the castle," Iris pointed out. "Why in the world would you build such a wall just to put doors in it?"

It was strange indeed. But there they were.

"Let's keep moving," Cameron said.

"This way." Matteo led the group down the road. "That's the Basilica di San Michele right there," he said, indicating the building in front of them.

The moonlight shined brighter once escaping the shadow of the castle wall. Cameron followed close as Matteo led them around a small iron fence to the front of the church. The building had been erected over the cave many centuries ago. It was white marble with a small frontal courtyard and an octagonal bell tower rising up in the east. There were two tall gothic archways on the front that led to the bronze doors. Above the arches was a statue of Saint Michael overlooking the courtyard. Professor Skull noticed how the portrayal of the archangel showed him as the guardian and protector with his hand raised above his head, holding the mighty sword.

"Beyond the doors is the Portale del Toro," Matteo said. "The Gate of the Bull." He stood still for a moment. "It leads down to the cavern." He turned to ben. "Tu e Adrian aspettate qui."

Ben was about to protest but Iris spoke first. "Your father is right," she said. "All of you should wait here."

"Actually," Cameron said. "You too." He looked around at everyone. "Let me go by myself first and see if I can get in."

Matteo raised a hand. "I am coming with you," he told him.

Cameron gave him a nod and waved for him to come along. Iris and Emily accepted the idea and leaned against the iron gate, but the four teenagers were not quite as accepting and paced around anxiously.

"There's no one here," Matteo said once they reached the doors. "We can't get in."

Cameron took a step back and evaluated the building. "Well, shit." He looked to Matteo. "Now what? Isn't there some other way?"

Matteo shook his head. "No, there is no other way. But maybe we should check out the castle."

CHAPTER 38

"There are nine of us," Cameron said. "We can't all go in."

"But you might need our help," Josh said.

They were standing back outside the small doorways along the back wall of the castle. The front entrance, Matteo already knew, could not be breached. Although the moat had been empty for many years, it was still a wide and deep trench that traced the front and side perimeter walls. There was only one bridge leading across it that lead to the main portcullis—and there was certainly no way of getting through that unless they wanted to try driving the truck through it like a battering ram.

Cameron turned to Samuel who was sort of becoming his right hand. "Can you run back to the truck and see if there's a flashlight in there somewhere? Maybe under the seat or in the glove box."

He loved being included and took off quickly down the trail towards the truck.

"I'll go with him," Adrian said, and ran off after him.

Cameron turned to Frank. "I think you and Iris should take Emily and the boys and see if you can find a place to lay low for a while."

"I think we'll wait right here," he said.

Cameron knew there was no changing Frank's mind. And actually, it was probably a good thing

Frank was there, otherwise Ben and Josh may have decided to go rogue and do something dumb. "Matteo, do you have any idea where these doors might lead?"

"The castle has many levels to it and there are also many underground tunnels. Since these don't seem to be guarded very closely, my only guess is that maybe they just lead into the center courtyard."

"Well at least that will get us past this wall," he said, looking up again at the mountain of mortared stone.

They waited a few more seconds until they heard Samuel and Adrian running back up the trail. Samuel carried a flashlight in his right hand, and it's beam broke through the trees before they did. He was out of breath when he reached the top and didn't say anything as he handed the light to the professor.

Cameron thanked him then started towards the open doorway with Matteo following. Just past the opening was another tunnel that reminded Cameron of the one he had been in inside the mountain, although these walls were dirt, not ice. He was also silently thankful that he didn't have to use his lighter again to see with.

Both men had to hunch over slightly to fit inside. "Let me know if you need to me to slow down," Cameron whispered to Matteo behind him.

"I'm alright. Keep going."

The tunnel turned several times, and twice

Cameron had hit his head against the dirt ceiling, grunting each time and sending back warnings to Matteo to watch out. Then the bluish-grey outline of moonlight coming through the end of the tunnel became visible from a distance.

They emerged into the center court of the castle. It was an open grassy area with a few modern sidewalks and railings crossing over it. Through the narrow glassless windows on the northern wall above them was a nighttime view of the endless hills leading out to the Adriatic Sea.

Cameron clicked off the flashlight. The light grey stone of the castle walls inside the courtyard reflected the moonlight enough to illuminate the grounds. On every wall it seemed there was at least one door and occasionally a window.

Matteo turned his head in all directions. "I guess we should just start trying them," he suggested.

Cameron had one of his "feelings" though. Something wasn't sitting right with him and he felt his guard going up. "What does the church want with this place?" he said quietly to himself. He began slowly inching his way back against a wall and out of the moonlight. "Psst. Hey. Matteo."

Matteo turned at his noise and noticed Cameron's new posture. The professor's instincts translated over to him and he suddenly felt vulnerable as well. He crouched down and met Cameron at the wall. "What should we do?"

It took Cameron a second to answer. He was

still scanning the area. "What reason would a church have for taking over a castle?" Again, he was mostly whispering out loud to himself, but he turned to Matteo with his next thought. "Does this castle have anything to do with Saint Michael, like the cave does? Do you think the sword may be here instead?"

"I doubt it," he answered. "This castle has nothing to do with Michael. It is old, but it was not here when Michael blessed the cave."

Something wasn't right. Professor Skull wasn't sure about anything else—but he was sure about that. "Let's see if we can get inside," he said. "Stay close."

Matteo felt his heartrate start to rise. He left the safety of the wall and followed Cameron across a small grass area to the closest door. It didn't budge when Cameron tried opening it. They moved on to the next door. It was locked as well but had not been replaced in recent years like most of the others had been. The wood of the door was splintered and warped from years of swelling in the rain and baking in the sun, and it rattled loosely against the worn rock around it.

Cameron looked around again and listened, then handed the flashlight to Matteo and shouldered the door with some moderate force to test its strength. It bowed inward but did not break. He looked around again, and listened again, then hit it again, harder than before. The lock cracked under the pressure and Cameron nearly fell in when it broke open.

"Here," Matteo said, handing him back the light.

He took it and clicked it on but kept one hand partially covering the lens to dim it as he pointed it into the open room of the castle. The ceiling inside was low and crisscrossed with stone arches and there was a large fireplace built into one wall. Several small antechambers branched out as well as a staircase leading down and two other doors. There were no signs of any people though.

Damn I wish I had my HK on me.

Any gun at all would have been acceptable though. This did not feel like the right situation to be unarmed in.

Matteo kept tight to Cameron's heels as he moved silently to the first door in the room. It opened, and beyond was yet another room, larger than the one they were currently in. Cameron took a step inside and noticed even the sound of his own light footstep echoing through the larger space. This time he decided to take a different approach. "You take that side," he said, pointing to the left. "I'll start searching this way."

"Are you sure that's a good idea?"

"Just do a quick sweep," Cameron told him. "Don't open any doors or anything, but listen for sounds and note anything useful, like staircases or even trap doors. We'll meet up at twelve o'clock." He pointed straight ahead in the direction of the hour, then handed him the flashlight. Matteo looked at him with curiosity, but Cameron pulled the BIC lighter out of his pocket again and sparked the flame. "All good," he said as both a question and a statement.

Matteo tipped his head then turned and started his sweep of the left side perimeter of the room. Nothing struck him as noteworthy until he turned the first corner. A sound was resonating through the walls, coming from somewhere deep inside the castle. An eerie sound like the low moan of an injured dog. He stopped and listened hard. There was a thud then the moan again, but this time it was more than one. Several moans of different pitches mixed over each other very softly through the walls. To drown out the frightening noises, Matteo began to pray. "Padre nostro, che sei nei cieli, sia santificato il tuo nome."

"Matteo," Cameron whispered loudly across the room. "Matteo, come over here."

Matteo stopped reciting the Lord's Prayer and looked in the direction of Cameron's small flame across the room. He swept his flashlight towards him and noticed that it revealed a hallway leading out just to the left of where Cameron was. "What it is?" he asked as he approached. "What did you find?"

"Do you smell that?" Cameron asked.

Matteo sniffed the air. "I smell something, but I don't know what it is."

"Me neither," Cameron said. "But it smells familiar to me." He sniffed again, moving his nose closer to the door in front of him. There was a metallic scent coming from behind the closed door.

"And there's something else," he added.

"What is it?" Matteo asked.

"Turn off your flashlight." Cameron also released the gas button on the lighter and let the flame go out.

Now, in nothing but the darkness of the room, Matteo saw it.

"I noticed it right after we split up," Cameron said.

There was a thin line of light glowing beneath the door. It was not a yellow shine or a warm fluorescent, but the dancing orange of a flame. "And the smell," Cameron whispered. "It's metal. But not just like iron or rust. It smells like molten steel."

"It's definitely not wood that's burning," Matteo agreed.

Cameron shook his head, although Matteo could not see it. Then he held his breath and pushed gently on the door. It was warm and it was solid. *Not going to be able to shoulder my way through this one,* he thought.

"Did you hear that?" Matteo asked. He had been focused on sounds ever since hearing the moans, but what he heard now was different. It was a footstep.

It happened again. "I did that time," Cameron said. "Go back." He pushed Matteo a little, guiding him back towards the doorway they had entered the room through.

They needed to get out of here and hide—quickly.

Someone was coming.

CHAPTER 39

The two monks brought the boy to Father Santé's room. Bastian greeted him. "How are you feeling?"

The boy was afraid. His wound from the surgery a few hours ago had healed completely and he was in no pain, but he was still scared. He was only 8 years old. And like any child would be, he was afraid of the unknown and he was terrified of the intimidation of a strange place and the strange man who had kidnapped him from his family. Bastian's kindness towards him now was only confusing, not comforting, and he did not answer Bastian's question.

Father Santé walked over to him and leaned over. "Do you know what you are?" he asked. He tilted his head in order to keep eye contact with the boy. "You are the answer. You are the arrow in the quiver, and I am the warrior. Just like the Psalm says."

The room around them was dark and musty. The only light came from somewhere behind Bastian, so the boy could not see his face well. He trembled and tried backing away, but the two monks stood behind him, blocking the way.

"I want you to have this," Bastian said. It was another gesture to try and calm the boy. Fear was just inevitable—but it was not Bastian's goal. He held out the short-sword. "You are the only other one who can carry this," he told him. "Only you and I." He pointed to the two monks still standing behind him. "Not even they can touch this sword."

The child gulped. His throat was still dry, and he did it a second time. He didn't want the sword. He just wanted to go home.

Bastian leaned closer and whispered in his ear. "You could kill them with it right now if you wanted to."

The two monks heard the whispered threat and tensed. But the boy still did not reach out and take the weapon.

Father Santé kneeled down completely. "This sword," he said. "Once belonged to an angel. His name was Phanuel. Now it is yours." He extended it out again to the boy and this time the child took it. He grabbed it by the handle and held it awkwardly, not knowing what was expected of him now. Bastian smiled. *He is actually holding it*. He hoped the results would be the same with the next sword though. The child was not safe just yet.

Bastian stood and spoke sternly to the monk on his right. "Go down to the vault and fill another box. The carrier will be here in an hour to pick it up."

The monk bowed his hooded head and walked away while the other monk remained. It was a weekly routine for one of them to fill a 10-pound box for the carrier to pick up—always at night. Bastian sold the boxes for 90,000 Euros each, making him a very rich man. They were then resold and distributed through the dark web for probably double that amount, making the carrier a very rich man as well.

He looked down at the boy again. "Shall we go?" He didn't give the child time to think, but stepped around him and out the door. The remaining monk also stepped around the boy and drove him from the rear, following Father Santé down the hall, then down the stairs.

—

Professor Skull followed Matteo quickly and ducked behind the doorway just in time to avoid being seen by the man approaching. Cameron stopped just outside, then turned and peeked back into the dark room. Matteo was further away but stopped as well, but did not try to signal Cameron. Instead, curiosity got the best of him and he went back and peeked over Cameron's shoulder and into the room as well.

They watched together as a cloaked figure carrying a lantern in one hand and a small box in the other emerged from the hallway. He walked to the locked door—the one with the firelight coming from under it—then set down the box and inserted a key. The door squeaked on dry hinges as he pushed it open. Immediately the glow of his lantern was washed away by the intensity of whatever was burning within the room.

Cameron and Matteo both pulled back further behind the cover of the doorway to keep from being seen. But their eyes remained fixed on trying to get a glimpse of whatever was inside the room. From their angle though, all they could see so far was the outline of the man's hood and tunic blocking their view.

The man bent down slowly and picked the box back up then entered the room, and Matteo had to shield his eyes from the bright light that flooded out until he got adjusted.

"What is that?" Cameron said very softly.

A dazzling array of sparkles and swirls of orange blasted out of the room like a disco ball reflecting the light of whatever was burning inside. The room itself glowed with a bright mixture of orange and yellow beams and there was a soft hissing sound like the pull of a vacuum—or the breathing of fire.

Cameron was mesmerized and stepped slowly and quietly back into the main room. He snuck closer to the open door then froze solid. What he saw stopped him dead in his tracks.

Matteo called to him with a quiet urgency. "Cameron. Professor Skull. What are you doing? Let's get out of here."

Cameron didn't move or even blink, and eventually Matteo was grasped again by his curiosity and snuck to Cameron's side. He gasped and motioned the sign of the cross over himself. *Nel nome del Padre, e del Figlio, e dello Spirito Santo.* "It is the sword of Uriel," he said.

"It's not just the sword," Cameron pointed out. "That is Nazi gold in there."

The monk inside the room was carefully filling the box in his hand with gold coins from an open crate. There were at least 20 more identical crates piled further back inside the small room—half a dozen of them with their tops removed. On the front of each crate was a faded, but recognizable, swastika.

What is that doing here? Cameron thought to himself. *How can it be?* But it did explain how the castle was being paid for.

The gold coins inside each open crate sparkled and reflected the light of the flame burning above them. Suspended in the air over the center of the room, somehow by its own power, the angelic steel of the archangel's sword burned intensely. Whenever the monks hand reached a little too far into the room, past the first segregated crate, the flames of the sword roared higher—seemingly defending the gold in the same way that it had once defended the Garden of Eden. The monk would pull back quickly each time.

A moment later the monk finished filling the small box and closed its lid.

"Go back," Cameron said to Matteo urgently.

They turned, ready to run, when another figure stepped in front of their exit—blocking them in.

"Shit!" Cameron turned, no longer concerned with silence or stealth, and tugged the sleeve of Matteo's jacket as he ran for the only visible exit—the open hallway. The monk carrying the box of gold sidestepped into their path, but Cameron ran into him hard, sending the box of gold flying from his hands and spilling across the large open floor of the room. "Where's the flashlight?" Cameron yelled, then stalled for a second to let Matteo take the lead.

Matteo clicked on the light and they ran in line with each other through the confined hall until coming to the Great Room of the castle. The giant space was the centerpiece of the medieval fortress and had a row of windows along one wall and connecting doorways on all three others. They hooked left and into the first and closest room. It was a laboratory of some sort, full of modern medical equipment and cold stainless-steel tables. "What the hell is this?" Cameron asked.

Matteo swept his flashlight around. There was a rack of distillation equipment, a microcentrifuge, an incubator and a refrigerator, and a small out-of-place fish tank on one of the tables. There was also a cart full of blood covered surgical tools—but, there was no way out.

Both men turned around and ran to the next open room. Matteo entered first then nearly crushed Cameron as he halted and scrambled to run back out. "Dear Father in Heaven!" he cried.

Skull was nearly trampled by him but caught his balance. The low moans that Matteo had heard through the walls earlier roared loud now in anger. Cameron grabbed him and held on—attempting to control the man's panic. They were both in danger and Cameron was nervous and full of adrenaline too, but losing complete control of yourself was the worst thing to do.

He took the light from him and shined it into the room and quickly realized why Matteo had reacted the way he did. There was a wall of bars that went from the left wall all the way to the right, turning the room into one giant prison cell. Dozens, maybe even a hundred of the zombie-like creatures that Cameron had encountered on the mountain stirred inside. They growled and scratched at each other trying to get through the bars. Corpselike hands reached out and desperately attacked the air between them and the two men who had just arrived.

Cameron suddenly had to hold back the urge to vomit from the smell. *This place is a living nightmare.*

"Oh no," Matteo said. "Here they come."

Cameron turned again quickly. The two monks, one still holding the lantern, were walking out from the hallway. They seemed to be calm— preying upon the two intruders with a relaxed composure. It was a discouraging sight. If the monks were afraid that the two men could escape, they surely would have been much more aggressive.

Matteo felt himself loosing hope. "What are we going to do?" he asked with a sadness in his voice.

Cameron did not give up so easily. He grabbed Matteo by the shirt sleeve again and pulled. "We're going to get the hell out of here. Come on."

Justin Hyde

There were still a few other doorways that connected to the Great Hall that they had not yet tried. One in particular was larger than the others and was arched at the top rather than squared. It had no door on it and was really more of a passageway than a doorway. Beyond the threshold it was pitch black, and without the flashlight Cameron would have never seen that just inside was a stairway leading down—he would have fallen for sure.

"Watch it," he said to Matteo as he quickly descended the first few steps.

Halfway down there was a sharp turn, then a long open room at the bottom. It was cold and had a musty smell. It was also quiet, and Cameron could now hear their own loud breaths. Matteo stopped short just behind him, and Cameron pointed the flashlight into the open space. The chilling sight was a lot to take in.

They were in the dungeon.

CHAPTER 40

"Help me."

"Who said that?" Matteo asked. The voice was soft and scared. It was also feminine and childlike. *A little girl.* "Where are you?" he asked as he walked past Cameron and into the darkness of the dungeon. His own fear was gone, replaced now with purpose. "I can't see you," he said.

Cameron caught up to him and aimed the flashlight at each cell, trying to ignore the dusty medieval devices still resting throughout the open room. There were pulleys and rope, a large wooden pedestal with some kind of medieval clamping mechanism on the top, and a tall iron cage suspended from the ceiling by chain. Inside the cage was the crumbled skeletal remains of its last victim.

Then there were two other torture devices that Professor Skull recognized—and even respectfully feared. Just the sight of them now in person caused his hair to rise. One was a rectangular wood frame with a large pulley at the top and another at the bottom. It had wrist and ankle straps and a crank that the dungeon master would use to stretch out the victim across the rack.

The other device he recognized was standing in the farthest back corner. An Iron Maiden. The worst and maybe most feared of all medieval torture devices. A sarcophagus of iron that stood upright over 6 feet tall and opened in the front by two swinging doors. Inside were hundreds of needle-sharp spikes that, when the doors were closed, would pierce through the victim from all sides and hold them until death. On the top of the device was a smaller section where the victims head would go. And like many Iron Maidens, the head portion of this one had been molded into the shape of a face on the front. But, on this particular one, the eyes had been removed, allowing whoever was inside to look out as they died—and to let the executioner look back in at them.

Over the years the outside of the iron had turned almost black. But even in the far corner of the dungeon and covered in dust and cobwebs, there was no missing it. The double swinging doors on the front of it were closed, and Skull had to force himself to not think about whether or not there was still someone inside.

"We're over here," a new voice said.

A large hand waved out of one of the last cells in the room. Cameron and Matteo ran up. Inside was a small girl and a big man. "Can you get us out of here?" the man asked.

The little girl with him looked up into the light of Cameron's flashlight with pleading tears in her eyes.

"*We* are trying to get out of *here*," Cameron said, indicating the space of the dungeon.

The big man behind the bars didn't look surprised by that. He pointed to the wall behind him. "There's a secret passage through that wall," he said.

"But I can't get it open by myself. Maybe if you both help me, we can lift it together?"

"There's only one problem," Cameron said. "You're in there, and we're out here." He took a step back and looked at the door of the cell, examining it and testing the lock. "We can't even get in there to help you."

"You can if you get the key," the man said. Cameron was about to comment back when the man added, "He's got it." Then pointed to someone coming down the stairs.

Cameron and Matteo both spun around. The two monks had entered the dungeon.

"You can't hurt them," the little girl cried.

"She means that they can't be hurt," the man said, trying to clarify what the girl meant. "We saw one of them take a knife to the side twice earlier and not even flinch. It's like they're bulletproof or something."

Oh great! Cameron shifted his weight onto his back foot, taking a defensive stance against the two hooded men approaching. One of the monks lifted his lantern higher, and as he did the light momentarily shined off the blade in his hand.

"They have knives," Matteo warned.

"Listen to me," Cameron said. "I'm going to need your help here." Already a plan was forming in his mind. Even if these two men were indeed bulletproof, the situation wasn't much different than the original knights of this castle who battled each other in armor—long before the invention of the gun. Once Cameron's initial shock from the statement wore off and he realized that fact, he was able to focus on how to deal with it. Medieval knights fought opponents all the time who their weapons were largely useless against. A sword was not a gun, but it could not cut through the steel plates of a suit of armor. So how did the knights overcome it?

Unfortunately, Cameron didn't know all the ins and outs of medieval combat. However, he did know enough about modern combat to make some justifiable decisions on the matter. A suit of armor had to have weaknesses—at the joints most likely—that a sword could penetrate. That wasn't likely the case with these two monks though, since they weren't actually wearing armor. Suits of armor could also be damaged, if not by a blade, then perhaps by a hammer. *A different weapon. Or a different approach.* There was one other thing that Cameron could think of. *A knight in armor could be restrained or immobilized.* He looked at the two monks who were getting dangerously close. *So can they.*

"Matteo," Cameron said. "I want you to circle with me. Pretend there is a pole and we are slowly walking around it. Always face them and move the circle in the direction I lead." Professor Skull's focus had already gone into what his old martial arts sensei had called, *Zanshin.* Basically, a mental state of awareness. He was no longer concentrated on just reactions and survival, but was calm and conscious of all his surroundings—actively preplanning every option and every move.

The monk holding the lantern was within striking distance now and in another second he would probably attack first—swinging or lunging with the knife. Matteo was the closest and Cameron sped up the motion of their circle until he took the place of the target. He backed up a step and mapped out the room next to him with his peripheral vision. "Matteo. When I say so I need you to pull that rope to your right. The one dangling above the floor."

Cameron suddenly stepped right, reversing the direction of the circle him and Matteo were moving in, and keeping himself in front of the first monk. The second monk, he noticed, was only a few feet behind, but also moving in slow.

Beneath the man's hood, Cameron could read the look in his eyes and knew the attack was coming. The monk lunged out with the blade and Skull dodged left, avoiding it and grabbing him by the wrist. The monks were not fast, but this was one was strong, and he did not let go of the knife. Cameron kept hold of his wrist then spun back around again and tucked the man's elbow under his arm then dropped to the floor on his knees, which brought the monk down too, belly first. As fast as he could he leaned forward and got the man's hand onto the lower part of the wooden frame next to him and under the loop of old rope on it. "NOW!" he yelled to Matteo.

Matteo bent over and pulled on the bottom of the rope. It cinched the loop down over the monk's wrist and locked him to the frame. "Get his other..." Suddenly a pain ripped into Cameron's bad shoulder—but not an internal pain like he had gotten accustomed to. The second monk had cut him open from behind and blood started running down the left side of his back. Cameron cried out then quickly tucked his shoulder in and rolled to his right and out of the man's reach.

Matteo used the distraction and the second monk's attention on Cameron to grab the other arm of the first monk before he was able to free himself from the binding. Matteo was strong too and was able to pull hard enough on the man to get his other arm under the second loop of rope and tighten it down on him. The monk was now locked by the wrists to the top of the medieval rack.

Sergio yelled something from the cell to Cameron's left, but only Matteo heard it clearly. "Get his keys!"

Matteo looked down at the restrained man. He was struggling and kicking with his legs. Given enough time he would probably be able to free himself. Matteo reached down. The ring of keys was hung from a rope tied around the man's waist. He tried pulling them away, but the rope held them to the man. Never in his life had Matteo used violence against someone, but now he walked around to the side of the monk, looked at him directly, and punched him as hard as he could in the face. The blow did not hurt the man, but his natural reaction had been to defend against it, and he open both hands, dropping the knife. Matteo grabbed it and slid it under the rope. It cut through easily and the keys dropped to the floor.

Now it was the little girl in the cell who called out. "Leave him alone!" She was not talking to Matteo. The second monk was closing in on Cameron.

The room around Professor Skull was an abstract mixture of dark and light. Sometime during the fight, both the flashlight and the monk's lantern had been dropped, and now cast blurry, unintentional spreads of light across the floor in random abstract patterns. The lantern was on its side and sent an elongated shadow of the monk towards Cameron as he approached him. With his free hand, the man reached up and removed the hood off his head. His features were shadowed as well but he didn't look like a monster as Cameron had thought he would. He looked like a man—just pale and expressionless.

"Not today, pal," Cameron said. He faked a jab then leaned back and kicked the man's kneecap, buckling it backwards. The monk dropped like a stone but attacked again quickly from the ground. Professor Skull jumped back then grabbed the iron handle on the door next to him. He pulled hard and the heavy door of the Iron Maiden swung open just as the monk was getting back to his feet. Cameron grabbed him by the front of his tunic and flung him around, slamming him into the spikes on the inside of the medieval torture device. Blood appeared in the man's mouth and his eyes opened wide—not from pain, but from astonishment.

Cameron slammed the door shut. He had to plant both feet firm to the ground and push hard. The years had made the spikes on the inside of the door dull and rusty and they didn't puncture through the man as easily as expected.

To the side, Matteo had picked up the flashlight and unlocked the dungeon cell already. Sergio and Becca now stood next to him as he pointed the beam back over to Cameron. Inside the Iron Maiden in front of the professor, they could all see the eyes of the monk trapped inside. He was still very much alive and staring out helplessly and ferociously. *He is not alive,* Matteo told himself. *He is something else.* "Professor," he said. "We should go."

Cameron kept his eyes locked with the man inside the iron box. *What in God's name is going on?* This monk wasn't even one of the zombie things. Or was he? *How is he not dead?*

"Professor," Matteo said again.

Cameron turned and looked at the three of them. "Yeah. Okay let's get out of here."

They went back into the cell and Sergio brought them to the back where the heavy steel door had fallen, locking him, Becca and Tony in earlier. "It slides up," Sergio said. "But I can't lift it."

"I hope there isn't some sort of spring locking mechanism above it," Cameron said.

Sergio shook his head. "I don't think so. Tony

and I were able to move it a little. But we couldn't hold it open enough to let either of us crawl underneath. It's just really heavy."

"Tony?" Matteo questioned.

"My brother. He's gone. Don't worry about him."

Cameron could tell there was some bad blood there and left it alone. Anything could have happened to his brother in this castle, and the details weren't important right now. "Maybe two of us can lift and the third person helps hold. If we take turns doing that, maybe we can all get out." He began looking around the ground. "See if maybe there's anything we can use to help pry it up or brace it once we get it off the ground."

"The knives," Matteo said. "We can use them to pry it up." He ran out with the flashlight to go find them. One was locked inside the Iron Maiden with the monk, but the other was still on the ground next to the man tied to the rack. He grabbed it and ran back.

Sergio took it from him and quickly jammed it underneath the metal door. With the strength of all three men they were able to lift the solid door a few inches when a voice shouted from the staircase at the dungeons entrance. "What's going on down here?"

It was one of the castle guards. One of the unaltered men who Bastian kept around for not much more than to make hourly foot patrols of the property. The guard yelled again. "Who are you?" He began running towards them with a flashlight and a taser gun.

Little Becca was quick to think, and her fear drove her into action. She ran a step forward and shut the cell door, locking the guard out.

"Stop right there," the guard ordered. But his taser had very limited range and the only one he could have shot from outside the bars was the girl. He did not.

Matteo guided the frightened child towards the passageway that Sergio and Cameron were now struggling to hold open. "It's okay," he assured her.

She went into the tunnel and Matteo followed, then switched places with Sergio and helped hold the door as he came through next.

Cameron turned to look at the guard before ducking in himself. The guard made eye contact, but then turned and ran fast for the stairs leading out of the dungeon. He had his orders, and knew what he was supposed to do in this situation.

CHAPTER 41

Emily and her boys had gone with Iris back to the truck in the lower parking lot, while Francesco and the two other boys were still waiting up near the outer wall of the castle. With nothing else to do with the time, Frank had of course taken to researching something, and was currently still pacing around in the dark and staring at his phone. He remembered Cameron mentioning something about zombies when they spoke on the phone earlier. A stupid comment—yet Frank knew that the professor would not have just blurted out something ridiculous like that unless that was truly the only word that he thought he could have used.

Initially it hadn't meant much to Frank. Even if Cameron really did think he saw a zombie, he obviously did not, so Francesco had dismissed it. But now, after having nothing else to do but think for a while, Frank's mind had begun to put bits of a puzzle together. The individual pieces didn't seem to fit quite right yet unfortunately, but a bigger picture was starting to take shape.

Francesco's sometimes wild imagination was always one of his best research tools, and often one of the leading causes of him sniffing out the right trails. *Why would Cameron have thought he saw a zombie? Everyone knows that zombies aren't real, obviously. What could it have been though? Something that looked like a zombie maybe? It definitely wasn't a dead person walking around. A burn victim? A crash survivor? No, the professor has seen plenty of those in his days. He wouldn't have made that mix-up. Maybe it was some weird experiment gone bad.* That thought had triggered something in him. Maybe what Cameron had seen was not natural, but manmade. *Why would someone want to make a zombie?*

At first, he could not come up with a good answer to his question, so he had shifted gears and started thinking about archangels and the Sword of Saint Michael instead. *I can't believe I missed all those clues. I didn't even catch that the sword of Michael was a geographical sword as well as a physical one. And I thought it was in Ireland. I wasn't even close! And then what? What was I going to do then? I was going to dig it up with Iris and I didn't even know that you couldn't touch it. I could have gotten us both killed!*

Another light went on in his head.

Unless I couldn't die.

The idea seemed impossible.

Could it be? Could someone be trying to artificially create a human with the ability to touch the weapons of the angels without dying? How else could you create your own army of warriors? We know that whoever this person is, has found at least two weapons so far. Maybe more. But—wait a second. This person CAN touch the weapons already. The man from the jungle never said anything about him being some kind of zombie. No, that can't be it.

Discouragement flooded over him once again. "Ugh!" he said out loud. "What is the matter with me?"

Josh and Samuel had both been sitting on a curb and looked up at him.

Think Frank. What if somebody WAS infecting people with some sort of zombie virus? How would they do it? But then a scarier thought crossed his mind. *How could we stop it?* That was the question that he had been working on and trying to answer for the last fifteen minutes now, until a scream came from down the hill.

Immediately him and the boys ran for the truck. "Iris," he yelled, as he came to the bottom of the short path. "What's wrong? What happened?"

Samuel answered first. "Professor Skull," he said. "How did you get here?"

Cameron, Matteo and two new people—a man and a young girl— were walking up the hill from below the parking lot.

"Sorry to scream, but you scared the heck out of me," Iris said to him. "How did you guys get down there?"

"We came out through another secret passageway from the dungeon," he answered. "We ran into some trouble in there though, and one of the guards ran off as we were escaping. It looked like he might have been going to alert people."

Matteo was dusting off his pants while Sergio and Becca stood uncomfortably off to the side, staring at the group of people gathering around. "Is everybody here alright?" Matteo asked.

"We're all fine," his wife said reassuringly. "Are you hurt?"

He shook his head, but little Becca pointed at Cameron and spoke up. "He is," she said.

All eyes turned to the professor. Iris could now see the stain of blood on his shoulder from the knife wound. "Cameron! What..."

"I'll be fine," he said, gently interrupting her. "It's not as bad as it looks."

"Are you sure? Because it looks bad!"

He nodded and forced a smile. "Is everyone here?"

"Yeah. We're all here."

Sergio caught a glimpse of two people walking away down the road though. "What about them?" he asked. "Where are they going?"

Cameron and Matteo both turned to see who the big Italian was talking about. "Who..." Matteo started to say to himself. He squinted to try and focus better on the couple. It looked like another man and child. The man was very tall and suddenly Matteo knew who it was. "Padre Santé," he whispered. He turned to Cameron. "It is Bastian Santé. The man who accused me of theft and stole my church from me."

Everyone was now looking, and Emily questioned who was with Bastian.

"I don't know," Matteo answered. "But they are headed towards the cave."

Cameron's eyes opened wide. "Matteo, let's

go." He immediately started for the church and Matteo followed.

"What about us?" Francesco called out after them.

Matteo and the professor were already concentrated on catching up with Santé and the child though and didn't answer him. They followed Bastian's trail to the entrance of the church, where they had been earlier, and crept back to the bronze doors at the Basilicas entrance. The door was closed. Father Santé and the child were already inside.

Cameron waited for Matteo to catch up, then looked to him for a sign of readiness before placing a hand on the door and pushing.

It opened.

—

Francesco turned back to Iris and the group and scratched his head. "I don't feel right just sitting here not doing anything," he said. "Maybe we should at least move closer to the church in case he needs our help suddenly."

Iris tended to agree, but there was one point she needed to make about it first. "Last time him and Matteo took off though, they ended up somewhere completely different than any of us expected. Maybe a few of us should wait here in case that happens again." She turned to Emily and her boys. "Emily. Would you, Ben and Adrian mind staying here at the truck? That way if your husband comes back and we don't see him first, there will be someone here to tell him where we went."

"Of course," she said. "We'll watch after the little girl too."

Adrian was happy to stay with his mom, but to Frank's surprise, Ben didn't argue either.

Iris turned to the young girl who Cameron and Matteo had rescued from the castle. She couldn't tell if the man with her was her father, but she didn't think so. If he was, he wasn't a very comforting one. She walked over to the girl and knelt down. The girl was still scared, and Iris spoke softly. "Are you alright?" The girl fidgeted with her fingers but nodded. "What's your name?"

"Becca," she answered.

"Becca, is this man your father?" Iris asked. The girl shook her head, no, and Iris looked suspiciously up at the man, then back down to the girl. "Will you wait here? This lady over here will watch out for you till I get back. Then we will find your mom and dad. Okay?"

"Yes," Becca said timidly, putting her trust in Iris and Emily.

Iris smiled. "I'll be back soon, and then we'll get you home." She gave Becca a quick hug.

Sergio walked over to Francesco. "Let me come with you."

Frank immediately shook his head. "You are free to leave," he said. "But I don't know you and can't take a risk on a new person right now."

"Your friend just saved my life back there by

getting me out of that dungeon" Sergio said. "I owe him one."

How could Frank stop him? Sergio was much bigger than he was, and if he was determined to follow, at least to the church, what could he do about it? So, he simply didn't respond directly and turned back to Iris. "Okay, let's go." Both Iris and Sergio could tell that the instruction was implied for both of them.

"Take good care of her," Iris said to Emily before walking away with the two men.

Emily waved a hand up, then put her arm around Becca's shoulder.

Frank took the lead as they approached the outer edge of the castle. The church was just in front of them now, maybe another thirty feet directly down the road, when a loud sudden—*Tang*—then the fast, metallic clinking of chain being spun around a pully came from the front of the castle to their right. All three of their heads turned.

Through the darkness of the night sky, Iris saw it first. The portcullis across the bridge at the front of the castle had opened and dozens of people were flooding out. Some seemed to walk calmly, while others ran about frantically like wild animals. A symphony of raspy, guttural cries filled the night.

Above their heads, looking down from one of the battlements at the top of the castle, was the guard who had just watched Professor Skull and the other three escape from the dungeon. He was now watching Santé's creatures run out to catch them.

Justin Hyde

CHAPTER 42

Inside Basilica Santuario San Michele Arcangelo

Cameron passed through the entrance doors and into the silence of the church. He glanced up momentarily at a carved inscription on the wall just beyond the threshold: *Daniel 12: At that time Michael, the great prince who protects your people, will arise. There will be a time of distress such as has not happened from the beginning of nations until then.* Cameron pulled in a quick involuntary breath through his nose then held it as his eyes scanned further down the bible passage. *Multitudes who sleep in the dust of the earth will awake. Some to everlasting life, others to shame and everlasting contempt.* Goosebumps rose on his arms.

"This way," Matteo whispered. He turned and led Cameron down the 86 smooth and empty steps of the Angevin stairs till reaching a pair of twisted columns at the bottom—framing the mystical Porta del Toro. "Once we enter the crypt of the Arcangelo," Matteo said, "you must show respect. Saint Michael appears to men here. If he chooses you to be one of them, do not forget that he is the commander of God's army, and the great leader of all of the angels."

Professor Skull had no trouble hearing Matteo's deeper meaning. *Be humble. You may think you're tough, but you are nothing compared to*

Michael. Cameron tipped his head in understanding.

"Good," Matteo said. "Let us go." He turned again and disappeared down the corridor.

Cameron did not have a flashlight of his own, and there were no more windows to let in the moonlight in the deep underground caves and tunnels of the church. He hurried down the next set of steps, catching up to the glow of Matteo's light. The walls now had become narrow and constraining. They were not finished here, as they were in the upper portions of the basilica, and the steps below Cameron's feet were now dirt. He noticed the goosebumps on his arms were still there, but no longer from the chilling accuracy of the passage from the Book of Daniel, but now from the cold subterranean air of the hallowed cavern they were entering.

Both men stepped with caution. The yellow beam from Matteo's flashlight did not spread well, and only illuminated a stream of light filled with speckles of dust, and a small circle on the crumbling stone walls around them. They crept slowly through the first room of the crypt, then stepped gently over a small mound of dirt piled on the floor beneath the archway leading to the second. Once entering, both men looked around. This room was smaller than the last, although still large enough in its own right. Two giant stone sarcophaguses sat in the center of the space, surrounded by broken up walls and sandy colored stone bricks covered with ancient runic inscriptions.

"Now what?" Skull whispered.

Matteo slowly swept the light around the room, searching for any sign of the priest and the boy. Then a fear suddenly rose in him at the thought that maybe he had been wrong and led himself and the professor to the wrong place. Maybe Santé had gone to the main grotto instead?

He brought the light back around, sweeping it over the top of the second sarcophagus deeper in the room, then jumped back in alarm. His light went up to the ceiling and he stumbled back, nearly tripping over something on the ground and falling.

Cameron reacted fast and caught him before he fell. "What's wrong?" he asked him quickly. "Are you alright? What happened?"

"I saw someone," Matteo answered, re-aiming the beam of the flashlight to the far end of the crypt. "Over there."

Again, Cameron went into a defensive position. "The priest?"

Matteo was calm. "No... No, I don't think so." He held the flashlight in both hands and moved slowly around the first of the two stone burial boxes, then deeper into the cave.

Cameron didn't move yet. He stood still, watching Matteo's strange new posture as the man walked heedlessly over the rubble on the floor, seemingly fixed on something near the back of the crypt. "Then who was it?" Cameron whispered a little louder.

Matteo could not say for sure. Whoever he

saw was gone now. Disappeared. But the man had been as real as he was just a moment ago. He had been shirtless under two straps of armor across his chest—all his muscles relaxed, but defined. He had had flowing hair almost to his shoulders, but Matteo could not see clearly the features of his face. He had been wearing leathery cuffs around each wrist and was pointing a hand at something beyond the back wall.

"San Michele," Matteo said softly. "Non eri tu?" *Is that you?* He could only think of one thing to say to the archangel—the prayer of Saint Michael.

Cameron watched in disbelief. He had not seen anybody but knew who Matteo was now talking to.

Matteo continued slowly, praying out loud as he neared the second sarcophagus. "Saint Michael the Archangel, defend us in battle, be our protection against the wickedness and snares of the devil. May God rebuke him we humbly pray. And do thou, O Prince of the Heavenly Host, by the power of God, cast into hell Satan and all the evil spirits who prowl about the world seeking the ruin of souls."

Just as he finished the prayer, he stepped past the large unopened stone box and saw the faint glow of a light coming from a small dug out hole hidden near the floor of the cavern wall. He turned back to Cameron who was still staring at him in wonder. "This way," he said confidently.

Professor Skull didn't waste any time. He joined Matteo at the back of the crypt, and then he saw the hole too. It was well hidden in the depths of the cave and easily missed. The soft light coming from inside it was the flicker of a distant flame— similar to what he had seen coming from under the door in the castle earlier, but there was no smell of molten steel here. Only the scent of dirt and his own sweat. He took the light from Matteo without saying anything, then got down to the ground on his knees and squeezed through the tiny opening first. Matteo followed right behind.

"This is a sacred place," Matteo said upon entering.

Cameron was about to respond but stopped himself. They had entered another tunnel, and there were soft voices now noticeable from the far end. Cameron clicked off the light. The tunnel was not long. Thirty feet ahead both Cameron and Matteo could see the tips of the torch flames as they burned in the room beyond.

Then there was a crying sound. "Please stop," a young boy's voice said.

Bastian spoke angrily. "Reach out and take the sword," he said to the frightened child. "You will pick up the Sword of Michael, or I will cut off your head with the sword of Phanuel. I will not tell you again."

Cameron shot forward like a lion, no longer caring who heard him. He came quickly to the open chamber and flung himself at the man standing over the boy. But Father Santé had heard his approach and spun around just before Cameron got to him. He swung the blade of the short-sword but wasn't fast enough to cut his attacker. He hit Cameron instead with his forearm. The blow caught Cameron in his wounded shoulder and knocked him away. He landed on his side, five feet from the man, but stood back up quickly.

It was too late. Bastian now held the boy by the arm now and pointed his angelic sword out at the two intruders. "You," he said, seeing Matteo. "I should have destroyed you a year ago. But I gave you a chance. I let you go." He pulled the boy closer to him. "You should not have returned."

Cameron was crouched and ready to leap at him. Between him and Matteo, they had two vantages on the false priest and could attack him from different angles. Matteo had already proved himself in a fight now, and Cameron was confident they could handle this.

Until Bastian turned the blade on the child. The two torches in the room blazed on both sides of them.

"Don't!" Matteo shouted, and held out his hand for mercy. "Bastian. Let the boy go."

Bastian laughed. "Never. This boy is the key." He slowly touched the flat of the blade in his hand to the side of the boy's face. "Do you see? He is not in any danger. He can survive! I have given him that gift."

"Then what are..." Suddenly Matteo realized. "Not even you can touch the sword of Michael," he said softly. "Can you? It is too powerful even for you, isn't it? Only a true angel can wield the great sword of Michael the Archangel."

"Not for long," Bastian said with conviction. "Once this child proves that what I have created works, then I will hold the strength of God in my hands." He kept his eyes on Matteo and his peripherals on Cameron, then pushed the boy towards the sword. "Pick it up," he commanded.

"Hold the strength of God? You hold *nothing*!" Matteo shouted. "You are *playing* God—with this child's life!"

Cameron was now looking at the mighty weapon and was stunned by it. Michael's sword was long and bright. Its metal was a sliver and blue color that melted together in a sea of flowing lines across the double-edged blade. It stood upright, sticking straight out of the ground like Excalibur. But more likely, Excalibur stuck out of the stone like Saint Michaels Sword, and Professor Skull had a momentary wonder if this was how King Arthur's legend had come to be. Even with the tip of it buried in the rock, the large cruciform hilt of Michael's sword stood almost as tall as the boy, and Cameron doubted if the child could even lift it—if he lived long enough to try.

"Do it!" Bastian shouted to the boy. Then his voice softened. "Or everybody in this cave dies."

The child was shaking and had to wipe away tears from his eyes. He then took the first step towards the sword.

Matteo was watching in fear. But then his

vision blurred, and he could no longer see the child. The figure he'd seen before suddenly appeared to him again and blocked his view of everything else. Michael stood before him. He had a radiance about him, but not from the flame of the torches. He reached out and took Matteo's hand and gently pulled it towards his sword. Matteo didn't resist, but a spark of fear lit him up from inside.

Michael stopped pulling and looked at him, sensing his inner discomfort, then nodded his head once and let go of Matteo's wrist. He turned and reached instead for his sword, and Matteo's eyes opened wide. On the back of the archangel were silvery wings tucked tight against him. They were covered in soft, delicate white feathers and reached almost to the ground. Time seemed to stop as Matteo stared at them in wonder and awe. *The wings of an angel.*

Michael grabbed a hold of his sword and lifted it from the earth, but the physical blade did not move, only its spirit. He held out the apparition to Matteo. Then his shoulders tensed, and his powerful wings shot open. He flew upward and was gone.

Matteo gasped, but knew what he was being called to do. He jumped forward unexpectedly and pushed Bastian out of the way, then grabbed the child and wrapped him in his guard. Bastian stumbled sideways and pushed himself off the cavern wall. He deflected into Cameron and grabbed the professor, throwing him now back around towards Matteo. Santé now had the advantage. He was no longer caught in a crossfire of men, but was facing them both directly. And—he stood between them and the caves only exit.

Santé was furious and yelled out loud as he brought the angels short-sword over his head and swung it down at them. Cameron reached up quick and blocked the attack—grunting and hitting Bastian's forearm with the knife edge of his right hand. Santé kept the momentum of the swing and arched the sword back around fast for another strike, and Matteo knew they were ultimately defenseless against such a weapon. *My life to God*, he thought. *And my trust in His angel*. He let go of the boy and turned, then closed his eyes and grabbed the hilt of Michael's sword and pulled. It lifted from the stone and Bastian froze in mid-swing. Cameron stopped as well.

Nobody moved except for the child, who lifted his head up at the man holding the powerful sword behind him.

A surge of panic and disbelief flooded into Bastian Santé. "How…"

But before anyone could understand, Bastian turned and ran out of the cavern.

CHAPTER 43

"Oh my God," Iris said. "Cameron was right."

Sergio and Francesco watched in horror as dozens of zombie-like creatures emerged from the castle—pushing and fighting each other as they crossed over the bridge. Several of them were knocked over the edge and into the dry moat surrounding the fortress. Most of them walked or limped, but a few were fast, and moved with a speed that was almost a slow run. They spilled out from the main doorway like the castle had sprung a leak, and scattered in every direction under the glow of the half moon.

"What are we going to do?" Iris asked. There was panic in her voice.

A night breeze swept in and carried their moaning sounds like it was its own. The wind itself seemed to be calling out in angry sorrow. With each new creature that emerged, the noise grew louder, and the other creatures became more aggressive, as if feeding off each other's rage. They began disappearing between buildings and down the side streets of Monte Sant'Angelo.

Sergio noticed first that they had been spotted, and half a dozen of the zombies were now headed in their direction. He started pacing back and forth in a short line. "We need to do something. Those things are going to tear up the city." Then he remembered the little girl back at the truck. "We have to warn the others."

Iris turned to Frank. "He's right. We need to get back to them."

The sounds of the creatures coming at them were getting louder and Frank didn't need to look to know that they only had a few more seconds before a decision was forced on them.

Suddenly the terrifying scream of a woman pierced through the moaning wind from somewhere down the street. Then the sound of glass shattering. Soon the entire town would be awake—and in a lot of danger.

"Rrrahhhh," Sergio grunted loud as he grabbed the first creature by the shoulders and wrestled to keep it off him. He used his strong back and arms to finally overpower the thing and lift and throw it to his side. It toppled over the edge of a gate next to him and tumbled down a small hill on the other side. Within seconds though it was back on its feet and moving again, although no longer an immediate threat. It struggled trying to climb back up the hill but would not be able to climb back over the fence at the top even if it made it there.

"We have to go, NOW!" Iris said again.

Frank was petrified, and his body shook as he forced out his next words. "You two go. Once you get back to the truck you'll have all four of those boys to help you, and you should be able to hold these things off. At least for a little while."

"Frank, what are you talking about?" Iris said. "Are you crazy? You're coming with us. Come on!"

Another creature was coming up on him from the side and Frank had to take a leap backwards to avoid it—putting some distance between him and Iris. The creature turned and followed after him and Frank started stepping back faster. He called out to his two partners. "Go!" he shouted. "I won't be able to help you down there. I have to find a way to stop this!"

He turned and ran in the opposite direction—and a tear fell down the front of Iris's cheek.

—

Bastian Santé burst through the doors of the Basilica and into the church's front courtyard. What he saw there angered him even more. All of his creations were loose in the city, running or pulling themselves up the main roads and down the narrow back alleys. Several townspeople were now up and coming out from their homes. An elderly shop owner carrying some sort of a wooden club stepped out from behind a door and swung his bat at the closest creature. The attack was futile, and the creature tore at him, shredding with its nails and biting with its jaws till the old man fell back through the doorway. His club rattled off the stone walk outside his home as the creature continued after him and they both disappeared from Bastian's sight.

Bastian ran to the end of the courtyard and out the gate. Another of his creatures was there, coming from up the street, already focused on him as its target. He held up Phanuel's short-sword and slashed it across the creature's throat, severing its head from its body, then started to run towards the castle. He knew he would have to face more of the creatures before getting there, but that was okay—he was not afraid. The creatures surrounding him did not scare him as much as Michael's sword did. He still did not know how Matteo had managed to hold it, and that infuriated him, but it was not over yet.

He sliced through the head of another creature without stopping as he ran further up the street. The castle was close now, and in all the commotion he didn't even notice the blur between the buildings to his right of Francesco Ferrari running in the opposite direction.

—

Cameron and Matteo ran out the front of Sanctuario de San Michelle less than a minute after Bastian Santé. They froze solid, taken aback by the sight of the city streets infested with the living dead. Neither of them wondered where Bastian had gone. They both knew he had gone to the castle, but the sleepy city that they had snuck quietly through earlier was now a screaming nightmare, and they could not just chase carelessly after him.

Professor Skull naturally went for a weapon but quickly realized once again that he was unarmed. Anything he had would have been useless against these things anyhow. But Matteo still carried the

Sword of Michael. The long heavy blade was surprisingly easy to control, and Matteo did not feel awkward wielding it has he would have thought. He was comfortable and determined. "We can make it to the castle," he said, bringing the sword up.

Cameron gave him a look of agreement. They jogged to the front of the courtyard and turned right. A lone creature was hobbling down the road in front of them, but it looked like the majority of the others had taken to the upper main street of the town. Matteo walked up to it and slid the tip of the sword into its belly. The creature's insides erupted in a glow from the touch of the steel and it fell instantly. Small streams of smoke came from it as it burned from the inside out.

Matteo stood still with his head down and Cameron saw the look of despair wash over his face. He walked up to him and put his arm on his shoulder. "He was already dead," Cameron said, trying to give some comfort and ease his guilt.

Matteo nodded, then held the sword back up. They ran cautiously to the next building but pulled back when another man-like form appeared from behind a wall in front of them. Matteo brought his arm back, ready to swing and cut down the creature, but Cameron ran in his way. "Hold it!" he shouted. Then turned to the figure who had emerged in the darkness. "Frank! What the hell are you doing here? Where is everyone else?"

Frank rested a hand on his hip while he tried to speak between deep breaths. "Iris and the man you rescued from the castle went back to the truck to help the others." He coughed once. "But I think I might know a way to stop these things," he said. "At least I hope I do."

Matteo held out the sword—careful to still keep it at a safe enough distance from Frank and the professor though. "This can kill them," he said.

"There's too many of them for just one man and one sword though," Cameron said. "But we need to stop Bastian. God only knows what else he's got going on inside that castle." He thought back to the laboratory he'd seen.

"I'll go with Francesco," a voice said, shouting from a distance.

The three of them turned to see Iris running towards them.

"Iris! Look out!" Cameron yelled.

She had been too focused on the men that she didn't notice the creature lurking half hidden by a bush to her right. It stepped out in front of her as she passed. She screamed as the thing took hold of her and snapped its teeth together trying to bite at the side of her face. Cameron ran up faster than Matteo could react and tackled the creature hard to the ground. He landed on his back and quickly rolled to get it off of him.

Matteo came up from behind and plunged his sword into the creature before it could rise again. He waited a second, then pulled the sword back out of its body and watched as the blood dissolved off the blade like water on a hot pan.

The commotion had drawn the attention of three more of them. "Are you two okay?" Frank asked.

Neither of them answered him. Physically they were okay, but mentally they were destroyed. "Iris," Cameron said, grabbing her by the shoulders. "You need to stay at the truck. Everyone..."

She cut him off. "Sergio and the boys can take care of the girls." She almost added, *And I can take care of myself,* but stopped herself, realizing that that may not be true after the attack she had just been rescued from. "Let me help," she asked instead.

"They're coming," Matteo said.

Frank knew that Cameron would have argued with her still, so he made the decision himself. "I can use her help."

Still Cameron's stubbornness tried to drive him to protect her. Everyone could see it on his face.

"We don't have time for this!" Iris said to him angrily. "I am going with Frank. You two figure out a way to stop that man." Her voice softened. "But be careful. Please."

Professor Skull sighed. "You too," he said. "Please."

Frank turned to leave but then remembered something and stopped. "Hey Matteo. You know this town pretty good right. Is there a power station around here?"

"A power station?"

"Yeah," Frank said. "An electric power plant or a utilities company or anything like that?"

Justin Hyde

"Come on you guys," Iris said from the side. "Hurry up! Those things are almost here!"

Matteo turned his head quickly and saw Cameron's back as he took on the role of their shield, facing down the creatures that were now only a few feet away. He thought for only a second, then answered. "Yes. There is a municipally owned power and gas company about a quarter kilometer from here." He pointed east. "Straight down Corso Vittorio."

Frank and Iris turned and ran, and Matteo brought up the sword. He turned again. The first creature attacked, and Cameron ducked and shoved it to the side then drove a fist into the next creature behind it. A third was coming at him from the side and reached out to grab him, just before the Sword of Michael ran him through.

placed the tips of her toes into another.

Frank wasn't as optimistic of his own climbing abilities but followed her lead as she slowly started inching her way up to the second floor.

A minute later she was able to stretch up her hand enough to grab hold of the bottom bar of the balconies railing. The muscles of her arm tightened and strained as she pulled herself up and over, then turned to reach down and help Frank. "Can you reach my hand?" she asked.

Francesco clung to the side of the wall and held tight as he looked up, hoping that he was only inches from the top, but felt suddenly worried, seeing that he still had several feet to go.

Iris stretched her hand down further, but Frank was still too far down.

Oh no...

The sounds of the dead were getting louder. Then came the scuffing noise of a foot dragging across the ground. "Francesco," Iris said. Her voice was shaky. "Concentrate. Breath. You can do this. Three points of contact," she said, reminding him of some of his training with Nightcorp back in the day.

He grunted and tried pulling himself higher. *Hurry Frank*, he told himself. He did not want to let go with his left hand but the only other visible place to grab above him was on that side. He forced himself to do it and reached up quick. His fingers caught the small edge, but his heart leaped when he felt some of the decayed plaster of the wall break and crumble under his fingertips. "Iris!" he shouted.

Two of the creatures rounded the corner on the street below him. They were not the disgusting or mutilated ones, but the lifeless look in their eyes and their evident rage towards him sent him into a panic. He pulled harder with both hands and scrapped the tip of his right boot down the wall over and over again trying to find a new foothold. The first of the dead men approached and reached up and grabbed Frank by the ankle.

"Give me your hand!" Iris screamed, stretching her own hand down as far as her body would allow her, until it felt like her entire arm was going to rip off her shoulder.

The second dead man came up behind the first and also started trying to get a piece of Franks leg.

I'm going to die, he realized. He looked up at Iris and she could see the surrender in his eyes, even through the fear.

"Don't you fucking give up on me, Frank." Her words were not a plea—they were an order. "You can do this. Just a little farther."

Tears and sweat were running down his face like he'd walked through a hot sprinkler. The two creatures were pulling hard on his right leg and he knew he couldn't hold on much longer, but he locked his jaw and shook the leg violently until it was free, then kicked the first creature hard in the face. It phased it for only a second and Frank knew that he had only one option—but if Iris didn't catch his hand it would be all over. He had to act now. His left foot was still on a ledge and he bent the knee just slightly, then pushed up hard and jumped with all the strength of that leg. His hand reached out and he closed his eyes. If he had the time, he would have prayed.

Then he felt the firm grip of Iris's hand latch onto his. He opened his eyes and sucked in a heavy refreshing breath of air. The two creatures below him relentlessly continued to reach for him, but he was being held safely above them now.

Iris smiled down at him. "I knew you could do it," she said, as she pulled him over the railing.

"I'm glad one of us did," he said.

"You don't give yourself enough credit, Frank." She turned to the window. "Now let's get inside this building where it's safe."

Francesco couldn't have agreed more. And a few feet away on the balcony was a baseball sized piece of rock that had probably fallen from higher up on the old roof at some point. He bent down and grabbed it, then chucked it at the window, smashing it out.

They both ducked inside.

"What are we doing here?" Iris asked, getting back to her question earlier.

Frank took out his phone and turned on its flashlight feature. "These things must be some sort of genetic mutation," he said, getting right to the heart of it. "I don't know what else they could be. "Probably the resulting side effects of some experiment gone bad."

Justin Hyde

Iris followed close behind him as he walked through the upper floor of the power plant. "What if they aren't though? What if this is what they were intended to be? Like an army of the dead."

"Well, I thought about that too. It is possible I guess, but I don't think that's the case. If it were, then we wouldn't see such variation in them. They would all share the same intentional traits. But their abilities and their physical characteristics are all different. Like you would see in lab trials." He scanned briefly over some loose paperwork on a desk in the room, then moved on. "But, either way, it wouldn't necessarily change things much actually," he continued. "Genetic modifications, and mutations, generally originate from proteins."

Iris now had her phone out too and was shining her light at the open door leading out of the room. Frank pointed his at the same place then led the way into the hall. *We need to find the control room.*

"DNA and RNA are made up of amino acids," he continued explaining as they walked down a hall. "Just like protein is. Actually, it's our DNA that tells our genes what kind of proteins to become. Basically our body's instructions—what color hair we have, the sound of our laugh, everything. RNA is similar, except RNA is like the messenger. It's what transports everything. So when scientists genetically modify something, they use our RNA to bring specific proteins to the genes and change the structure of the DNA."

Iris ran a hand through her hair. "Sometimes I forget that you were a scientist back in the day."

Francesco's background was actually in nuclear science. After graduating with his masters from Cornell University in New York back in the nineties, he had gone to work at the Savannah River Nuclear Site in South Carolina. His job had been to study and test rapid radiochemical separation of tritium isotopes from meteorites, with an end goal of furthering the use of the extraterrestrial material in nuclear weapons. Everything he had just said about DNA to Iris though, went right over her head.

They came to a stairwell at the end of the hall and Frank suspected that the control room and generators were probably on the ground floor, so he led the way down.

"Frank," Iris said from behind him. "What do we do with that information now?"

Frank stopped at the first door on the lower floor. "This is it," he said. The door was locked, but it wasn't a strong lock and he leaned back and kicked the front of the door and it popped right open. He went straight for the main power grid and operations distribution center. "What we need to do is extract whatever protein was introduced to cause this outbreak." He sat in a chair and started running fingers over switches and around knobs, getting a feel for the controls. "But technically you can't just separate protein. It doesn't work that way. But there is a process called *cell lysis* that can break open cells. It is the first step in protein extraction. In a lab it is typically done through physical grinding or pounding, like with a mallet; sometimes freezing the sample with liquid nitrogen first to create brittleness. But since we can't obviously do that to all those creatures out there, we need to take a different approach."

Iris looked over his shoulder as he paused for a minute to concentrate on the controls in front of him. She kept silent, giving him space and time to think.

Finally, he sat up a little straighter. "Those things out there are tough as nails though. Grinding on them or freezing them probably wouldn't even do anything. So, we need to think beyond that. If they can't be hurt, then their bodies are probably strong at the cellular level. Which means that in order to harm them we are going to have to use something that a cell would not be naturally resilient to." He turned and looked at her. "I use the word *naturally* because the easiest way to mutate something is to cross it with something else that already has the traits you are looking for."

"Just like any GMO," Iris said.

"Exactly. Just like most food at the grocery store has been modified with the desirable traits from something else." He turned back to the panel of electronics in front of him. "It happens all the time. Humans have introduced a spider silk gene to goats to make them capable of spinning a web protein. We've added the poison of a scorpion to lettuce, making it venomous to other crop damaging insects.

There are rabbits that glow in the dark and pigs with mouse DNA. But all of these mad-science experiments use already existing DNA as the splice. So, we need to come at those things outside with something that their cells, whatever they are, would not have encountered enough in nature to build up a resistance to."

"And what is that?" she asked.

"It's called sonication," Frank answered. "It's how electronic animal deterrents work. They emit an intense ultra-high frequency sound wave that is inaudible to humans, but wreaks hell on animals or anything with sensitive acute hearing. Adults are typically impervious to it. On a cellular level we can handle it—to a point. But if those creatures out there are the results of some failed genetic experiment, then maybe whatever they have been introduced to does not have that same resistance. They obviously can handle physical things like cuts and blunt trauma, but can they handle super high harmonic energy?"

He flipped on a switch and the panel of instruments on the desk lit up. Iris took a small step back. "And we can do that from here?" she asked.

"Honestly..." He turned and looked at her again. "I'm not completely sure." There was a bit of unease in his voice. "But I think so." *And I don't have any better ideas*, he added to himself.

"How?"

"Well," he began. "Believe it or not, this damn town only has one traffic light. Just *one*!

Unbelievable right?" He held up his hands in astonishment. "But maybe we can use it. It's just past the castle to the west. I saw it when we were near the truck earlier. From what I could tell, it's pretty new. Probably installed just recently. And if so, then it might use ultrasonic technology to control it."

He flipped another switch then put his hand on a large round dial. "A lot of new traffic lights use ultrasonic sensors to send out a sound wave to detect cars and tell the lights when to change from red to green, and vice versa. Kind of like SONAR on a submarine. If we can massively increase the wattage to the sensor and send a surge of power through it, we might be able to blast the entire town with an ultra-high frequency sound wave that technically we should not be able to hear, but will hopefully overload the mutated cells of those creatures out there enough to break the cells apart and extract, or at least weaken the new foreign protein in them."

CHAPTER 45

Matteo and Cameron walked the bridge to the main gate of the castle. Down in the dry moat below them several creatures became agitated and extra aggressive from the sight of the two men walking freely above. One of them bumped another and lashed out, igniting a small war amongst themselves.

Once past the gatehouse and inside, both men stepped lightly as they tried to get a feel for the new environment suddenly surrounding them. To the right was the magazine, and a few stables, and to the left was a more open area—perhaps the banquet hall. They crept through the large room nervously. It was cold and dark inside, with few places to hide or take cover quickly if they needed to. Matteo handed his flashlight to Cameron who clicked it on, exposing several doorways at the opposite end of the long room.

"It's too quiet in here," Cameron said softly.

Matteo agreed, but wasn't sure which was worse: the growls and moans of the living dead, or the suspenseful silence of the unknown. "They're all outside now," he said. He was trying to convince himself of the normality of the stillness around them.

Professor Skull shook his head. "I doubt it," he said. His instincts were warning him against each next step that he took, and his eyes barely blinked as he investigated every inch of the medieval space around him. "We're not alone in here."

Matteo knew he was referring to more than just Bastian Santé wandering the halls somewhere, but he didn't say anything back. The thought scared him too much to speak anymore. He followed behind Cameron down the side wall of the room.

"It looks like there's stairs through that doorway," Cameron whispered, pointing the light at what he was talking about. He sped up a little, not because he was in a hurry, but because subconsciously the pain that kept stabbing at his lower back was prodding him forward. He slowed again, then felt the pain stick into him again. He turned to look behind him. *What is that?*

Matteo stopped. "What's wrong?" he asked.

"I... I'm not sure. I keep feeling something, but..." He was confused. "Nothing. Never mind."

"We should keep moving," Matteo said, taking a step forward.

Cameron jumped away from him, suddenly feeling the same pain in his stomach now. "It's the sword," he said, all of a sudden realizing what was happening. "When you get it too close to me, I can feel it."

Oh no, Matteo thought, feeling bad for not being more careful. "I'm sorry," he said, and pulled Saint Michaels sword in towards his own body.

Cameron turned back around and kept moving. Up ahead they came to the first in a series of doors leading out of the hall. He stopped outside and peeked around the corner. Then, seeing it empty, he entered the small space at the bottom of the stairwell and began to climb.

Sounds of footsteps started becoming noticeable from somewhere up above, but both men continued up. This is what they had come here for.

"Professor," Matteo whispered.

Cameron paused and turned around, looking down at Matteo.

"Let me go first." He lifted the Sword of Michael a few inches to remind Cameron that he had the only weapon between them.

After a second's hesitation, Cameron leaned back against the cold stone wall of the stairwell and let Matteo pass.

They continued up, and the noises in the space above them grew louder. Soon they could hear the commotion of another person scurrying about like a giant rat, then some faint voices, although too quiet to hear clearly.

Matteo placed his right foot onto the upper landing and brought the sword up to his waist— pointing the tip of the blade out in front like an arrow leading the way. Moonlight shown in through two narrow windows on the far wall of the room and there were flames burning in torches hung from the walls. One of the long torches had been taken down and was now in the hand of a man wearing a monk's tunic. Next to him, Father Santé walked out another doorway just after Cameron reached the top step.

This is the room I was in earlier, Cameron noticed. The other room to the left, that Bastian was now facing, was the one loaded with Nazi gold. It glowed almost brighter than the torches on the walls.

"Bastian," Matteo said. "Stop whatever this is you are doing." He took a step towards the man. "It's over. I have Michael's Sword."

Santé got an evil look in his eyes. He paused, then began creeping sideways towards the room of gold, while keeping his gaze on the sword in Matteo's hand.

"Bastian!" Matteo said louder. "What you are doing here goes against God. Surely you see that." He let go of the sword with one hand and pointed behind him, indicating the army of the dead terrorizing the town outside. "You have ruined the lives of so many people. Why? What good is this sword to you anyways?"

Santé still did not speak, but Cameron noticed that he was no longer carrying the short-sword that he'd had back in the cave. He was however, inching closer and closer to the room full of gold. Cameron slowly started moving in that direction too—hoping to get in his way if he decided to make a run for it.

Firelight danced ominously over Bastian's face. "How is it that you can hold that sword?" he asked in an angry monstrous voice.

I don't know, Matteo wanted to say. But he said something else instead. "What you have done to all those people... It's the work of the devil."

Bastian chuckled. "Let Isaiah remind you: *'I form the light, and create darkness. I make peace, and create evil. I, the Lord, do all these things.'*"

"But *YOU* are not the Lord!" Matteo shouted. "You are playing God! And you are perverting the gospel of Christ!—like Paul said to the Galatians: 'Even if an angel from heaven should preach a gospel other than the one we preach to you , let them be under God's curse!'"

The monk holding the torch took a step forward and Matteo and Cameron's eyes both shifted to him. Bastian seized the opportunity and ran into the golden room.

"NO!" Cameron shouted. He had let himself get distracted and didn't react in time. "Shit!"

Matteo ran after Bastian, but Professor Skull grabbed him by the arm. "Wait," he said. "There's another…"

Santé came flying back out of the room. He was now holding the sword of Uriel and slashed it across the air, barely missing the bellies of both men. The sword burned with terrifyingly intense flames. They roared and blazed with each move of the steel, but no smoke came from them. They were clean and bright. Bastian lifted it again and swung it back around, this time aiming directly at Matteo, who brought up the Sword of Michael just in time to block the attack. Embers and sparks erupted into the room and rained down as the two angelic weapons clashed together.

Cameron charged Bastian from the side to tackle him to the ground but was stopped hard as though he'd hit a wall of daggers. The power of just Michael's sword was enough to hurt from a distance.

But the power of *two* angelic blades so close to each other was impossible to pass through. The pain was too great. Another step closer and he knew he would be destroyed by them instantly.

Like two titans, Santé and Matteo battled across the room, filling the space with the ringing sounds of metal each time the blades met. Bastian's speed was ruthless, and one blow after another came crashing down. But Matteo was strong, and Michael's blade did not bend or break. He countered and deflected each attack.

On the other side of the room, the monk holding the torch approached Cameron. But without even thinking, Skull grabbed him and flung him into the fight between the two men. The monk's body was strong, and the man did not cry out as a normal man would have, but the power of the two swords dropped him to the ground. His body landed on its side and Matteo's foot caught one of his outstretched lifeless arms and he tripped—falling backwards and also landing on the ground.

A great fear suddenly arose in him. He had dropped Michael's sword. It was laying on its side, 5 feet away—out of his reach.

Bastian knew that Skull could not pick it up either and laughed. He approached Matteo slowly, pointing the burning tip of Uriel's sword to his face. He stood still for a moment, savoring the sight of the doomed man cowering below him. "You are going to show me how you can touch the sword," he said with determination.

Cameron watched the scene helplessly from the side.

"I will do nothing but pray for you," Matteo said.

Bastian grinned. "I'm not asking for your cooperation," he clarified. "I only need your body, not your life." He raised the sword above his head till the flames brushed the ceiling above.

Matteo closed his eyes.

CHAPTER 46

Cameron pictured his daughter in his mind. He missed her so much, and he would miss her forever, until the day finally came that they met again on the other side. His heart ached. And for the first time in years—he cried.

Saint Michael's blade gleamed on the stone floor beside him. He saw it, then watched as Bastian raised the long fiery blade of Uriel above his head, and Matteo prepared for death.

Dear God, please watch over my family, Cameron prayed. He had a moment of regret that he had never asked Iris to marry him, but surely God knew that he loved her too. And Frank—the man who he loved like a brother. *I will see you all again someday.*

It felt like everything moved in slow motion as he bent over and wrapped his hand around the hilt of Michael's sword. He closed his fist around it tightly, grinding his teeth hard against the awful pain it sent through him. The metal of the blade scraped across the stone as he swung it around. He let go, throwing the long weapon at the chest of the evil man in front of him, then collapsed.

Santé yelled out. The mighty sword of the archangel spun through the air. It hit him from the side, and he let go of the burning sword above his head and grabbed his wounded ribs. The blade had not pierced him, but sliced him open, and the blood instantly began flowing. The power of the sword burned like a thousand knives were still inside him.

Matteo was horrified by the sight—but not out of concern for Bastian Santé. Cameron's body had dropped and was now motionless on the floor. He knew he had to stop Bastian once and for all though, and he rolled over and again picked up Michael's sword.

Bastian was still in shock and clinging to his own side. He saw Matteo reach back for Michael's blade and he panicked. Keeping one hand over his ribs, he bent down and also picked back up his weapon. But instead of facing off again, he took Uriel's sword and ran out of the room before anything could stop him.

Matteo quickly slid over to Cameron's body and rolled him onto his back. He prayed to God and to the archangel to save him, but there was no sign of life left. *Please no.*

He stood. The glow of the flaming sword was still flickering but fading in the stairwell and he shot up and ran after it. He leapt down the last of the steps then ran back through the Great Hall and caught up to Bastian at the main gate. "Bastian, STOP!" he commanded.

Santé obeyed—knowing deep down that he needed to end this here. There was nowhere else for him to go. He stopped and turned around slowly. The arched portcullis of the castle door framed him in a box of blue-grey moonlight. The sword in his right hand hung low and burned bright against the backdrop of the night. Its orange flame exposed the dark stain of fresh blood growing on the man's side. Behind him, beyond the bridge, Matteo could see the small dark shapes of some of the creatures still lurking in the distance.

"All can be forgiven through Christ," Matteo told him. Even through his anger, and despite all else, Matteo still found mercy in God. He took the first step forward towards Bastian, who again grinned and shook his head.

Matteo stepped closer again. "Lay down your weapon, Bastian." Another step, and his voice grew passionate as he preached. "Remember the two thieves crucified with Christ," he said. "They were led out to the place called Skull with Jesus to be executed. One on his right, and the other on his left. And Jesus said, 'Forgive them, father, for they know not what they do.'"

Bastian lifted his head and looked at the man approaching. Matteo still carried Michael's sword, but held it down to his side.

"One of the thieves mocked Jesus," Matteo continued. "He said to him: 'If you are the Messiah, then save yourself!' But the other condemned man, the penitent thief, defended Jesus and said back: 'Don't you fear God? Since you are under the same sentence? We are punished justly, for we are getting what we deserve. But this man has done nothing wrong.'"

Bastian listened quietly, and Matteo stepped forward yet again, now only a few feet from the man holding the burning sword.

"Do you remember what happened next?" Matteo asked him. "The penitent thief asked Jesus to remember him in heaven." His voice lowered. "And Jesus answered him: 'Truly I tell you, today you will be with me in paradise.'"

They looked into each other's eyes. "You see," Matteo said, now standing directly in front of him. "It is never too late. You have never gone too far or waited too long to receive God's love. That is the eternal gift He has given us through his son Jesus Christ." He slowly reached out to take the sword of Uriel from Bastian's hand.

Bastian lifted his chin a little higher. Ultimately, he did want salvation, but his greed for mortal power was stronger than his greed for eternal love. He pulled his arm back. His elbow bent, then straightened. His hips turned back, then forward, and his shoulder rolled as he swung the burning sword with all his might at the neck of the weak man in front of him.

Matteo's heart filled with sadness. But with little effort he raised the blade of Michael with one swift smooth motion to protect himself. The two swords erupted in sparks as they clashed together. Bastian leaned forward trying to drive him backwards, but Matteo shifted his weight and turned. Santé lost his balance and stumbled, then spun and tripped and fell over the edge of the bridge and down into the dry moat of the castle. Uriel's sword landed below as well, but not within his reach.

Justin Hyde

The creatures that were trapped down in the moat immediately converged around him. They moaned and growled loudly as they slowly encircled the unarmed man.

Pray, Matteo thought for him. *Now is the time to pray.*

Bastian was still on his knees. He turned his head towards the weapon. The ring of deathly faces was getting smaller around him, and hands were beginning to reach out. But if he fought hard, he was sure he could make it through the creatures and reach the sword. He lifted one leg and put his foot flat on the ground, preparing to run for it.

Then everything stopped. Matteo kept Michael's sword at his side but held his other hand to his head. He felt a pulsing. Not just in his head but throughout his whole body. It was like a bomb had been dropped, or a drum was beating inside him, sending concussions of humming energy through him. It wasn't painful, but it wasn't natural. What it was, was uncomfortable and concerning.

Bastian felt it too. But his creatures felt it most of all. They cried out in agony and scrambled like disturbed ants around the confined valley floor of the moat. The sensation lasted only a few seconds, then stopped. But it had left damaging repercussions on the creatures—the men and women whom Bastian had infected. They fell where they stood. All was silent and still throughout the town. Then, slowly, one by one, they began to move again. New life resurrecting inside them.

Matteo watched from above. Bastian saw them all starting to rise again too, and he stood and quickly ran to the sword. He leaned over and grabbed it, picking it up and holding it out in front of him defensively. Then he felt it. An unimaginable pain began flowing through his hands and down his arms. His heart raced with fear. *What is happening?* He had lost his ability and could no longer hold the angelic steel. The pain worsened and spread into his shoulder. He dropped the sword, but it continued. "No!" he cried. The feeling reached his heart and he felt it expand under his chest. He tasted ash in his mouth and his body began to smolder and char— then he dropped to the ground—dead.

CHAPTER 47

Matteo watched Bastian fall. He felt no remorse and no pity. Only a reassurance in his own faith in God as the only true path to salvation.

Down at the bottom of the moat below him, Bastian's body lay on its side. His legs were tucked in and one armed was outstretched, and Matteo wasn't sure if the man's eyes were open or if the moonlight was giving that illusion. Uriel's sword still burned beside him.

He stood there on the edge of the bridge, watching for a moment as Bastian's deathly creations stirred. A few remained on the ground, but most were beginning to stand. Although their movements were less feral now than they had seemed before. Instead of wandering about like lost and injured souls, they moved about with something that almost resembled confusion.

One of them grabbed its head with both hands, and Matteo thought he could almost hear the sound of a sigh. Another of the fallen creatures was still lying in the dirt. It had been one of the broken ones—its skin torn and bruised. But as easily as if the wounds were nothing more than dirt, they washed away in a slow wave of light sweeping over it. The body was healed.

At first glance Matteo was overwhelmed with emotion at the sight before him. But then he fell into a state of peace. The Lord's work be done.

To the east, the first break of the morning sunrise was beginning to appear over the horizon. It crested over the ridge and shined its light onto two figures walking up the street to Matteo's right. The two looked around in amazement and wonder at all the other men and women suddenly wandering about.

Iris turned her head to Frank. "It worked," she said with a smile. "You did it, Frank."

"We all did it," he said back.

She stopped walking for a second and waited for him to stop as well. "Look around us," she said. "This is a miracle. You didn't just find a way to stop those things. You saved them."

A woman in worn and dirty clothes overheard them talking and approached nervously. Her hands fidgeted and trembled in front of her and her eyes were open wide. "Where am I?" she asked. Tears began to flow down her cheeks. "What happened?"

Iris pulled the woman in and wrapped her arms around her. "You have been saved," she whispered. "We all have."

The corner of Francesco's lip raised up in a small grin. He turned and looked back towards the castle, squinting now against the sun. There was a man standing alone on the bridge. "I see Matteo," he said, stealing Iris's attention back.

She let go of the healed woman and went to stand beside Frank. Matteo was looking back at them and raised a hand in the air. Iris and Frank both raised theirs back.

"Come on," Frank said, leading the way.

They reached the bridge and Iris peered over the side. There was Bastian, curled up and gone. The flames of Uriel's sword burned beside him. But the fire was no longer burning in defense or protection—but was roaring in triumph. "How?" Iris asked, still looking at the body below.

Matteo shook his head. "The Lord certainly works in mysterious ways," he said.

Francesco was equally stumped. The shockwave of the ultrasonic sensor should have weakened the creatures, perhaps even partially extracted or broken up whatever alien protein had been introduced in them, but he could not understand how it could have healed them. Nothing about a low frequency harmonic, no matter how strong, should have been capable of restoring cell integrity or repairing cellular damage. And what had happened to Bastian Santé? "You killed him," Frank said to Matteo. There was no judgement or criticism in his voice. It was a statement of congratulations and gratitude.

Matteo shook his head. "No. Bastian killed himself."

Frank and Iris were both confused. "What do you mean?" Iris asked.

"He fell over the side," Matteo told her. "Then something happened in the air." He raised an eyebrow at them. "I'm guessing you two may have had something to do with that?"

They looked at each other momentarily but

Matteo continued before giving them a chance to figure out how to answer. "Whatever you did," he said. "However God worked through you. It changed these people back. And it seemed to have changed Bastian as well. He lost his ability to touch the sword. And when he did, God punished him"

Frank spoke something quietly to himself. "He never was one of the Nephilim," he said, suddenly realizing.

"What do you mean?" Iris asked.

Frank understood now. "Bastian never was able to touch the sword. He was not descended from angels like we thought. He must have been the original experiment. That's how he gave himself that ability. Somehow Santé must have discovered a formula to alter his own genetic code enough to allow him to touch angelic steel." His voice got a little louder. "But Saint Michael's Sword was still too much for him. Michael is the great leader of all the angels. He is the commander of God's army! His sword must still have been beyond his reach."

Iris was intently listening but playfully scowled at Franks pun.

"So," Matteo said, adding some of his own thoughts. "He must have then changed his recipe and experimented with it first on all these other people before trying it on himself again."

"Exactly what I was thinking," Frank said. "That would make sense. So then whatever DNA was triggered by the ultrasonic sound wave right now had one effect on all these people, but a totally different effect on him, since his altered code was unique"

"How could that have healed these people though?" Iris asked.

Frank scratched his chin. "What if Santé had used some sort of protein that could actually be reversed or regenerated? Like a starfish or a salamander. And instead of extracting it with the sound energy, we actually hyper-stimulated it?"

"Or a jellyfish?" Matteo asked from the side.

Francesco turned to him slowly.

Matteo added: "I saw a small aquarium full of jellyfish in Bastian's lab inside the castle. Professor Skull and I..."

"Oh my God, where is Cameron?" Iris screamed.

Frank felt his own heart sink when Matteo bowed his head. "He is upstairs," Matteo said sadly.

Iris took off for the castle door. The two men followed behind and into the Great Hall. "Up those stairs," Matteo said, pointing towards the far end of the long room.

They ran and climbed up to the second floor, then stopped. Iris fell to her knees and cried out. "God, no!"

The body of the monk lay in the center of the room—and Cameron's body just beyond. Matteo knelt beside Iris and put his arms around her. She sobbed and cried, then tried to stand but had trouble, and he had to help her.

Frank was already a few feet ahead of them,

moving slowly towards his fallen friend. Just a day ago he had thought that Cameron had died on the mountain, and now he was afraid that his brush with death had only been a tease to a fate soon to come. He felt his bottom lip and his chin start to shake a little, and he knelt by his friend's side and put a hand on his shoulder.

Iris was crying loudly and came up beside him—also putting a hand atop Cameron's body, then leaning over and laying her forehead on him as well, letting her tears flow onto his chest. Matteo stood behind them both, bowing his head in grief.

Then from the eastern wall of the room, the sunrise hit the bottom ledges of the narrow windows. A ray of yellow sun landed on Cameron's body. Iris could feel its warmth on her hand and on the back of her neck. She took in a breath and forced herself to calm down but did not move from her spot. She was held to him—unsure if she could ever even leave this room now, knowing that he would not be going with her.

Matteo closed his eyes and prayed. When he reopened them, he saw the back of Iris's head lift and fall ever so slightly, and he knew she must have started to cry again. But she was not making any sounds. Her head went up again then slowly back down again, and Matteo realized it was not her crying after all. It was air filling Cameron's lungs and raising her head on his chest. Iris still didn't move. She waited for it again, to make sure she wasn't dreaming, and a few seconds later, it happened.

She picked her head off him quick. "He's breathing!" she cried. "He's alive!"

Matteo stooped down. "Let me in," he said, squeezing between her and Frank. He gently lifted Cameron's chin and tilted his head back to open the airway, then bent over and listened for the sounds of breathing. But instead of a noise, he felt a soft puff of air on his cheek from Cameron's exhale, and his heart filled with joy.

"Why are you laying on me," Cameron suddenly asked, then coughed.

Matteo and Frank smiled, and Iris bent down again and wrapped her arms around him as best and as tight as she could. She was still crying, but now also laughing. "Stop dying on me," she said in his ear. "Please."

He was still too weak to hug her back, but she could feel it anyways. She raised her head again and looked down at him. He smiled. "I promise I'll try," he said.

She leaned over and kissed him.

Frank was overjoyed as well. "Good to see you, my friend."

Cameron looked at him. "You too, Frank."

"Think you can stand?"

Professor Skull tightened his stomach and tried to sit himself up, but it pained him, and he laid back down. "Yeah—in a minute."

CHAPTER 48

Frank, Matteo, Iris and Cameron walked out the front of Monte Sant'Angelo Castle and around the side till they reached the back path that led down to the truck in the small lower parking lot. The town was wide awake around them now and hundreds of people were walking about the streets. Emergency crews had been called in and where trying to make sense out of the situation, but no one had any answers. The dozens of men and women who had been saved and changed back were confused and scared, and the townspeople who had come out before the blast of the sound wave were relieved, but equally confused.

One man walked towards a tent that was being erected for triage and medical treatment. Matteo recognized him as the man who he himself had impaled with Michael's sword earlier, and he was now forever grateful to see the man alive.

"I'd keep that thing down," Iris said to him, pointing at the long sword that he still carried.

They had left Uriel's sword at the bottom of the dry moat. It was still burning. There was no scare of it disappearing though, since no one could even get close to it without being injured. Once things settled down in a few hours, Matteo would go back and get it. But right now he still carried the sword of Saint Michael the archangel close to his side as the truck became visible through the trees.

Emily looked up and saw her husband as they got near. She choked in a breath and put her hands to her mouth. Then Ben and Adrian saw him too. "Daddy!" Adrian shouted, and ran to his father.

Matteo wrapped him in his arms then pulled Emily and Ben into the embrace. Joshua and Samuel sat happy, but exhausted, on the back flatbed of the truck.

Cameron looked around at everyone. He saw the young girl and the man who he'd helped rescue from the dungeon. Sergio was now talking to another man though who Cameron did not recognize, and who was crying like a baby. Professor Skull walked over to them.

"Please God, forgive me," the man said. "I swear that I will never do bad things again!"

Sergio looked at him with sorrow, but also with hope. "God has given you another chance, Tony."

Tony? Cameron thought? He remembered Sergio mentioning something about his brother back in the dungeon, and that his name was Tony. He had said that something had happened to him in the castle, and that he was gone, but that was it. *A second chance indeed,* Cameron thought. *For me too.* He turned and let the two brothers have their time together to sort out whatever they needed to sort out.

A few feet away, Iris was talking to the young girl. Becca seemed terrified of the man, Tony. "Don't you worry about him," Iris told her as Cameron came up from behind. "You are safe with us. We are going to get you home. And I won't let you out of my sight until we do. Okay?"

Becca sniffled and nodded her head. Then Iris stood and took her by the hand.

"Is she okay?" Cameron asked.

Iris turned. "She will be. But a terrible experience like this is something that no child should ever have to go through." She lowered her voice a little. "I hope we don't have trouble finding her parents."

"I'll make a call to the director in a minute and get a team at Alpha-Meridian working on it. The director still has some pretty strong connections with the FBI from our old days as Nightcorp. And I'm sure some of their hands can easily reach across borders. We'll find her parents. Don't worry."

Matteo and his family walked over. "Mister Skull," Emily said. "We all want to thank you for everything you've done. And for bringing Matteo back to us safely."

Cameron looked at the family. "You're welcome. But I'm not the one anyone should be thanking. You're husband..." He paused and looked into the faces of the two boys. "And your father," he said to them. "He is the one who saved *me*. I owe him my life." He paused again. "And Frank." Frank was talking to the other two boys, Josh and Samuel, over by the truck. "Frank is the one who figured out how to stop this thing and change all these people back."

Iris still held Becca's hand, but put her other arm around Cameron. She smiled at Emily but then noticed Emily flinch. *That was weird.* Iris thought. She had a brief moment of jealously as though maybe Emily's reaction could have been because of the affection towards Cameron. *Does she like him?*

Matteo took his right arm off Adrian's shoulder and extended his hand to Cameron in thanks. Cameron reached out to take it, but then noticed something too—and it scared him. Matteo had stuck the sword of Michael through his belt. It now hung from his side as naturally as if it belonged there and had always been.

"Wait a second," Cameron said with alarm, and pulled his hand back. "How do you still have that sword? How can you still touch it?" Then his eyes widened in shock. He looked at young Adrian next to his father. The sword was literally brushing against his side too and he acted as though he hardly even noticed. "And how is he…?"

Emily smiled and spoke up first. "They can both touch it," she said, putting a hand on Ben's bicep.

Cameron looked at Matteo who nodded at him in agreement.

It was then that Iris realized it too. Emily's flinch a moment ago had not been a reaction to her or Cameron at all. She had flinched because Matteo had turned the right side of his body a little too close, and the sword had hurt her.

Professor Skull was still surprised. "All of

you?" he asked. "So, you're…"

"No. Not me," Emily said, confirming Iris's suspicion.

"Michael," Cameron said. "You're Saint Michael?"

Now Matteo's eyes widened in shock. "What? No!" He laughed. "I am not Michael!"

"Then…" Cameron shook his head back and forth several times. "I must be more tired than I think," he said, embarrassed and not understanding what was going on yet. "If you're not Michael." Then he figured it out and was surprised all over again. "You're a Nephilim," he said softly. It all made sense now that way. Bastian Santé had not been descended from angels—but Matteo was. Therefore, so were his children. The three of them were all capable of holding the weapons of heavens angels.

Matteo nodded. "I didn't know either, until today."

Iris smiled at Emily, then looked at Matteo. "Do you know that the name Michael means, 'One who is like God'?"

Again, he nodded. "I may not be a language specialist like you are, but I was the priest of Sanctuario San Michele Arcangelo for six years," he said with friendly sarcasm. "I think they would have thrown me out long before if I didn't know at least that."

"Good point," she said with a laugh. "Okay, well do you know what your name means then?"

"I believe it is the Italian form of Matthew,"

he said. "But no, beyond that, I'm not sure what it means."

Cameron looked down at her beside him, also waiting for the answer.

"It means," she said. "Gift from God."

2 Days later

CHAPTER 49

November 22, 2019
60° N, 0° Longitude
Alpha-Meridian
11:35 a.m.

Director Kestner walked into his office and opened the blinds over the window to let in some of God's light. Outside he saw Ethan walking across the yard below, carrying a long wooden pole with a metal ball on one end. The huge man had finished up with the mornings field training class already and was now on his way to practice for the *Hammer Throw* event at next year's Highland Games. He looked up at the director through the window and raised the huge hammer in greeting as he walked past.

Francesco appeared in the doorway behind him. "Director," he said. "Good morning." He walked into the room with an arm full of papers. "I've finished reviewing the lab results."

James turned to face him and offered Frank a seat at the desk. "Should I call in Cameron and Iris?"

"I already did," Frank said. "They should be here in a minute or two."

The director sat down at the desk across from him while they waited. He picked up two new student applications and looked them over. They were for two brothers, Josh and Samuel, who Cameron had given the referral for yesterday.

Frank noticed the director's breathing seemed a bit hard as he sat there and wondered if he was still having some chest pain, but didn't want to say anything about it, sensing it might still be a sore subject.

A moment later, Professor Skull and Iris arrived together and walked in. "My class starts in twenty-five minutes," Iris said. "But I can send someone over to fill in for a few minutes if you think this will take longer than that?"

Frank shook his head. "No, I don't think so. I just wanted to share with you the results of the lab tests we did on the samples taken from the castle." Everyone listened as he opened one of the folders he had brought. "It turns out that Bastian had combined a protein known as DSUP with the somatic cells of a Turritopsis dohrnii, also known as the Immortal Jellyfish. The DSUP protein is what gave his test patients their durability and strength. It is an acronym for *Damage Suppressor*, and is most commonly found in Tardigrades. Basically, it created a virtually indestructible barrier around their individual cells, making them extremely resistant to things like fire, blunt trauma and radiation. But not to vibration. It turns out that the surge we sent through the traffic light sensor had a frequency of somewhere around 15 to 17 hertz. For comparison, your eyeballs can only handle down to about 18 hertz before they start wobbling around in your head like a raw egg. And just like an egg, the DSUP protein had created a hard outer layer around their cells like a shell. But when we blasted those people with the ultrasonic sound wave, it was able to crack through and dissolve the protein. Exactly the kind of result I had hoped for."

He flipped through some of the other papers in front of him, although he really didn't need to. He had a pretty good understanding now of what had happened. "The part that was not expected was the affect the sound wave had on the mRNA of the jellyfish."

"Does that have something to do with how they were healed?" Iris asked.

"Yes, exactly," Frank said. "The immortal jellyfish is one of the most unique creatures on earth. Its name is not an exaggeration. In the wild they are capable of not just regeneration, but of actual transdifferentiation. Meaning that their cells can actually reverse age. If they become sick or injured, their somatic cells can revert back to an earlier stage of their life. To a time before the sickness or injury. Even going all the way back to a polyp stage. Kind of like a stem cell. It's sometimes known as lineage reprogramming, and the Turritopsis can do it immediately and indefinitely."

"But why wasn't that destroyed with the sound wave like the DSUP was?" Cameron asked.

"In a way, it was," Frank said. "The blast of ultrasonic energy hyper-stimulated it, causing it to defend its host by instantly jumping back in time. It reverted the cells back to a time before it was even present in them—wiping itself out. And since the

DSUP protein was also weakened, it couldn't do anything to stop it."

"Wow," Cameron said. "So, then that must have also been at a time before Bastian mutated any of them."

"That's right. When the cells biologically reversed, they went back far enough to a time before the injuries. Causing the miraculous healing that we saw."

"Oh, speaking of which," Cameron said to Director Kestner. "Were you able to set something up to recover the snow tank and the trailer that I abandoned in the mountains?"

"I was," James replied. "I had to go through a few different channels in order to arrange it without blowing it into a national headline, but an EVAC team went out early yesterday morning. The five men locked in the trailer were brought to Aviano Air Force Base and are now in the care of the 31st medical squadron."

"We were able to use a more refined and controlled version of sonication on them," Frank added. "They are all recovering exceptionally well now and are expected to be released in a few days once they have been fully screened and cleared."

Cameron nodded. He had been leaning against a wall and now stood up straight. "Good to hear. I guess that's it then?"

"For now," James said.

Cameron took Iris's hand and started walking out of the room. He stopped just outside the door.

"Oh, James, one more thing," he said with his back still to him. "You might want to send that EVAC team back in."

Oh boy, James thought. "And why would I might want to do that?"

"Probably have them start somewhere around the base of the Matterhorn. Tell them to be on the lookout for a really beat-to-crap zombie wandering around in the snow by itself somewhere."

"Beat to crap?"

"Yeah," Cameron said. "Beat to crap. It fell off a mountain a few days ago and landed on a train."

Iris nudged him with her hip and they both started walking away down the hall.

"But don't call *us* for a few days," Cameron yelled back. "We're taking a vacation!"

EPILOGUE

November 24, 2019
21° N, 159° W
Approaching Manawaiopuna Falls, Kauai
1:31 p.m.

"This is paradise," Cameron said through his headset. The wash of the helicopter's rotors was deafening; but him, Iris, the two other passengers and the pilot all had on the same headsets with radio communications between them. Their tour had taken them offshore into the Pacific then circled back into the island and traced the flight path that Dr. Hammond had taken Alan Grant and his team when first bringing them to Jurassic Park in 1993. The iconic theme song played in the background through their headsets as the majestic 400-foot tall waterfall became visible out the helicopter's front windshield.

Cameron winked at Iris next to him and she smiled.

Sitting in the seats across from them, Kekoa and Lea Awapuhi both stared out the windows at the lush jungle below them. Iris leaned forward. "Kekoa," she said loudly. He turned to her and his face was pale. "Are you okay?" she yelled.

It was not being back in the jungle that frightened him. Even after his encounter with Bastian Santé—the man he had known as Makehewa—the rainforest was still his home, and he was more comfortable there than anywhere else in the world. But that was on the ground. Being thousands of feet in the air above it was *not* comfortable to him, and he felt his stomach turning and bubbling as he tried to keep his lunch from coming up.

"Ladies and gentlemen," the pilot said dramatically as the helicopter started descending. "Welcome to Jurassic Park."

They landed, and one at a time they all got out. Cameron was the last to duck under the whirling blades of the helicopter as he stepped out into a tropical mist from the bottom of the falls that sprayed lightly over them. The air was rich with the smell of flowers and the surrounding ancient untouched geology. Another tour guide was already there waiting for them. "This way," the man said. "We'll follow the path upstream. If you want, we can go all the way to the top." He pointed to a rise. "There's a spectacular view of the island and the Pacific from there."

"I've seen it," Lea said. "It's pretty incredible. I say we do it."

Kekoa nodded. He had obviously seen it before as well. Probably many times. But he also obviously had a little crush on the Sergeant, and probably would have ran circles around the entire island if she asked him to.

"All right!" Iris said excited. "Let's do it."

They climbed through the jungle for about 45 minutes. It was a little strenuous, but nothing any moderately experienced hiker couldn't handle.

Once reaching the summit all of them stood quiet. They each turned in slow circles, marveling at the magnificent view surrounding them. The sky was clear, and a few birds soared gracefully over the jungle canopy, occasionally chirping as they sailed the skies. Deeper in the rainforest beyond they could see breaks through some of the green trees where streams cut through and more waterfalls dropped majestically over the edges of cliffs. Along the island's beach below them, white-capped waves rhythmically washed ashore. The faint sound as the water rolled onto sand, then pulled back out to sea, reached up to them. Far off in the southern distance, the island of Oahu gently rose over the otherwise endless blue of the ocean.

Iris spoke first. "This is beyond beautiful," she said. "It really is paradise."

Kekoa whispered something to Lea, but neither Cameron nor Iris could hear it. The tone and their body language seemed to suggest that that was the way they wanted it though, so Cameron and Iris gave them some privacy and stepped a few feet away.

"Pretty incredible, huh?" Cameron said, staring out over the rainforest and the ocean.

A small sailboat could be seen in the distance and Iris watched it as she answered. "It's not hard to believe that this was once the Garden of Eden," she said, turning to face him. The afternoon sun was shining down on them both. "Bastian was playing God," she continued. "But how could someone ever think that they could compare to this?" She swept her hand over the glorious horizon.

"You can't," Cameron answered. "And Bastian found that out the hard way. In the end, God brought everything full circle. Just like He always does. Bastian was taken out by his own vanity and stubbornness. His attempt to play God is what ultimately killed him."

Iris nodded. "And all those people he hurt were saved by the same thing that had been used to hurt them."

Cameron held her gaze. "There is only one God," he said. "And He doesn't make mistakes."

Her eyes were locked on his just the same. They sparkled in the sun. "Just like how we are on this mountain together right now."

Cameron smiled and she smiled back. Then he bent down and kissed her. They remained that way for 10 full seconds before Cameron finally pulled his head back. "You are an angel," he whispered to her.

She blushed but shook her head. "No sir. *You* are the angel."

—

They got back to the hotel about an hour before sunset. Cameron had last-minute booked one of the oceanfront suites at the Ko'a Kea Resort at Poipu Beach. The luxurious suites were close to a thousand dollars per night—way more than Cameron could normally ever afford. But he had been declared the lawful finder of over 50,000 pounds of lost Nazi gold. And while he couldn't legally keep the treasure, he was able to sell it. The value had been set by an independent board of antiquities, but in the end, Cameron had taken far far less than even the gold's weight value. However, it was still a very considerable sum. And the truth was, he would have gladly gifted the treasure if it wasn't for the insistence of several people, including a few curators and diplomats.

It ended up getting split three ways between the International Museum of World War II in Massachusetts, the Documentation Center for the History of National Socialism in Munich, and the largest portion going to the National World War II Museum in New Orleans.

"Shall we get a drink," he asked after they all got out of the car.

"That sounds amazing!" Iris and Lea both said.

Again, he smiled and put his arm around Iris's shoulder as the four of them started walking to the pool bar. As they approached, Cameron's small SAT phone suddenly vibrated in his pocket. Only a few people had the number, and he was glad to see that it was his daughter Kendall who was calling this time. "Order me a Jack and Coke, will you?" he said to Iris real quick as he answered the call. "Hi honey!" he said. "Everything going okay? Did I forget something?"

Cameron and Iris had detoured and stopped back home in Oregon for half a day on their way out to the islands. Kendall had been so happy to see them, but the joy that she brought to her father was incomparable. Kendall had also been pretty upset about her dad and Iris taking off to Hawaii without her though, but junior high midterms were in a few weeks and she could not afford to take a vacation. Her counselor had *strongly* advised against it. She did however make them both promise to take her somewhere great once winter break started. And they had of course happily agreed.

"No, you didn't forget anything," Kendall said. "At least I don't think you did."

Cameron went to check his watch, but he wasn't wearing one. He suspected it was maybe close to 5 o'clock though. "What time is it there?" he asked her.

"It's almost eight," she said.

"Oh, okay. What's up? Is everything okay? Are you just calling to hear how much fun your old man is having?"

"You wish!" she said jokingly. "And you don't need to rub it in that you're in paradise without me."

He laughed. Both at her teenage sarcasm and at the unknowing accuracy of her metaphor.

"I just wanted to call and tell you about my doctor's appointment today really quick."

"Oh yeah how did it go? Did you see Doctor Stadler?"

Doctor Stadler had been Kendall's

Neurologist since she was 8 years old—ever since she had had her first seizure. Since then she had had 2 more. Doctor Stadler, and Doctor Willers—her clinical psychologist—had diagnosed her with mild autism, claiming that epileptic seizures can sometimes be a common side effect. Thankfully nothing had ever been life-threatening, but they were scary nonetheless. But her autism often put hard social restrictions on her. Besides unexplainable mood swings that Cameron sometimes just attributed to a *teenager*, and not necessarily an *autistic teenager*, Kendall struggled a lot in school and with simple conversation with anyone outside her home. She also was extremely sensitive to certain sounds and noises.

"Yeah," she answered. "I saw Doctor Stadler."

Cameron could hear some excitement in her voice.

"He said that they want to try a new treatment on me next month. He has really high hopes for it and says that it's showing good results in other people. Remember when he told us about the *FMR1* gene?" She didn't give him a chance to respond. "He said that that's what the treatment can fix!"

Cameron was always a bit skeptical about his daughter and new treatments. She was his baby, not a lab rat. But he wanted help for her more than anything. "What is the treatment?" he asked a little apprehensively.

Her voice rose with optimism. "It's called

Justin Hyde

CRISPR."

.

Author's note

Dear reader,

Thank you once again for taking this journey with me. It is for you, and because of your support that I can continue to write these books.

As always, I tried very hard to write a story that was as historically, scientifically and geographically accurate as possible. Although, my understanding and explanation of many things in this novel do not even begin to scratch the surface of their full detail.

In Science: CRISPR technology is a very real advancement in genetic modification today. Although, I admit that even after many hours of research I am still no scientist or molecular biologist, but I do hope (for those of you who are) that I explained it at least accurately enough to understand, yet not so detailed as to turn this book into a science textbook rather than a fiction novel. It's a fine line to walk, and if I stumbled on it here or there, I hope that you were still able to engage in the story and enjoy the excitement of both this adventure and of the real things to come.

In history, religion and locations: Most of (if not all of) the historical and religious mentions in this book are based off of truth. The geographic Sword of Saint Michael is also real, and fascinating, and I

Justin Hyde

would love the chance to visit some of the places on it at some point in my life. I did however try very hard to accurately describe each of them as best as I could.

The lost train of Nazi gold: As I investigated and researched this I was certainly intrigued at the thought that there might be a hoard of lost gold out there, but the kid in me was even more excited about the fact that there could be a really cool old German war train buried out there somewhere!

The Garden of Eden: In this book I have made a case for the location of the garden. Do I believe what I wrote to be true? Yes, I do. Should you? That is up to you.

Thank you all again so much for your time and your support!

Until the next adventure!

Justin Hyde

Made in the USA
San Bernardino, CA
14 May 2020